Perfect Timing

BRENDA JACKSON

Perfect Timing

www.kensingtonbooks.com

DAFINA BOOKS are published by

Kensington Publishing Corp.
119 West 40th Street
New York, NY 10018

All Kensington titles, imprints, and distributed lines are available at special quantity discounts for bulk purchases for sales promotion, premiums, fund-raising, educational, or institutional use.

Special book excerpts or customized printings can also be created to fit specific needs. For details, write or phone the office of the Kensington Sales Manager: Attn.: Sales Department. Kensington Publishing Corp., 119 West 40th Street, New York, NY 10018. Phone: 1-800-221-2647.

The Dafina logo is a trademark of Kensington Publishing Corp.

First Dafina Hardcover Edition: May 2002

ISBN-13: 978-1-61773-416-8 (ebook)
ISBN-10: 1-61773-416-0 (ebook)

ISBN-13: 978-1-4967-3791-5
ISBN-10: 1-4967-3791-1
First Kensington Trade Paperback Edition: April 2003

10 9 8 7 6 5 4 3 2

Printed in the United States of America

ACKNOWLEDGMENTS

To the love of my life, Gerald Jackson, Sr., and to my sons, Gerald Jackson, Jr. and Brandon Jackson.

To all those who attended the 1971 Class of William Raines High School 30-Year Class Reunion Cruise aboard the Carnival Jubilee. Thanks for the wonderful memories and all the fun.

To Sheryl Muraca of Cruises and Tours Unlimited, Jacksonville, Florida. Thanks for making our 30-year class reunion cruise to the western Caribbean so memorable.

To a very special little girl, Mya Ki'Shae Sheppard.

To an avid reader and friend, Brenda Woodbury.

To fellow authors, Carla Fredd, Maggie Ferguson, Francis Ray, and Rochelle Alers. Thanks for listening to my plot and providing your feedback.

To Denise Coleman and Pat Sams. The beginning of our friendship was definitely perfect timing. Thanks for giving me sistah love and support when I needed it most.

To Randy and Andrea Watts, Terry and Dawn Johnson, Daryl and Tonya Knox, and Ben and Nina Davenport. I couldn't resist because you're all very loving couples.

To my Heavenly Father. I'm everything I am because you love me.

Prologue

"**W**hy are you so sad?" Seven-year-old Maxine Chandler pushed the long braids covering her head away from her eyes to get a better look at the girl sitting alone watching the other kids play. Just that morning the teacher had introduced her as Mya and said she was new at school and had moved to town from someplace where it snowed all the time. Maxine wondered if the reason she looked sad was because she was missing the snow.

"I want my mommy and daddy," the little girl answered in a voice that sounded like she was about to cry.

"Where are they?" Maxine asked curiously, feeling herself about to cry too, although she didn't know why.

"They went to heaven and left me behind. Now I have to stay with my granny," the little girl answered.

Maxine nodded as she looked down at the girl thoughtfully. She shoved her hands into the deep pockets on her dress and asked, "Don't you like your granny? I like mine."

The question made the little girl lift her head up and push her chin out. "I like my granny just fine, but sometimes I miss my mommy and daddy awfully bad. I get lonely."

Maxine nodded knowing that if her parents went away she

would miss them too. She suddenly felt really bad inside. "Do you want me to sit with you for a while so you won't be lonely?"

Mya looked up at Maxine and then, after a short while, she scooted over. "If you want to."

Maxine sat down on the bench next to Mya. Silently they watched the other kids in the schoolyard who were running around having fun. After a while Maxine said, "I'll share my parents with you. My momma said my daddy always wanted another child."

"You're the only one?"

"Yes."

"So was I," Mya said softly.

Neither said another word for the longest time. Then Maxine asked. "Well, do you want to be my parents' other child or not?"

Mya thought about Maxine's offer. "Does that mean I'll have to leave my granny and come live with you?"

Maxine pondered Mya's question then answered. "Yes, more than likely you'll have to live at my house. My daddy says he only feeds what's living under his roof, so you'll have to come live with us if you want to eat."

Mya tossed Maxine's words around in her mind. Blinking away more tears she looked at her. "But I don't want to leave my granny. She needs me now that my mommy and daddy are gone."

Maxine nodded. "All right, but if you change your mind let me know. But we can be friends can't we?"

Mya wiped away her tears and smiled. She was glad she didn't have to leave her granny and go live with someone else for now. "Yes, we can be friends."

"Best friends?"

Mya's smile widened. "Yes, the very best. For the rest of our lives."

Maxine scrambled to her feet and reached out her hand to her new best friend. "Come on, let's go play."

Evelyn Jerott, the girls' teacher, watched as they rushed off with their long braids flying in the wind behind them. Standing not far away while watching the other kids in her care, she had overheard the two little girls' conversation. She smiled. Maxine Chandler's approach to Mya Ross had been perfect timing. Evelyn had been concerned whether Mya would sit by herself all day or whether she would eventually mingle with the other kids. Mya's grandmother had explained the situation to her that morning regarding Mya's parents' death in a car accident. Her heart had gone out to the little girl but now she had a feeling she would be okay. Mya was laughing and running around with a new friend.

Evelyn sighed. She had a feeling that the friendship that had just been made between Maxine and Mya would be a special bond that would last a long time.

A very long time.

PART ONE

*When the clouds are heavy, the rains come
down; when a tree falls, whether south or
north, the die is cast, for there it lies.*

—Ecclesiastes 11:3

CHAPTER ONE

Maxi
Twenty-one years later

Maxine "Maxi" Chandler hated the smell of a doctor's office. It was the same scent one found in a hospital—a medicinal, antiseptic, and sterile odor.

Since she was Dr. Frazier's last patient for that day, the waiting room was empty. She'd had consultations scheduled earlier with four of her students and had appreciated the late appointment time. The side door opened and Pauline Warren, a lady in her early sixties, appeared. It seemed Mrs. Warren had been Doctor Frazier's nurse for years.

Maxi took a deep breath. Pauline had called her yesterday to let her know that the results of her tests had come back. In a few minutes she would know if the medication the doctor had prescribed for her a few months ago had improved her medical condition, or if the worst-case scenario was what she was now up against.

"The doctor is ready to see you, Maxi," Mrs. Warren said, smiling.

Maxi stood, returning Pauline's smile. That same smile had had a calming effect on her frazzled nerves when she had undergone her first GYN exam before leaving home for college at eighteen, almost ten years ago. Also, that same smile had offered sympathy to her four years ago when Jason had gotten killed.

"And how is your mom?" Pauline asked as she led Maxi to one of the empty examination rooms.

"Mom is fine and wanted me to tell you hello."

Pauline nodded, closing the door behind them. "I take it that she and Mr. Hudson still haven't made any wedding plans?"

Maxi laughed. "No, they haven't." Her mother, a widow for nearly ten years, and Walter Hudson, a widower for probably just as long, had been seeing each other for years. "Do I need to undress?"

"No. The doctor just wants to talk with you and go over the results of your tests."

Maxi nodded. She'd had a queasy feeling in her stomach ever since receiving Pauline's call.

"Dr. Frazier will be with you in a minute" were Pauline's last words before turning and exiting the room.

Maxi sat down in one of the chairs. No matter what Dr. Frazier had to tell her, she had to believe that she could handle the news. How many times had her mother told her that the Lord never put more on you than you could bear and trouble didn't last always? Taking a deep breath she glanced around the room. For the second time that week she thought about Jason and how his death, which had occurred a week before their wedding day, had nearly destroyed her. He had been on his way to pick her up for dinner when a drunk driver crossed the median and hit him head-on, killing him instantly at the age of twenty-six. He had moved to Savannah seven years before from Ohio to open an insurance agency.

Maxi's thoughts came to an end when the door opened and Dr. Frazier entered. Although she studied his features for any tell-tale signs, there weren't any. There was nothing about him that gave anything away. Not even a small hint. He appeared jovial as usual.

"How are you, Maxi?"

"I'm fine, Dr. Frazier, and you?"

He chuckled. "I have one year, three months, and twenty-four days before retirement, so I'm doing pretty good. I talked to Sonja last night and she's making plans to go on your class reunion cruise. What about you?"

Maxi inhaled deeply. Dr. Frazier's daughter Sonja, now a gynecologist herself in Atlanta, had graduated from high school with her. To celebrate their ten-year class reunion, a seven-day cruise to the western Caribbean had been planned. "I've decided not to go. This summer will be much too busy for me." As a college professor teaching African-American studies at Savannah State University, she had agreed to instruct several classes during the summer term.

"Everyone can use some R and R every now and then, Maxi. Always remember that. There's nothing worse than working yourself to death. Vacations are things people should strive to have at least once a year. Besides, I'd think you'd want to go to the reunion. According to Sonja you were the most popular and most well-liked girl at Beaches High, and were friends with just about everyone."

Maxi nodded. And that was one of the main reasons she didn't want to go. Five years ago she had attended her five-year reunion with Jason, as an engaged couple. Although she had gotten over losing him, she didn't want people who didn't know about his death to open old wounds by asking her about him. "I'll keep that in mind, but I know you didn't summon me here to talk about my high school class reunion."

"No, I didn't." Dr. Frazier took a seat across from her. "The results of your tests came back." He opened the chart he held in his hand. "I'm sorry to inform you that the medication I placed you on isn't working like I had hoped, and there's no other alternative now but surgery."

Maxi took in a deep breath. "Which means if I want a child I need to get pregnant before the surgery." It was a statement and not a question. She bowed her head. It had always been her dream to have children. But then she'd always wanted a husband too. Now it seemed that both were lost to her forever. "Is there any chance the test results are incorrect?" she asked, knowing she was pulling at straws but pulled at them anyway.

"No, Maxi, I'm sorry, but then deep down I think you knew surgery would have to be the answer, didn't you?"

"Yes." She tried smiling. "But a girl can have hope, can't she?"

"Yes, she can." For the longest time he didn't say anything else but continued to look at her with concern on his face. "I still think you should consider going on that cruise. Being around old friends will do you good."

Not if I have to put up with them pulling pictures out of their purses and wallets, displaying their perfect families, she thought. After ten years most were heavily involved in careers and families. More than likely they would want to talk about both. Although she had the career she'd always wanted, she didn't have the family she'd always dreamed about having.

She stood. "I'll think about it," she said, knowing deep down that she probably wouldn't. She checked her watch. "I'd better go. I'm sure it's been a long day for you. Thanks for everything, Dr. Frazier. You will be the one doing the surgery, won't you?"

"Yes, if you decide to do it."

"Do I have a choice?"

"Not if you want to be completely well."

"Then I guess that's that. But I want to put off the surgery for as long as I can."

"All right, but if you begin having problems I want you to re-think that decision. Your monthly cramps will only continue to get worse until the matter is taken care of."

Maxi nodded. "I'll be in touch, Dr. Frazier." She walked out of his office thinking that somehow she would deal with what lay ahead. Somehow she would find the strength to do so.

* * *

Later that evening after enjoying a quiet dinner alone, Maxi went through her closets in search of her high school yearbook. Her conversation with Dr. Frazier had made her think about her former classmates. Many of them had moved away after graduation to attend college, never returning except for occasional visits. Out of a class of over two hundred students, only half of them still made Savannah their home. Although she had left to attend Howard University in Washington, she had returned to the historic coastal town that she loved.

She flipped a few pages of the yearbook, most of them now yellow with age, and checked the section where all the seniors' pictures were. She studied the pictures. The class of 1992 had graduated students who were now doctors, lawyers, federal judges . . . there was even a movie star or two in the group, as well as a few living the life of crime. She knew for a fact that George Buford was in jail for armed robbery. At one time he had made the FBI's most wanted list for robbing more than fifteen banks.

Maxi turned to her senior picture and smiled, grateful the hairstyle she had worn back then was no longer stylish. Her gaze then moved to the photo of the young man next to her—Christopher Chandler. She'd had a big-time crush on him during their entire senior year. Because they'd had the same last name it seemed they had always been in some of the same classes throughout their entire twelve years of school. He had come from an area of town that some considered ghettoville and was always known for getting into trouble. Rebellious, wild, and filled with anger and bitterness because of how society had treated him, Christopher had taken pleasure in being the town's bad boy. Raised by a mother with a reputation of sleeping around, who had enrolled him in school two years later than she should have and only after the school officials had threatened her with legal actions, he had barely made the grades to graduate. She couldn't help but recall the scandal

that swept through Savannah during their senior year of school
involving Christopher's mother and the city's mayor. To this
day Maxi believed the reason their science teacher, Mr. Thompson, who'd for some reason had taken a liking to the rebellious
Chandler, had teamed him up with her for their science project
was because he had known Christopher's hidden potential.
And giving him something to do that required a lot of concentration would take his mind off what was being exposed in the
newspaper about the high profile affair. The project had taken
first place at the Science Fair. Christopher had surprised even
her with his hard work and dedication to the project. And she
had found out something about him during the six weeks they
had worked closely together on the project. It had been something the other students and some of the teachers had not
known, and probably never discovered. Underneath his undis-
ciplined bad boy exterior, Christopher had a brilliant mind. It
wouldn't surprise her if the boy who'd been voted "least likely
to succeed" had become a success. It would serve them all
right, those who had snubbed him and had considered him
nothing more than a thug. Although his name had come up at
the last class reunion, no one had heard anything about him
since the day he left town after graduation. His mother had
committed suicide a week before graduation and he claimed
when he left that he would never return to Savannah.

Maxi then turned the page and glanced at a picture of the
guy who had been captain of the football team and the girl who
had been captain of the cheerleading squad. Childhood sweet-
hearts, their love had been the ultimate storybook romance.
Both had left to attend college in Texas. After college they had
married, and he had begun playing professional football. Mya
and Garrett Rivers were still happily married and living in Dallas. She and Mya had been the best of friends all through
school, each other's confidantes. But due to a misunderstanding they rarely stayed in touch. The last time she had seen Mya

had been two years ago when Mya's grandmother had died and Mya had returned to Savannah for the services. Before then the last time she had heard from her had been when Mya had called offering condolences after hearing about Jason's death. Jason.

Maxi closed the book and a feeling of loneliness washed over her when she thought about him. They had met at the birthday party of one of her co-workers, Sandra Miller. He had been a neighbor Sandra had invited. Maxi had liked him from the very beginning. He'd been a dynamic conversationalist. And he'd been pretty pleasing on the eyes as well, with his handsome features. He had asked her out and from that night on they'd become almost inseparable. They had enjoyed each other's company just that much. They'd been dating a little more than a year when he had asked her to marry him. Everyone thought they were the perfect match. And they had wanted the same things out of life—marriage and a big family.

Maxi sighed deeply. The sudden loss of Jason had been a brutal blow. So was the thought that after her surgery, she would never be able to give birth to a child. She shook aside the brief moment of depression, not wanting to bring back into focus her conversation with Dr. Frazier. The last thing she needed was to feel sorry for herself. Seeing those red check marks under some of her classmates' names, indicating those who were now deceased, had reminded her that at least she was still alive. Five people in her class had died since their last reunion five years ago. So no matter how big you think your problems are, someone else's problems could always be bigger, which makes yours relatively small.

Dr. Frazier had been right. Maybe she should consider going on her high school class reunion cruise. She had always enjoyed the friendships of former classmates and, maybe at this time in her life when all seemed bleak, being surrounded by friends was what she needed. Besides, there was a good chance

Mya would be going and maybe they would be able to spend some time together, renewing their deep friendship that had somehow fallen by the wayside.

Before she had a chance to change her mind, Maxi picked up the phone to call the travel agency that was handling all the arrangements. Since the trip was only six weeks away, she hoped it wasn't too late.

CHAPTER TWO

Christopher

Christopher Chandler stood in the doorway of his bedroom and gazed upon the naked woman who was lying in his bed. Soft light from a nearby lamp cast shadows over the bed, making the long, slender form that much sexier.

He had spent the biggest part of his day behind closed doors with his top management teams. Everything was finally in place with the Landmark Project. He smiled. He enjoyed working deals, making lucrative investments, and being a mastermind when it came to major construction projects. Those things had made him a fairly wealthy man. And because of his dirt-poor beginnings, he'd sworn never to do without again.

But it seemed that money, especially his, was like a magnet. It attracted a lot of people, some he could just as well do without. Like the woman sleeping naked in his bed. A part of him was angry and upset that she was there and wondered how she had gotten past security. Evidently she had convinced the guard at the gate that she had a right to be there. He shook his head. With a body like hers she could probably convince any man of anything.

He walked toward the bed, deciding that since she had entered his private domain uninvited he may as well make it worth his while before tossing her out on that sweet little behind of hers. Pamela Carlyle was determined to get under his skin and he was just as determined to make sure she didn't.

No woman got under Christopher Chandler's skin.

He went into his bathroom and moments later returned stark naked. He walked over to the bar in the room and poured a drink of brandy before walking over to the bed to stand over the sleeping woman. "Pamela," he said huskily. "Wake up."

He sipped his brandy and watched as the sound of his voice made her open her eyes. She smiled up at him, stretching against the pillows as her gaze took in as much of him as she could see from her position. "I know what you want, Christopher," she purred softly, unfolding her naked body in one sensuous curve.

"And I know what you want as well, " he said before tilting the glass he was holding and dripping a small portion of the dark liquid onto the upper part of her body, wetting her breasts. He grinned. "I guess I'm going to have to lick that off you."

"Yes, I guess you will."

And he did. But that was just the beginning. One thing Christopher Chandler knew was how to please a woman in bed and went about doing just that. He gave her just what he knew she had come for. She clawed his back, screamed his name over and over again, and bucked against his every thrust before finally reaching a climax that sent her over the edge.

And he followed her, glorying in the feel of being inside a woman who knew just how to work her body to make a man revel in the power of "groan-deep-in-your-throat" sex. This was not lovemaking. This was hot, lusty sex. The satisfying of hormones, the ravaging of passion. It was a good thing he was wearing a condom or else she would have been filled to capacity with his semen. Something he wanted no woman to take into her body since he did not intend to have children. Ever. He would never marry and he refused to have a child labeled a bastard like he'd been while growing up.

Feeling completely spent, he pulled out of her as the aftershocks of both their orgasms still trembled through them. He rose from the bed and went into the bathroom to dispose of his condom. When he returned wearing a robe, she had curled up in his bed and was drifting off to sleep. He walked over to the bed and nudged her awake. "It's time for you to go."

She slowly opened her eyes and looked up at him with a languid gaze. "Can I stay tonight?"

"No. I like sleeping alone."

"I'll make it worth your while, Christopher," she promised in a soft, sexy voice, one that no doubt brought most men a quick hard-on.

"You've already made it worth my while. Now I want you to leave. After I return from taking my shower I want you gone and the next time I come home and find you here in my home uninvited, I'll do more than give you a good screw. I'll toss you out on your naked behind."

Anger flared in Pamela's eyes and she reared up at him. "Why you bas—"

"That's exactly what I am and don't ever forget it. It describes me perfectly since I have no idea who my father is." He crossed his arms over his chest. "I like choosing the woman I want warming my bed. Don't ever put too much stock in anything when it concerns me, Pamela. Understand?"

She angrily tossed her long, shapely legs over the bed. "Oh, I understand, perfectly. But one day you'll get yours, just you wait and see."

Christopher smiled. "Besides being a good lay, I take it you're also a fortune-teller as well?" Not giving her a chance to respond he turned and headed for the bathroom, then stopped and turned around. "Remember what I said, Pamela. Don't ever show up here again uninvited."

He then entered the bathroom, closing the door behind him.

* * *

Twenty minutes later when Christopher walked out of the bathroom freshly showered he heard the doors to his kitchen cabinets opening and closing. Thinking that Pamela had not left like he'd told her to do, he tightened the sash of the robe around his waist before angrily leaving his bedroom and walking into the kitchen. "I thought I told you to—"

He stopped upon seeing the person in his kitchen was not Pamela but his best friend Gabriel Blackwell.

Gabe lifted a dark brow. "You thought you told me to do what?"

Christopher frowned. "Nothing. I thought you were someone else."

"Someone like who?"

"Pamela. She evidently talked the guard into letting her inside here. When I got in she was asleep, lying naked on my bed."

Gabe grinned. "Must have been some sight."

Christopher couldn't help but return his best friend's grin. "It was." He then studied Gabe. They had been together the better part of the day going over things at the office and in a long string of meetings. In addition to being his best friend, Gabe was also his business partner. "What brought you by? I wasn't expecting you."

"I'm sure you weren't. I decided to pay you an unannounced visit to make sure you hadn't brought any work home from the office. You work too damn hard, Chris. What you need is a vacation."

"A vacation?"

"Yes, a vacation. I order you to take some time off."

Christopher smiled shaking his head. "You order me?"

"Yes."

"That's cute, Gabe. Real cute." Christopher gazed at the man standing before him. Their friendship had spanned nearly ten years. After leaving Savannah he had made his way to Detroit where he'd had the good sense to apply for work at a construction company that Gabe's father owned. The older man had taken him under his wing and later, he had talked him into furthering his education right alongside his son. Christopher decided on a degree in industrial design and Gabe in structural engineering. Then they both graduated with MBAs at the top of their class. Omar Blackwell, who had since retired, had signed ownership of the business over to Christopher and Gabe. Christopher, who never had anyone take an interest in him before, other than a former teacher, Mr. Thompson, had felt nothing but gratitude and appreciation for the Blackwell family; a family he'd been adopted into.

"No, Chris, I'm serious about you taking a vacation. Mama's orders. She's worried about you. When you were at the folks' house for dinner on Sunday, she picked up on how tired you looked. And you know Mama. She likes worrying about us."

"Why didn't you explain to her that the reason I looked tired was because I've been staying up late working on the Landmark deal?"

Gabe shook his head. "That would have only verified her claim that you're overworked. Do yourself a favor, don't argue with Mama. Take some time off and go somewhere or you'll have her breathing down our necks and constantly checking up on us."

Christopher nodded, knowing Gabe was right. Joella Blackwell was a force to reckon with and they knew when she spoke she meant business. "I'll call her and promise to take a trip somewhere in a few weeks. There's no way I can leave now with the Landmark Project nearly finalized."

Gabe nodded, knowing just how much that particular deal meant to Christopher. "But you do promise to take time off soon? And I mean a real vacation and not one of those 'let's make a deal' business trips."

Christopher thought for a minute. He had received a newsletter that had been forwarded to him from Mr. Thompson advising him of his high school reunion, a seven-day cruise to the western Caribbean. He had a mind to go just for the hell of it, since most of his former classmates probably thought he was in jail serving time, or even worse, dead. "Yes," he finally replied. "It will be a real vacation."

"Okay, then please let Mama know so she'll stay off our backs." Gabe laughed. "At least until she decides to stick her nose into something else. She's still intent on marrying us off so don't be surprised when she starts sending those single church women our way."

CHAPTER THREE

Garrett and Mya

Mya Rivers looked across the room at her husband who was surrounded by an army of beautiful women. She had long ago learned not to get jealous when it came to Garrett. Some women it seemed liked athletes and cared less for their marital status. In fact they were challenged by it. That was one of the reasons she was paying close attention to the woman standing on Garrett's right. The brazen hussy had patted him on the butt when she thought no one was watching.

Stopping a passing waiter, Mya took a glass of champagne from the serving tray and took a sip. To toast the beginning of the new football season, the owners of the Dallas Cowboys had thrown this extravagant party. The players would be reporting to training camp next week.

Deciding she had seen enough of women throwing themselves at her husband for one night, Mya took another sip of champagne and walked toward him. Even she had to admit that at twenty-eight and six-feet-four inches of delectable dark meat, Garrett Rivers looked good. After all these years she still enjoyed looking at his well-proportioned body and its masculine yet graceful curves.

The closer Mya got to him the angrier she became. The woman had boldly fondled him again. That was one fondling too many. Mya eased up beside him, on the same side where the woman was standing. Upon seeing her Garrett automatically slipped his arms around her waist and pulled her closer to his side and made introductions. "This beautiful lady is my wife, Mya," he said. "Sweetheart, you do remember these ladies, don't you? They used to be part of the Cowboys' cheerleading squad a few years back."

Mya dutifully smiled at the women. "Yes, I remember them," she said. "Nice seeing you all again." She then turned her attention to the woman who had patted Garrett's backside twice that night. The smile on Mya's face wavered slightly. The woman was young, probably in her early twenties. Unlike the other women who'd been Dallas cheerleaders in the past, this sistah who'd been introduced as Paige Duvall was too young to be a "has been" and was probably a part of the current squad. "Are you a Dallas Cowboys cheerleader?"

The woman smiled. "Yes, I'll be joining the squad this season and I'm definitely looking forward to it," she said, throwing Garrett a flirty grin. It bothered Mya when he grinned back. Turning to Garrett, she said, "Do you mind if we leave now? I have an early flight out in the morning and need to pack."

"Sure. I'm ready to go whenever you are." He turned his attention back to the ladies. "It was nice seeing you all again." He then gave the younger woman a warm smile. "Welcome to the team, Paige. The players appreciate the cheerleaders out there on the sidelines cheering for us."

"The pleasure will be all mine," she said, her gaze never leaving Garrett's face. She then forced her gaze from Garrett and looked at Mya and smiled. "It was also nice meeting you, Mya."

Mya said very little on the ride back to their place. Their three-year-old twin sons, David and Daniel, were spending the night with friends. The boys had been named after their grandfathers. David Rivers was Garrett's father and Daniel Ross had been hers.

"Okay, let's have it, Mya. What's bothering you?" Garrett asked the moment they had entered their home.

"Nothing is bothering me," she snapped, walking straight to their bedroom. She had promised herself not to bring up what she'd witnessed at the party, making too much of a big deal out of it. She had been with Garrett long enough to know women threw themselves at him all the time and in the past she'd always been able to handle it. But for the first time tonight she had felt threatened. That young bimbo had all but made her intentions clear. She intended to do more than just cheer for the Cowboys on the sidelines. She had her eyes set on one player in particular.

When Garrett entered their bedroom moments later, he found his wife sitting in a recliner chair near the bed. Although she had told him that nothing was bothering her, he knew something was. He leaned back against the doorjamb and stared at her, thinking just how long they had been together. Just how long he had loved her. He had fallen head over heels in love with Mya from the time they had been in junior high school. Mya and football had been the two things that had always dominated his life.

He slowly walked over to her. "Come here," he said softly, pulling her to her feet. He then sat in the recliner and pulled her down into his lap. "There *is* something bothering you so let's talk about it. Remember our promise? There would never be any secrets between us."

Mya nodded, remembering that promise they had made long ago while still in high school. She took a long breath before saying, "She touched you. I saw her do it. She touched you twice and you seemed to have liked it."

Garrett didn't say anything for a moment. He knew who and what Mya was referring to. He had hoped she hadn't witnessed Paige's boldness. "Yes, she touched me, honey, but it meant nothing to me. Women have touched me before. You know how bold some of them can get about men they consider super jocks. The most important thing is that I don't touch back. The reason I didn't react was because I hadn't wanted to make a scene. However, had she done it a third time, I would have said something to her about it."

He looked down into Mya's face. "You do trust me, don't you?"

"Yes, but I don't trust her. There's something about her that I don't like. For some reason she—"

Garrett touched his lips to hers. "Don't ever feel threatened by any woman, Mya Ki'Shae Rivers. Ever. You are the only one who has my heart. You should know that. You're the one I come home to every night and the one who sleeps in my bed. You and the boys are all I want and all I need," he said before bringing his mouth down and fully kissing her.

Garrett was an accomplished kisser. And as far back as Mya could remember he always had been. Moments later, after he had thoroughly ravaged her mouth, she snuggled against his warm chest while he held her in his arms.

"Do you have to leave tomorrow, Mya?" he asked softly, a few moments later.

Meeting his gaze, she noted the quiet disappointment in his voice and didn't answer him for a while. She knew he was still trying to come to terms with her working outside the home. Her management position with a well-known investment firm required occasional travel. Although she'd always made sure the boys were taken care of in her absence, she knew Garrett didn't like the idea of her working. He came from a generation of Rivers who believed a man took care of his family, and the woman's place was in the home, taking care of her man and her children. Her and Garrett's biggest arguments had been about her wanting to utilize her degree in Finance. Even while she was home there was little for her to do since they had a housekeeper who doubled as a babysitter. She had felt the need to get a job, not that she needed one financially, but because she wanted to feel useful.

"Yes, I have to leave tomorrow, but it's just an overnight trip. I'll be back before you know it."

His arms tightened up around her. "I'm going to miss you."

"And I'm going to miss you and the boys." After a few moments she said, "Did you talk to your coach about getting time off in June for the class reunion cruise?" She knew that during the summer months the players were hard at work preparing for the fall football season.

"Yes, and he said it's okay. That happens to be the same week he'd planned on giving the players time off to relax anyway, so it works out fine."

Mya smiled. "I'm glad. It will be good seeing old friends again. I hope Maxi is going. It will be good seeing her. I hope the two of us can spend some time together."

The corners of Garrett's eyes crinkled in a smile. He remembered just how close Mya and Maxine used to be. Thick as gravy. "Yeah, it will be worth it, won't it." Moments later he began nuzzling her throat. "Umm . . . as always, you smell good."

She looked up at him. His gaze was frankly seductive. "You smell pretty good yourself."

He chuckled. "Let's go into the bathroom and start smelling soapy."

"Are you suggesting that we take a bath together?"

"Yes." Garrett rose with her in his arms. "That's exactly what I'm suggesting."

Across town, Paige Duvall shared a cab with another cheerleader, as they made their way back to their apartments.

"I couldn't happen but notice your interest in Garrett Rivers. You're new so I'll give you some advice," the other cheerleader said to Paige. "Don't waste your time on him. He's a real family man who's tied to his wife pretty tight. I understand he loves her very much."

Paige smiled. "Most of them do . . . in the beginning. But a man being in love with his wife has never stopped me before. I like Garrett and intend to have him."

The other woman shook her head frowning, not liking what she was hearing. "You're pretty sure of yourself if you think that. Garrett Rivers is too dedicated to his wife and sons to let anyone come between them. You'll just be wasting your time."

Paige's smile widened. "Maybe . . . then maybe not. Every man has a weakness. The key is finding out what that weakness is and using it. Which is what I intend to do."

CHAPTER FOUR

The hospital's elevator doors opened and Maxi stepped in and pushed the button that would take her to the fifth floor. She thought about the woman she was on her way to see.

Bessie Johnstone was someone Maxi had known all of her life; a woman who had been her grandmother's closest friend. When Maxi's grandmother had passed away fifteen years ago, Bessie had made herself Maxi's surrogate grandmother. There was nothing Bessie wouldn't do for Maxi and vice versa.

Moments later when Maxi entered Bessie's hospital room she couldn't help but smile. A broken hip had rendered Bessie immobile, and from the expression on the older woman's face as she lay in bed looking out the window, she wasn't too pleased about being forced to stay in one place. Anyone knowing Bessie knew just how much getting around meant to her.

"Okay, you can stop sulking," Maxi said, making her presence known. "It doesn't become you. Besides, this will teach you not to be hardheaded."

Bessie made a snorting sound as she glanced at Maxi. "There was nothing wrong with me wanting to change that light bulb."

Maxi frowned. "Yes, there was if you had to get on a ladder to do so. You could have waited for your neighbor Mr. Ellerby to come home. He would have gladly helped you. Or you could have called me. You know that I would have come by."

"I don't like being a bother, you know that."

Maxi nodded. Yes, she did know it. "You deserve to be a bother, Ms. Bessie. Look at all the things you've done for so many people over the years. I don't know a soul in Savannah who would not have come to your aid had you only asked."

Bessie shook her head, knowing that was true. She had lived a long life and at seventy-four, a number of people had touched her life and she had also touched theirs. Maxi Chandler was one of them. In her book, Maxi had always been a good child. Respectful to her elders, a good student and thoughtful and giving, which was evident by the beautiful arrangement of flowers she carried in her hand.

"Maybe my being here, although it seems I'll be laid up a spell, is for a good cause. I think I found just the right man for you, Maxi."

Maxi grinned as she placed the vase of flowers on a table near Bessie's bed. Ever since Jason's death, Bessie had tried fixing her up with a number of "right" men. There had been Charlie, the painter, Aaron, the meat cutter, Paul, the shoe salesman, and Theodore, the man who had recently moved to town and opened a slew of dry cleaners.

"I think this one is special, Maxi."

Maxi lifted her brow as she took the chair opposite the bed. She decided not to tell Bessie that was what she'd said of the others. "And what makes this one special?"

Bessie's face lit into a smile. "He has a child. He's a divorced man with a twelve-year-old son he is raising by himself. I think that will solve all your problems."

Maxi sighed. She didn't have to ask Bessie what problems she was referring to. There wasn't any doubt in Maxi's mind that her mother had told Bessie about her visit with the doctor, so chances were Bessie knew of her pending surgery and what it meant.

"Just think, Maxi," Bessie continued saying. "That's a way to get the child you've always wanted but can't have after your surgery. You know I never had any children of my own but raising Dasha and Martin was the next best thing. I never regretted ever having married Solomon and raising his children. In no time at all they had become my children."

Maxi stared into space and after a few minutes she nodded. She knew from what she'd been told that when Bessie had been in her twenties, she had married a widower with two small children. Dasha and Martin, who were both in their late forties now and living up north, considered Bessie as their mother and would do anything for her.

"And after talking to the man," said Bessie, breaking into Maxi's thoughts, "it's apparent that he's lonely and would love to meet a decent woman. Raising a child alone isn't easy, especially for a doctor."

"A doctor?"

"Yes, dear. He's my doctor. Although he's a little older than what I had in mind for you—he's probably in his late thirties—I think he's the answer to your prayers and there's no doubt in my mind that you're going to like him."

"Ms. Bessie, you know how I feel about your playing Cupid."

"Yes, but then you know how I feel about your being alone. Jason's been dead for four years. You need to move on."

"I have moved on. I'm just not ready to get seriously involved with anyone yet."

"But life's passing you by and so are rare opportunities for you to meet someone special. Now is the time for you to start seriously thinking about finding the right man for you."

"And Mrs. Johnstone has taken the notion that I'm him."

Maxi's head jerked toward the husky voice and her gaze met that of the tall figure of the man casually leaning in the doorway. She lifted a brow and decided she couldn't lie. He was extremely nice looking and the slow smile that spread across his face made her feel completely at ease—given their awkward situation. From what he'd just said, Maxi knew that Bessie had been feeding him a bill of goods about her just like Bessie had been doing her about him.

Faced with the inevitable, Maxi stood and crossed the room, offering him her hand in a warm greeting. "Hi, I'm Maxine Chandler."

He took her hand and she noticed how warm it felt in his. "And I'm Dr. Reginald Tanner." He released her hand but continued to look at her. The look in his gaze indicated he liked what he saw. "I've heard a lot about you, Ms. Chandler."

Maxi chuckled. "I'm sure you have and Bessie has been telling me about you as well, Dr. Tanner."

Now it was his time to chuckle. "I find that Ms. Johnstone is one determined lady when she makes her mind up about something."

"Trust me, she is."

"And I'm sure that you are aware that she won't let the matter rest until I ask you out."

"Probably not."

"So, Maxine Chandler, how about going to a movie with me this weekend?"

Maxi stared up at him, immediately liking him. No doubt Bessie had already obtained all the pertinent information about him besides his name, rank, and serial number. Knowing Bessie, she probably knew something about every member of his family. Although the older woman was intense about fixing her up with someone, she took time to make sure any man she sent Maxi's way was law-abiding and God-fearing.

"I'd love to go to the movies with you."

Dr. Tanner's smile widened. "How about if I pick you up Saturday evening around six? We can do dinner first and then a movie."

"That's fine. Do you need my address?"

He chuckled. "No, Ms. Johnstone has given it to me already. Several times in fact." He straightened his stance from leaning in the doorway. "I have to continue making my rounds so I'll see you on Saturday."

"All right."

And then he was gone.

"Well, what do you think?" Bessie asked from behind Maxi.

Maxi turned around and faced the older woman. "He seems nice."

"He is and he's also a good doctor. He's taken good care of me since I've been here but like I said earlier, Maxi, he might be just what you need since he already has a child—a child who from what I gather needs a mother."

Maxi's expression was reflective as she thought about the man she'd just been introduced to. A part of her looked forward to Saturday.

"This will be your first cruise?"

Maxi looked across the table at Reginald. He had taken her to a nice restaurant in Savannah that was known for its seafood. She had just finished telling him about her ten-year class reunion cruise and her plans to go. "Yes, and I'm looking forward to it," she said smiling. "It will be so good seeing so many classmates again."

He nodded. "How do you like being a college professor?"

Maxi took a sip of her wine before answering. "I really enjoy it. I always wanted to become a teacher but I didn't decide on a career on the college level until later." After a few moments her expression was thoughtful when she asked. "And do you enjoy being a doctor?"

He smiled nodding. "Yes. My ex-wife Margie and I are both doctors so it made our married life kind of hectic, but being a doctor was all I ever wanted to be. I enjoy it immensely." His smile widened. "And it affords me the opportunity to meet people like Ms. Johnstone. She's quite a character."

Maxi couldn't help grinning. "Yes, she is."

Dinner was good and Maxi and Reginald continued to engage in pleasant conversation. He told her about his twelve-year-old son and how he was adjusting to Savannah, after having moved from Connecticut a year ago.

Outside, as they were leaving the restaurant, the night air was kind of chilly and Reginald placed his arm around Maxi's shoulder as they walked to his car. "I'm enjoying your company, Maxine. I usually don't take time to enjoy myself like I'm doing tonight. Now I find I'm in Ms. Johnstone's debt."

Maxi smiled thinking she was in Bessie's debt as well. Reginald truly seemed to be a nice person. He was a great conversationalist and had kept a steady flow of dialogue between them all evening. She was surprised to learn that although he appeared to be in his late thirties, in actuality he was forty-two. The only thing she'd noticed that bothered her was the number of times he mentioned his ex-wife. From what he'd said earlier, they had been divorced for two years yet Margie Tanner's name had crept into their conversation numerous times.

The movie, a new Eddie Murphy comedy, had kept them laughing. Afterwards, they decided to stop by a café for a cup of coffee before heading home. It was a little past midnight when Reginald walked Maxi to her door. Since they had just finished drinking coffee there was no reason to invite him in. Besides, although she had enjoyed his company, Maxi was tired. She had helped out at the church earlier that day in their food drive.

"Thanks, Reginald, for a delightful evening. I enjoyed myself."

He smiled. "I enjoyed myself as well. Maybe we can get together again soon. I'm working next weekend but I'm free the following weekend. Can I call you?"

"Sure."

"All right." He softly seized her hand then leaned down and brushed her lips with his. His kiss was light at first then after a few moments it became hungry. Maxi quickly pulled back when he boldly deepened the kiss. She was not ready for the level of intimacy he was about to take the kiss to. "Goodnight, Reginald."

He looked down at her and for a moment she wondered if he planned to try and kiss her again. For some reason the look in his eyes said he was thinking about it. Then after a few moments he said, "Goodnight, Maxine, and thanks for a wonderful evening."

Maxi watched him walk back to his car before opening the door and getting inside.

The following week while out shopping at the mall for clothing to take on the cruise, Maxi ran into Reginald. He was with another woman and a boy who appeared to be eleven or twelve. She knew without being told that the boy was Reginald's son. The resemblance was uncanny. She found out later, after introductions were made, that the woman was his ex-wife.

"Margie decided to surprise us and come down for the weekend," Reginald said to her in way of an explanation. The expression he wore reminded her of a boy who'd gotten caught with his hand in the cookie jar.

Maxi nodded, figuring he really didn't owe her an explanation, nor did he need to feel guilty about anything. They had dated that one time and, although he'd definitely shown signs of being interested in her, she had picked up on the fact that he still had feelings for the former Mrs. Tanner. So to Maxi's way of thinking, Margie Tanner had nothing to fear and was definitely wasting her time with the icy coldness in the gaze she was giving her.

"I'll call you," Reginald said softly breaking into Maxi's thoughts.

"Okay," she responded, although she had a gut feeling that

he wouldn't, but then she knew it would be for the best if he didn't call her. Although she had liked him, he had issues he needed to resolve before becoming involved with anyone.

Dismissing him from her thoughts, she continued her shopping. She had to believe that somehow things would eventually work out for her.

CHAPTER FIVE

Christopher was on his way out of the office to join Gabe for lunch when his phone rang. "Yes, Mary?"

"You have a call from a Ms. Smithfield, sir."

Christopher smiled as he checked his watch. "You can put her through." He then sat back down in his chair, relaxed. Tori Smithfield was a journalist for CNN who traveled around the country quite a bit. They had met three years ago while she'd been in Detroit on business. Their one night stand had led to numerous others after that, and she made it a point to always look him up whenever she was in town. She had a body that was stacked in all the right places and she knew how to use it, always giving him intense sexual pleasure. And that was just what he needed. He hadn't slept with anyone since Pamela and that was almost three weeks ago. He was beginning to get that constant ache in his lower mid-section, a sure sign that he was overdue for a tumble between the sheets.

"Christopher?"

His smile widened at the sound of the ultra sexy voice. It had been six months since he'd last heard it. "Tori, I take it that you're back in town."

"Yes," the sexy voice responded. "I got in yesterday. I should have all my business finalized by tonight and was wondering if I could see you. There's something I have to tell you."

He raised a brow, curious. "All right. Are you staying at the Hilton?"

"Yes. I'm in suite 410. Can we get together about seven?"

"Yes, that won't be a problem. Do you want to go to dinner?" he asked her, then got turned on from the sound of her small, sensuous chuckle when she responded. The ache in his mid-section deepened.

"Let's decide when you get here."

Christopher bit back another smile. Talking was the last thing on his mind. "Sounds like a winner. I'll see you later." He leaned back in his chair after hanging up the phone. Tori was something else and no doubt she would make his evening un-forgettable as usual.

Tori took a deep breath, ran a quick caressing hand through her short, curly hair and stepped back to let Christopher enter her hotel room. Closing the door behind him she turned and let her gaze move over him from head to toe. He was a fine specimen of a man and perfect by her and most women's stan-dards.

She knew a man as good looking as Christopher could have any woman he wanted—and probably did. But she was of the opinion that she could compete against any of those women mainly because she wasn't a threat. What the two of them shared whenever they saw each other was hot, mind-boggling sex with no strings attached.

Although she didn't know a whole lot about Christopher's past, she knew from the one time they had spilled their guts after having too much to drink one night that like her, he had been born illegitimate and also like her, his mother had been the town's slut. In fact it had been one of her mother's boy-friends with whom she'd had her first sexual experience at the age of sixteen. Her mother had almost flipped when she'd discovered that Rick Dover had been bedding both mother and daughter.

"You look good, Tori," Christopher said, as he pulled her into his arms.

"And as always, so do you," she replied as a slow smile touched her lips.

"So, what do you have to tell me?"

All thoughts of telling him anything had fled her mind the moment he had taken her into his arms. It had been six months since she had last seen him and she didn't want to waste time talking. Taking his hand she led him over to the bed. "We'll talk later."

The smile he gave her let her know she didn't have to make the suggestion twice.

Christopher rode her like a madman yet she refused to put an end to such excruciating pleasure. This was high-intensity lovemaking, uncontrollable sex and her body jerked again, for the third time that night, as the pleasure inside her reached its maximum exploding point.

She screamed out with the force of her climax from a throat already raw from earlier screams, as she clawed at his shoulder, his back, and his buttocks, whatever part of him she could grab. She then felt his body reaching its own orgasm as he thrust deeply into her one last time before finally collapsing on top of her.

As routine, he only lay on top of her for a few seconds before rising from the bed and going into the bathroom to discard his condom and put on a new one. She smiled. He took birth control seriously. He'd once told her that he had no intentions of ever fathering a child, which was fine with her since she had no intentions of ever mothering one either.

She inhaled deeply. It had become her intention to tell Christopher that she had gotten married since the last time they'd been together. But once she had seen him and he had taken her into his arms, the only thing she could think about was making love with him. And now as she thought more about it, she decided that maybe she shouldn't tell him anything and run the risk of him ending the relationship they shared. There were some men of the mind not to be involved with a married woman and Christopher might be one of those men. He might not understand, nor even care that her husband, who was thirty years older, could not fulfill her needs in the bedroom and that the only reason she had married him was because he had money, lots of it, and being his wife afforded her the respectability she'd always wanted.

Moments later Christopher came out of the bathroom, walking toward her naked with a body that was lean, sleek, and superbly toned. He was in outstanding shape, she thought, as he sat on the bed beside her. "So, what is it you have to tell me?" he asked.

"Umm," she murmured, still barely able to catch her breath as she thought of what she could tell him since she'd decided not to tell him that she had gotten married. Not when her body was primed to make love with him again. "That piece I was working on about Blacks living in Europe has gotten the attention of a major publisher." At least that wasn't a lie.

He smiled. "Tori, that's great news. I know you must be pleased about it."

"Yes, I am."

"I think that calls for a celebration. We'll order champagne with our dinner."

She nodded. She had worked up an appetite. "Champagne with our dinner sounds fine."

Tori was stretched out on the bed. Her skin was still warm, glowing and sweaty from the sex marathon they had just participated in. And just looking at her was turning him on again, which he was sure was her intention. He was tempted to give her just what she wanted again but decided they needed to eat. "I'll order room service while you shower."

Tori nodded as she watched him cross the floor to the closet, slip into one of the hotel's courtesy bathrobes before walking out of the room into the sitting area to use the phone.

Christopher stared across the table at Tori and wondered what made women tick. Especially the highly independent, high-sexual-maintenance ones like she was. They were the kind who believed that they did not have to depend on a man for anything other than a good night of sex. That night when they had met at a business function, and their gazes had met across the room, he had known that she'd only wanted one thing from him like he had only wanted one thing from her. Once they had gotten to her hotel room they'd mated like two wild animals. Now three years later, nothing had changed. Between them it had all come down to sex. But then . . . wasn't that the same with every woman he came in contact with? Going on the class reunion cruise would do him some good since he intended to use that time to rest and relax.

"Why are you staring at me like that, Christopher? You're not thinking about taking me back to bed, are you?"

Tori's question brought Christopher out of his thoughts. A smile played at the corners of his mouth when he answered huskily. "Could you handle it if I were?"

She gave him a lazy grin. "I'd like to think that in the morning I'll be able to walk out of here to catch my plane and not have to be carried out on a stretcher."

Christopher laughed. "Making love to you again isn't what I was thinking about, although it sounds like a wonderful idea. I was thinking about the western Caribbean cruise I'll be taking."

Tori lifted her brow and took a swallow of her champagne. "A cruise? For business again?" She remembered he had taken a business cruise to Alaska sometime last year, almost four months ago. It had been about the same time she had gotten married.

"No, this is strictly for relaxation purposes." He saw no need to tell her that it was for his ten-year class reunion, guaranteed to give some of his former classmates the shock of their lives when they saw him.

"When is the cruise?"

"Next month."

Tori gazed at him thoughtfully. An idea suddenly popped into her head. Umm, she wondered . . . It would definitely be a gamble but as far as she was concerned well worth the risk. She could tell her husband that she had to go on a cruise to cover a story. Chances were he would probably believe her since he was such a trusting man. "I haven't been on a cruise in a while. Would you like some company?"

She could tell from the look in Christopher's eyes that he'd been momentarily taken aback by her question. Their relationship had never been any other than what they spent in a hotel room.

He downed the contents of his wineglass, set it back on the table and slowly stood. "No, I don't think that would be a good idea." He then checked his watch. "I have to go."

Tori released a deep breath when she realized her mistake. The one reason their relationship had lasted for nearly three years was because of distance, no demands, no strings, no expectations. She'd never hinted at the possibility that she wanted anything beyond their chance meetings every four to six months.

Until tonight.

Her heart accelerated and she had a sinking feeling he intended this to be the last night they spent together. "Can I call you the next time I'm in town?" she asked as she watched him put on his jacket.

A faint smile tugged at the corners of his mouth, making him more handsome than ever. "Yes, you can do that."

But Tori knew that didn't necessarily mean he would come and see her. She slipped out of her chair and walked across the room to stand before him. Rising on tiptoes she placed a light kiss on his lips. A hint of regret was in her smile. "Goodbye then, until the next time."

He let his gaze linger on her for a few moments before saying, "Yes, until the next time. Come walk me to the door."

She did and when she opened it, they gave each other what she knew was a farewell kiss. She would definitely miss their quiet dinners, their intimate evenings—but more than anything, she would miss him.

She arched her body into his as he kissed her in an exchange that she would remember for a long time. Moments later when the kiss ended her hand reached up and her fingers rubbed softly against his cheek. "Take care of yourself, Christopher."

"And you take care of yourself as well, Tori."

He then stepped back and turned around to leave. Tossing one final glance over his shoulder, he walked down the corridor toward the elevator. Tori closed the door when she could no longer see his tall form.

Both Tori and Christopher were so caught up in their own individual thoughts that neither noticed the slow opening of another hotel room door, nor the small lens from a miniature high-powered camera that had captured their heated kiss on film.

CHAPTER SIX

Mya Rivers's mind went blank. She couldn't believe what her boss, Mr. Lee, was saying. She looked at the man again. "Excuse me, sir. Would you repeat that?"

She shifted uncomfortably in her chair when he smiled. Mr. Lee never smiled. "Why certainly, Ms. Rivers. I said the reports from the past six months have been so impressive that my partners and I agree that you should be promoted, and we've decided to do just that. Therefore, effective today you are now senior financial analyst. Congratulations."

Mya took a deep breath. Mr. Lee had just handed her the position she'd been aspiring to since coming to work for the company, and one that normally took two years at least to achieve. And that was only if you had landed and retained some big name accounts.

"Can I assume that you're happy about this promotion, Ms. Rivers?"

A smile covered Mya's face. "Yes, yes. I'm very happy about it, sir. You'll never know how much."

"I'm glad to hear it. As you know, with this promotion comes a new territory."

The smile on Mya's face dimmed. The territory she was

presently working included New Mexico, Oklahoma, and Louisiana. They were states that weren't too far from Texas and required little travel time. "Do you have any idea what my new territory will be?"

"Yes, we're assigning you to handle one of our newest accounts on the east coast. The company is located in Orlando and is an account we want to give special attention to and feel you're just the person to handle things."

Mya nodded. She didn't want to think about how she would break the news to Garrett about an increase in travel when he really didn't want her traveling at all.

"Will the increase in travel be a problem for you, Ms. Rivers?"

Mr. Lee's question interrupted her thoughts. Evidently the expression on her face had been a dead giveaway. "No. I'll have to make arrangements with my children's nanny. As you know my husband plays major league sports and sometimes he has to be gone away from home a lot, especially when football season begins. I need to make sure the lady who keeps my sons will always be available."

Mr. Lee nodded. "And if she isn't, you may want to find someone else. With this job comes a fifty thousand dollar increase in your annual salary, not to mention the bonuses you'll be able to earn."

Mya nodded. The promotion was a dream come true. She stood. "I appreciate the company's faith in my abilities." She then turned and walked out of Mr. Lee's office.

Later that evening Mya heard the hollering and crying the moment she entered the kitchen from the garage. She took one look at the kitchen and knew the Rivers boys had misbehaved. Tonight was Mrs. Butler's night off and Garrett had come straight home from football practice to feed the twins dinner. Evidently while he'd been preparing their meal, the two precious darlings had decided to throw the eggs she had boiled that morning against the wall.

"I'm home," she called out.

Garrett entered the kitchen with one son under each of his arms, like a sack of potatoes. The angry look that met hers challenged her to say something, anything. She refused to do so. She didn't even walk across the room to take her screaming sons from their father's clutches.

"Just look at the mess they made, Mya."

She glanced around. "I see. And I think the best thing to do is to make them clean it up. Don't you?"

Her voice had been soft and calm. So soft and calm that her sons immediately stopped screaming. Thinking it safe to do so, she walked over to Garrett and kissed his cheek. "Rough day, huh?"

"You don't know the half of it."

She looked up at him. What he wasn't saying and what he was probably thinking was that she should have been at home cooking dinner and watching the boys. He always claimed they behaved a lot better for her anyway. "How about if you leave these two with me and just go in the bathroom, run water in the tub, and relax. Let me finish dinner."

Garrett studied her for a moment. He was tempted to do just what she suggested. But then he glanced around the room and looked at the mess the twins had made. "No, that wouldn't be fair. You worked today just like I did. We'll clean this up together, then I'll help you fix dinner." He leaned over and whispered in her ear. "And once these two hoodlums are fed and in bed, you and I will both get in the tub and relax. How does that sound?"

She smiled at him. "Sounds like a wonderful idea," she said taking their sons from his arms. "You may want to consider the fact that the reason David and Daniel like throwing things is because they watch you throw footballs all the time and think it's okay to throw whatever they can get their grubby little hands on."

Garrett smiled at the thought of his sons trying to imitate him. "You think so?"

"Yes, but don't get all giddy over it. We have to find a way to explain to them the difference between throwing a football and throwing other things."

Garrett nodded. "Yeah, you're right." He reached out and took one of the twins, David, from out of her arms. "How was work today?"

Mya decided that now would not be a good time to tell him about her promotion. She wasn't sure when would be a good time. Since she wouldn't start traveling for another month or so, she decided to wait until after the cruise. "Work was fine. How was practice?"

"Things went okay. I think we're going to have a good season. We're going to try like hell to make it to the Super Bowl."

"And you will."

After David and Daniel had been placed in their chairs at the table with strict orders not to touch anything, Mya went into her husband's arms for the kiss she knew awaited her. She didn't like keeping secrets from him but the one about her promotion was a secret she was keeping in the name of peace.

CHAPTER SEVEN

Maxi Chandler buried her head in the pillow feeling sick. The ship had barely left dock and already queasiness had settled in her stomach. This was her first cruise and if she didn't start feeling better it would definitely be her last. She hoped she wasn't like some people who were sick the entire while. Seven days was a long time to be miserable.

She was counting on the medication the ship's doctor had given her taking effect before dinnertime. If nothing else it was making her feel drowsy. She had not seen any of her former classmates and she was grateful for that. She didn't want anyone to see her looking like she had a foot in death's door.

Evidently the ship had given her an upgrade since the cabin was larger than she had expected. And she couldn't help wondering why there was a double bed instead of two singles when she would be sharing it with a cabinmate, although she had no idea who the person was. That information had not been available when she'd checked in a few hours ago. Whoever the woman was, she must have decided to join the Bon Voyage party being held on deck. A party was the last thing on Maxi's mind. Surviving this cruise was.

She buried her face deeper into the pillow when another

bout of queasiness settled deep in her stomach. She hoped she wasn't about to throw up. She doubted she had the energy to make it to the bathroom if she was. She tightened her eyes shut and hoped and prayed for relief, and at the moment she thought that nothing could get worse than this.

Christopher stood in the doorway of his cabin and gazed upon the woman who was in his bed. Lying flat on her stomach with her face buried in the pillow, he couldn't see her features. But his gaze did a quick study of the delectable curves the shorts and tank top she was wearing couldn't hide. Not a bad view, he thought.

He then shrugged. It seemed that women getting into his bed uninvited were becoming a norm. He walked into the cabin closing the door behind him and glanced around. The cabin was modest by most means and he had selected it that way intentionally. His former classmates not knowing that he was now pretty well off financially would make the cruise interesting.

When he heard a slight moan he remembered the woman asleep on his bed. Or had she passed out from too much to drink? She must have begun partying before the ship had left Tampa. Somehow she had made it to the wrong cabin, and he intended to get her out.

He walked over to the bed, leaned over and tapped her on her shoulder. He thought about tapping her on her curvy backside, then decided against it. "Hey, you. Wake up. I think you're in the wrong cabin."

Getting annoyed when he didn't get a response, he tapped her again and repeated himself. *Finally,* he thought, when he noticed her body shifting as she tried raising her head off the pillow but had a hard time doing so. Christopher lifted a brow wondering just how many drinks she'd had. "Look here, lady, you can indulge in your hangover someplace else. I'd like to enjoy my cabin alone."

When she didn't give any type of response he decided to take matters into his own hands and flipped her over onto her back. He frowned. Even with her eyes tightly shut, her features looked awfully familiar. His gaze studied the roundness of her face, the firmness of her cheekbones, and the fullness of her lips. Christopher was caught off guard when at that very moment she forced her eyes open and looked up at him, straight into his direct gaze. Even after ten years recognition hit him immediately. It was hard for a guy to forget the girl he had fancied himself in love with through most of his adolescent years. "Maxi?"

Barely conscious from her drug-induced sleep, Maxi continued looking up at the man towering over her. She blinked once, then twice. He seemed to know who she was but at the moment everything appeared foggy and she couldn't make out who he was and why he was in her cabin.

"Maxi, are you all right?"

The sound of his voice was soothing, assuring. She attempted to nod but couldn't. She tried getting words out of her mouth but settled on the one word that described exactly how she felt. "Sick."

"You're sick?"

She tried nodding again but couldn't. She blinked a third time and the blurring in her eyes began clearing as her gaze stayed focussed on the man. She took in his facial features. Although she felt half-dead, and probably looked it as well, she could definitely make out the fact that he was attractive. Very attractive. And he looked very familiar.

"Like what you see, Maxine Chandler?"

She blinked again when she remembered that same husky voice and those identical words spoken to her one day years ago in school when she'd been caught staring. She forced herself to study his features more intently. "Christopher Chandler?"

He smiled down at her. "Yes, in the flesh."

She wished she had the energy to tell him he wasn't in the flesh when he had clothes on. Questions immediately began flooding her mind. But then another bout of queasiness hit her, this one worse than the others. She closed her eyes after mumbling softly. "I'm going to throw up, Christopher."

Her words prompted him into action when she placed her hand over her mouth. He quickly picked her up in his arms and carried her into the bathroom and lowered her in front of the commode where she immediately released her lunch from earlier that day. When her stomach was completely empty the first thing she thought was that maybe she would live after all— if she didn't die of embarrassment first. Of all the people to find her in such a sickly state and come to her aid, it had to be Christopher Chandler, the boy she'd had a crush on during her entire senior year of high school.

All thoughts fled from her mind when she heard the sound of the toilet being flushed, and felt strong firm hands picking her up off the floor and a warm washcloth wiping her face.

"Feeling better now, Maxi?"

"Yes, much better, thanks," she replied, as she looked into the face of the man who had been her rescuer. It had been ten years since she'd seen it last but those years seemed to have agreed with him. He was handsome as ever. "Christopher, what are you doing here?"

"I should be asking you the same thing."

She frowned. "I'm here for the class reunion cruise."

"So am I."

That information surprised Maxi. In fact if she hadn't been feeling so bad she would have laughed out loud at the absurdity of what he'd just said. He would have been the last person she would have expected to attend the class reunion since he'd never gotten along with the majority of their classmates. Most of them had been outright mean to him which made him retaliate with his anger, fists, or both. She'd always thought their mistreatment of him downright cruel and on numerous occasions had told them so, especially Ronald Swindel who'd been the class bully and who'd gone out of his way to make Christopher's life at school a living hell. Local rumor claimed that Christopher's mother had gotten pregnant from some sailor passing through town. Deborah Chandler, who had always lived on the wild and reckless side, found solace in other men, staying out late at night and at times gone for days, leaving Christopher to fend for himself. Since the kind of life he'd been born into hadn't been his fault, Maxi had never treated him the way the others had. Therefore, she felt completely comfortable in saying her next words. "I'm glad you came. It's good seeing you again, Christopher."

Christopher smiled as he stared down at her, looking for signs that somehow she'd changed over the years. But deep down he knew she'd remained, as she'd always been—a person who'd gotten along with everyone. A part of him felt the sincerity of her words. "It's good seeing you too, Maxi, but what's wrong with you?"

Maxi was grateful he had gotten her to the bathroom before she had thrown up on herself. "Motion sickness. I've never been on a cruise before. The ship's doctor gave me some pills to take and—"

"Why are you in my cabin?"

Maxi blinked. "I'm not in your cabin. This is my cabin."

Christopher frowned. "Are you sharing it?"

"No, I have a cabinmate. What about you?"

"I'm alone. That's the reason for the one bed."

"Oh. Do you think there could have been some sort of a mix-up?"

He couldn't help but grin. "Possibly. It wouldn't be the first time where you and I were concerned now would it?"

She shook her head, remembering. "Like the time the substitute teacher sent me to the principal's office to get a paddling you were supposed to get because she got our names mixed up?"

"Yeah, and like the time Mrs. Meadows gave you my grades and gave me yours. Boy, was that comical," he said laughing. The one thing he remembered about Maxine Chandler was that she was different from any of the kids in school. She had been one of the smartest but she had never acted stuck-up like the other kids had. Nor had she ever treated him like he was some sort of disease that might be contagious. He remembered the day Mr. Thompson had assigned the two of them to work together on a science project in their senior year. The other kids had teased her by saying working with him was an automatic zero. Instead of asking the teacher for another partner, she had ignored their classmates' words and jotted down the directions to her house for him, like there was nothing wrong with bad boy Chandler from ghettoville visiting her side of town where most of the middle and upper-class Blacks lived. Because Maxi had not put him down or asked that he be removed from the project, he had worked his butt off to make sure they had gotten a decent grade. He'd been just as surprised as she had when they made first place. Of course everyone figured she had done all the work and said as much. She tried convincing them otherwise, stating it had been a joint venture. But just the thought that she didn't try taking all the credit for the project had earned her his respect and admiration. It had also made him that much more infatuated with her. Leaving town after graduation had been for the best. There was no way that Maxine Chandler, the smartest girl at school—and he'd always thought, the prettiest—would have gotten involved with him.

"Let me get you back in bed while I find out what's the deal with our cabins."

Maxi marveled at how easily he was able to carry her in his arms as he gently placed her on the bed. She watched him cross the room and pick up the phone, thinking how good he looked in his designer jeans and shirt. They were a far cry from the tattered and worn-torn clothes he used to wear to school.

She studied his transition from boy to man. He had changed. Grown older. In her opinion his features had always been chiseled masculine perfection. Now they were even more so with his high cheekbones, strong chin, full lips, and straight nose. And there were lines around his eyes that hadn't been there before. He had gotten taller and the breadth of his chest and shoulders radiated power and strength. And as impossible as it may seem, he was more handsome than ever before. He'd said he was on the cruise alone. Did that mean he was still single? He wasn't wearing a wedding ring but that didn't mean anything these days.

He was so absorbed in making the phone call that he didn't look up for a long moment. It was long enough for her to continue her close study of him. His nose was slightly crooked from the time Ronald Swindel had broken it. Some say the two had been fighting over Lorraine Brown. Christopher had gotten a broken nose and Ronald had gotten a broken arm.

Maxi's gaze moved over him, downward. He was firm at his stomach and hip, and his muscular thighs were like tempered steel and looked like the type that could wrap themselves around a woman's waist and hips real tight while they made love. A deep tint covered Maxi's face. This was the first time she'd thought of a man in a sexual way since Jason's death. She inhaled deeply, thinking her racy thoughts must be the result of the medication she'd taken.

She forced her mind back to the real issue at hand—the mix-up of their cabins. From the conversation he was having on the phone with the cruise ship director, she got the distinct impression that he was a man who was used to being in authority, in control, and having his concerns taken care of to his satisfaction immediately.

"What did they say?" she asked when he had hung up the phone. She could see the frustrations outlined in his features. Evidently whomever he'd spoken to had told him something he hadn't wanted to hear.

"There was some sort of computer glitch. Since we have the same last name and were booked under the class reunion group, the system apparently assumed we were married and placed us in the same cabin."

"Oh," Maxi said. "But they are finding me another cabin, right?"

"They indicated they will try but according to the person I spoke with, this ship is booked to capacity. Their only hope is if there have been 'no shows,' and they won't know that until later this evening."

Maxi lifted a brow. "And if there aren't?"

Christopher sighed deeply before answering. "Then they will check to see if anyone who is paying for a single cabin wants a cabinmate."

"And what if no one does?" she asked, desperately.

He shook his head. A lot about Maxine Chandler hadn't changed. She still believed in asking a lot of questions. She used to drive their teachers batty with her constant stream of inquiries. But her endless questions had never bothered him. In fact those were the times he'd actually paid attention in class because he'd always liked hearing the sound of her voice, low-pitched and smooth. And then when he'd gotten to the age where he appreciated the opposite sex, he would enjoy watching her mouth move when she would ask her questions. Her mouth had the most delectable set of lips that he had ever seen on a woman. They were full, luscious, and soft and he'd always imagined, kissable. Even now the sight of them was holding his gaze captive.

"Christopher? What if no one does?" Maxi repeated, re-claiming his attention.

Then I guess we're stuck with each other for the next seven days. He felt a sense of panic surge through him as soon as that thought popped into his head. He didn't want to be stuck with Maxi or any woman for seven days. That fact had become crystal clear in his mind when Tori had made the suggestion to join him on the cruise. He didn't want any woman to invade his personal space and especially not the one lying on his bed watching him with those same gorgeous brown eyes he used to drool over in school. He needed to distance himself from Maxine Chandler and fast. Step away. Regroup. Get the hell out of there.

"I'm sure they'll find you adequate accommodations for the duration of the cruise," he heard himself say as he slowly began walking backward to the door. "I wouldn't worry about it. They should have at least one cancellation." He opened the cabin door. "I'm going to go personally talk to the ship's director. I'll take it to the captain if I have to. Don't worry about a thing. I'll be back later."

He then quickly left the room.

CHAPTER EIGHT

Maxi released a deep breath, unaware she'd been holding it until the door had closed shut behind Christopher. A part of her wondered if she had just dreamed the whole thing. Was bad boy Christopher Chandler actually here for their high school class reunion?

Although he'd always been nice to her in school, she had seen him in action with other students several times to know that he could be hell on a stick when he wanted to be. He'd carried a chip on his shoulder, a rather big chip; one placed there because of circumstances beyond his control and he had fought back the only way he'd known how. He had trusted no one and believed in nothing. And he had fought with a society that had scorned him. When he'd left Savannah a number of the locals had said "good riddance," but she had sadly thought, "what a loss," because during those six weeks they had spent working on their science project, she had gotten to know another side of him. It had been a side that had wanted to belong although he'd tried hard not to show it. And because of the time they had spent together and becoming what she thought of as friends, it had hurt when he'd left without saying goodbye.

She couldn't help wondering what he was doing after ten

years. Was he still fighting society or had he gone on to make something out of his life regardless of his less-than-desirable childhood?

Closing her eyes she began feeling drowsy again. She would let Christopher deal with getting them separate cabins since he didn't seem too pleased with their predicament. Right now all she wanted to do was sleep. She would deal with Christopher Chandler when she woke up.

Nancy Watson, the cruise ship director, thought that even her worst days hadn't prepared her for the likes of the man whose brooding dark eyes were boring into her. She held his gaze unswervingly, determined not to let him intimidate her any more than he already had. She had apologized for the computer mix-up at least a half dozen times but he still wasn't satisfied. And telling him that there were no vacant cabins had only fuelled his anger.

"Mr. Chandler," she said with smooth politeness, hiding with a plastic smile the aggravation that was eating her up. She refused to lose her cool, which could possibly mean losing her job as well. "I understand what happened has placed both you and Ms. Chandler in a very awkward situation. However, at the moment there is nothing we can do. We did contact a few of those with single cabins and the ones who have responded indicate they prefer their arrangements to remain as they are. We haven't heard from a few others yet, but will let you know as soon as we do."

Placing him in an awkward situation wasn't the half of it, Christopher thought. As a kid in grade school Maxine Chandler had fascinated him. As a teenager in high school she'd made him aware of his raging hormones. Now as a man there was no doubt in his mind that she could be the one woman who could get under his skin, and he wasn't about to let that happen.

"And what am I supposed to do in the meantime?" he snapped.

Nancy Watson didn't think he was a person who would appreciate being told what to do, but since he'd asked, she would oblige him. "You and Ms. Chandler evidently know each other since you're both in the same class reunion group. I suggest the two of you work something out. Although we don't make a habit of assigning opposite sexes to the same cabins, coed sleeping arrangements are common practice and maybe it will work for the two of you."

His gaze became hard as stone. "It won't work for the two of us. I'm a person who likes my privacy. Had I wanted a cabinmate, I would have requested one. Since I didn't I would appreciate it if you do whatever you can to see that I spend my time on board this ship the way I had intended. Alone."

Satisfied that he had made what he wanted absolutely clear, he walked out of the woman's office, then headed for the nearest bar, feeling the need of a stiff drink.

As he slipped onto a barstool he couldn't help wondering if someone up there didn't like him. The bartender came up to take his order. "Yes, sir, what would you like?"

"Brandy."

The bartender nodded and walked off. Christopher rested his arms on the counter and wondered what he would do if the ship's director wasn't able to find Maxi another room. The possibility of sharing a cabin with her was too much to consider. He hadn't been prepared for the sight of her, and he hadn't been prepared for those protective instincts he'd always had where she was concerned kicking in. And more than anything, he didn't like the way his body had responded to her when he had carried her into the bathroom. The last thing he wanted was to feel any kind of attraction to her.

And that was the crux of his problem.

It seemed he had known Maxi forever, and with each passing year as he got older and older, he couldn't help noticing things about her that went beyond the obvious sexual ones. Like the way she would always have something nice to say to him when the other kids did not, or the way she would try including him in school activities when the other kids would not have dared. And she never appeared intimidated by him like some of the other girls, at least the ones who weren't trying to talk him into taking them to bed. It had been amusing how during the day they would ignore him around school but then at night, some of those same girls would come around to where he lived and try and talk their way into his pants. And usually he would oblige them just for the hell of doing so. But not once had he allowed anyone to get close to the real Christopher Chandler.

Except for Maxi.

He sat there, listening to the faint sound of music in the background while he remembered that one particular night. After six weeks of spending the majority of their evenings together doing research on their project, they had done a test run on their experiment to make sure it worked. It had. Deciding to celebrate their success, Maxi suggested that they go grab a hamburger or something. However, not wanting to ruin her reputation by being seen out with him, he had talked her into ordering pizza instead. While sitting on her parents' back porch under a moonlit sky eating pizza and sipping Cokes, he had shared a side of himself that no one else knew. He had told her how he wanted to leave town and make something of himself and would work like hell to achieve that goal. She had said something to him that night that had forever touched him. *"Anyone can say what they want, but it will take hard work and sacrifices to actually get what you want. You'll have everything you want, Christopher, because you are strong and determined. I truly believe that because I believe in you and what you are capable of doing."*

She never knew how much her words had touched him. Throughout most of his life his dreams had been torn away from him. As a child he'd felt ashamed of who and what he was—the son of the woman who'd been known as the town's whore; a dirt-poor illegitimate kid that none of the other parents wanted their children to associate with. And then after the scandal involving his mother and the mayor broke out, things had gotten even worse. He would never forget reading the newspaper headlines about the sordid, sleazy affair. But with those words Maxi had spoken to him, she had given him pride. Not only pride but hope and deep determination to prove her right by becoming successful.

Although he'd left town the day after graduation without even telling her goodbye, he'd kept her words in the back of his mind all the while he'd worked part time while attending college full-time. And later when he and Gabe had taken over Regency Builders and later changing the name to The Regency Corporation, he had worked hard day and night to make it even more successful. So in a way he owed a part of his success to her.

But a part of him didn't want to feel beholden to anyone in Savannah, not even to Maxi. Sharing space with her was dangerous territory. That was the main reason he wanted her out of his cabin. Around Maxi he would need every ounce of his mental faculties. She had a way of making him not think straight. She had a way of making him remember things best left forgotten.

His thoughts were interrupted when the bartender returned with his drink. "Is there anything else I can get for you, sir?"

"No, this will be it." Christopher rolled his shoulders, aware of his tense muscles and wondering if he would get the relaxation on this cruise that he'd been counting on. For some reason he didn't think so.

Maxi groaned upon waking, accepting ruefully that she had not dreamed the entire thing and that a mix-up in the ship's computer had her and Christopher sharing a cabin . . . at least for the time being. Hopefully, he was getting the matter resolved and the ship would be able to accommodate her elsewhere.

She stretched, wondering how long she'd slept. Whatever

medication the ship's doctor had given her had certainly worked. She was feeling much better. Getting out of bed she went into the bathroom to wash out her mouth and brush her teeth, knowing doing both would make her feel even better.

Standing in front of the mirror she caught her reflection and thought of the situation she was presently in. *Christopher Chandler.* She shook her head incredulously. Of all people. But what she'd told him earlier had been true. She had been glad to see him and was glad he came. She hoped and prayed that during the last ten years their fellow classmates had matured, faced a few of life's challenges of their own, and were beyond holding anything against Christopher because of his less than humble beginnings.

She frowned. She knew for a fact that Ronald Swindel hadn't changed. He was still the egotistical jerk he'd been ten years ago, and even after three wives he still tried coming on to her whenever she ran into him in town. For some reason someone had fed him the lie that he was God's gift to women and he believed it. As a police officer he made it a point whenever he was in the vicinity of the university just to drop by and flirt with her when he could catch her in between classes. It had gotten to the point where she would dodge him whenever she saw him coming. He was intent on being the man to replace Jason in her life and had told her so on more than one occasion. What he refused to accept was that even if she was ready for anyone to replace Jason he would not be her top pick. The one thing she dreaded about this cruise was the fact that Ronald was somewhere on board. She knew it was highly unlikely their paths would not cross since they were scheduled to attend the same functions.

Maxi's current avenue of thoughts was interrupted with the ringing of the phone. Leaving the bathroom she moved across the cabin to answer it. "Yes?"

"Maxi, hi, this is Mya."

Maxi's face broke into a wide smile. "Mya, hey girl. It's good hearing your voice. It's been too long. How have you been?"

"I've been doing fine."

"And how are Garrett and the boys?"

"They're fine, too."

"Are you and Garrett all settled into your cabin?"

"Yeah, just about. What about you?"

"There's been a mix-up with my roommate assignment but I'm hoping the matter is cleared up soon." She decided not to tell Mya that she and Christopher Chandler had been assigned the same cabin by mistake. Being her best friend in high school, Mya had known about her infatuation with him during their senior year.

"If things aren't cleared up you can always stay here in the cabin with me and Garrett. We have a suite so it's plenty big enough."

"Thanks but I refuse to impose on the two of you. Things will work themselves out. Are you and Garrett going to the welcome reception tonight?"

"Yes, you?"

"Yes, now that my bout with motion sickness has passed."

"Garrett and I have decided to stay in and order dinner in our cabin. How about if the three of us meet on the upper deck to chat before the reception starts? Let's say thirty minutes before."

"Sounds like a wonderful idea. I'll see you then."

"All right. I'm looking forward to it."

"Same here."

As soon as Maxi hung up the phone there was a soft knock on the cabin door just seconds before it opened and Christopher walked in. Her breath caught in her throat. Now that she was feeling better and could see more clearly, the hard jolt of seeing him hit her. He was an imposing figure, but not an intimidating one and was even more handsome than she'd thought earlier. She actually felt herself feeling weak in the knees and her jaw went slack. His sable brown coloring brought everything about him into focus. His cheekbones were sharply defined and made his mouth all the more fascinating and provocative. His eyes were deep, dark, riveting. And his nose was decisively masculine and blended well with the strength of his jawbone. The combination of all his features reflected his African-American heritage and was totally male. She tried to downplay the quivering tension that began coiling in her stomach.

For years after he had left town she'd fantasized about him returning and how she would react if she were to accidentally bump into him one day on the streets of Savannah. But as time went by she knew he would never return and had accepted as much. She'd often wondered if he had remembered anything about the six weeks that they had spent working close together, sharing dreams and becoming what she had considered as friends. But when he'd left town without saying goodbye and never hearing from him again, she had accepted that the brief friendship they'd shared had meant everything to her but nothing to him.

Christopher paused as he stood in the doorway, studying Maxi as intently as she was studying him. Again he wasn't prepared for the sight of her. Earlier when he'd seen her, her features had been flushed from motion sickness. But now it was obvious that she was feeling better. Her face had a healthy glow. Her chocolate-brown features were clear, radiant, sculpted perfectly, and more beautiful than ever before. Maxine Chandler had grown up to be quite a looker.

Gone was the long, wavy hair that used to fan her shoulders. Her hair was cut short in a style that boasted sass and sophistication. And over the years her slender hips had filled out with nice womanly curves. He drew in a deep, steadying breath. His attraction to her was stronger than it had ever been before. He thought that was strange since ten years had passed since they had spent any time together. And during those ten years he had met and dated countless other women, but he'd never had to get a firm grip on himself or his emotions for any of them. As far as he was concerned, they were easy come, easy lay, easy go. Therefore, nothing could have prepared him for the emotions that were spiraling through him now. Emotions he'd thought a glass of brandy would straighten out. He hadn't been tormented with thoughts of Maxi for a good five years now. At least not since Mr. Thompson had written to tell him that Maxi had gotten engaged. Evidently something had happened since she was still using her maiden name and there wasn't a wedding band on her finger. Had she gotten a divorce?

He hoped not. In his opinion she was a woman who should be happily married. All she had ever talked about during those six weeks when they weren't working on the project was getting married and having babies. At the time he had thought that she deserved a man who could give her everything she wanted. A man who was solid, tender, loving, and respectable. Everything that he wasn't. That stark, cold realization was one of the reasons he'd known he had to leave Savannah. Not only to pursue his dreams but to put as much distance between him and the one woman he'd always wanted and could not claim as his.

Finally closing the door behind him he entered the cabin. He took a tentative step toward her, then stopped at what he considered was a safe distance between them. He couldn't allow what he'd felt upon opening the door and seeing her get next to him. However, as much as he wanted to deny the possibility, as much as he resented the fact, it seemed that fate had intervened and they were in trouble.

Deep trouble.

He decided the best way to deal with it was to make her aware of that fact as well.

"We have a problem, Maxi," he murmured finally.

CHAPTER NINE

Maxi's chest rose and fell with each labored breath as she met Christopher's unwavering gaze. Inwardly, she told herself that her attraction to him wasn't such a big deal. After all, she had lusted after him during her entire senior year of high school, probably even before then, but he'd never paid her any attention. However, what she couldn't dismiss was her sudden feeling of vulnerability. To be this attracted to a man you hadn't seen in over ten years couldn't be normal. And to make matters worse, she couldn't ever think of a time with Jason that he'd made her feel this tense to the point where she ached with an emptiness she hadn't known existed. As far as her encounter with Dr. Reginald Tanner, and any other men she'd dated since Jason's death, whatever attraction she'd felt for them didn't compare to the attraction she was feeling now for Christopher.

Several seconds ticked by before she realized she hadn't given Christopher a response to his statement. Wrinkling her brow, "What's the problem?" she asked in a voice that didn't even sound like her own.

Christopher paused before saying anything when he sensed

her uneasiness and nervousness. For a quick moment he wondered if he had been wrong about her. Had she been putting on a front all those years when she'd acted like she hadn't been afraid of him? Had she believed all those stories that had circulated around school about him that had been more fiction than fact? Had she thought he'd been nothing but a shiftless thug like everyone else did? There was only one way to find out.

"According to the ship's director there aren't any more cabins. So it looks like you and I are it," he responded in a clipped tone.

Maxi lifted her brow. "What do you mean we're *it?*"

"Just what I said. The ship can't correct their screw-up, which means you and I will have to share the cabin." He continued to watch her intently. "Unless you know of someone you can move in with for seven days."

Maxi released a deep sigh as she wrapped her arms around her body, clasping her elbows. "Mya and Garrett. You remember them don't you?"

At his slow nod, she continued. "They have a suite and Mya indicated it's big enough for another person but I don't want to intrude on them. But then I don't want to intrude on you either."

Christopher's eyes widened just a fraction. "You're concerned about intruding on me?"

"Of course. You evidently intended to spend time on this cruise alone, otherwise you would have gotten a cabinmate. The rates are certainly cheaper doing so."

He narrowed his eyes at her. "And that's the only reason you wouldn't share a cabin with me because you think you'd be intruding?"

Maxi shrugged. "I'm not sure. Are you married?"

"No."

"Engaged?"

"No."

"Wanted by the police for any reason?"

Christopher lifted a brow. "No."

"Okay, now I'm sure. My not wanting to intrude would be the only reason."

Christopher shook his head, not sure whether to believe her or not. He decided not to. He took a step forward and grabbed her shoulders. "Tell me the truth," he said, gritting the words through clenched teeth. "Admit the reason you wouldn't think of sharing this cabin with me is because you're afraid of me. After all, I was scum in school. What makes you think I'm any different now?"

Christopher felt a hard fist punch him in the gut, literally knocking the air out of him. He released Maxi immediately. "Why the hell did you do that for?" he barely got out through his lungs.

Maxi took a step forward and got all into his face. Her eyes flashed in anger. "Because you've never acted like an ass around me before, and I would appreciate if you didn't start acting like one now. The very idea that I'm afraid of you is ludicrous, Christopher Chandler."

Christopher shook his head. This was a side of Maxi Chandler he'd never seen. Around him she'd always been sweet, meek, and mild. She certainly never went around punching guys in the stomach when they got her pissed off about something. "And why is it ludicrous?"

"Because it is."

"Why?"

Instead of answering Maxi took a step back and gave them space. However, it was space Christopher didn't intend for them to have. He took a step forward and stood directly in front of her. "Why is it ludicrous, Maxi?"

Maxi's lips parted slightly on an indrawn breath, filled with apprehension. The tables had been turned. Now he was all in her face—eyeball to eyeball.

"Answer me and I want the truth," he said, his eyes darkening just a fraction as he stared at her.

"Because," Maxi snapped, reaching what she felt as her limit with him. "I know you would never hurt me or take advantage of me. So why should I be afraid of you?"

Christopher paused for a moment. Maxi's voice had been filled with such conviction that he became edgy with the notion that anyone thought they knew him that well, especially someone who hadn't seen him in ten years. "You don't know me, Maxi. For all you know I may not be the same person. I could be a rapist, an axe-murderer, a con-man, or a—"

"I asked if you were wanted by the police didn't I?" she asked, spitting mad as her brown eyes flared with mesmerizing intensity.

Christopher's jaw twitched in anger. Totally frustrated, he dragged his hand across his face. Did she actually believe he would have admitted to having a criminal record even if he had one? He then shook his head. "Are you this trusting with everyone?"

"Only with people I know," she responded easily.

His eyes narrowed. "And you think you know me?"

Hers narrowed right back. "Yes."

His gaze held hers. She was right. She did know him. Even after ten years she could still see beyond his outward appearance and look deep within, right into his very soul. That was something no one else had ever done or had ever tried doing. In their senior year of high school, she had discovered more about him than people who'd known him all his life, because she hadn't been judge, jury, and hangman. Instead she had offered him something no one else had—friendship. Whether she knew it or not, during the time they had spent working close together, she'd become the closest thing to a best friend he'd had before Gabe. And that was the main reason he'd left Savannah. He had wanted more than just her friendship and had known he hadn't deserved to even think of anything more.

"Ten years is a long time," he finally said. "I could have changed, Maxi."

She refused to buckle to the intensity of his stare. "You have changed, Christopher. Everyone changes with time. But with some things we remain the same. You haven't changed in the ways I believe count the most."

"How can you be so sure?"

A part of Maxi was getting fed up with his line of questioning. Although she knew he wasn't the same person she had fallen hard for in their senior year of high school, like she'd told him, there were certain things about him that were the same. "For one reason, because of the way you handled me earlier, when I was sick. You could have been rude to me but you weren't. And I know the only reason you weren't was because even after ten years you still consider me a friend. Right?"

Christopher knew that he could tell her she was wrong and end her goody-goody-two-shoes beliefs about him then and there. But what good would that do when she *was* right? In fact she didn't know just how right she was. He would never, ever hurt one single strand of hair on Maxine Chandler's head and he wouldn't stand by and let someone else do it either.

"Right, Christopher?" Maxi repeated.

He crossed his arms over his chest and gazed down at her. "I'm not sure. Are you married?"

She lifted a brow. "No."

"Engaged?"

He knew he had asked the wrong question when faint lines of pain appeared around her eyes and mouth. "Not anymore. Jason was killed by a drunk driver a week before our wedding," she said softly.

He said nothing for a few moments because frankly he didn't know what to say. The man she had planned to marry had died a week before doing so. For that reason, and that reason alone he didn't really feel bad because a part of him was still possessive where Maxi was concerned. But then again, by losing the man she intended to marry evidently set her back with having the family she'd always wanted. And because he knew just how much having a husband and children meant to her, for that reason alone he was sorry for her loss. "I'm sorry. That must have been hard on you."

"Yes, it was," she said softly. "But it happened four years ago. Jason was a very special person. You would have liked him."

Christopher shrugged. He doubted it but decided not to tell her that. He knew for a fact he would not have liked any man Maxi had loved enough to share her life with forever. "So, are you wanted by the police for any reason?" he asked.

Maxi blinked at the abrupt change back to their earlier topic of conversation. He was interrogating her like she had done him earlier. After concentrating on his question she thought about Ronald Swindel. "Yes, I'm wanted by the police but not the way you think."

He lifted a dark brow. "Is there any other way?"

"Yes. Ronald Swindel, remember him? He's a police officer and for some reason he's envisioned the two of us having a future together," she said smiling faintly.

Christopher frowned. "Don't tell me he's still sniffing behind you like he used to."

"He never sniffed behind me."

"Yes he did. Your face was too buried in books to notice."

Maxi raised eyes heavenward. "But you noticed?"

"Damn right I noticed."

Her brows drew together. "Why?"

"Because," he said quietly as a smile tilted the corners of his mouth. "My face wasn't too buried in books not to notice."

He decided not to add that during that time his face was too busy watching her. Unfortunately, he hadn't been the only one. Ronald Swindel had been watching her too. One day they both caught the other watching. Each had read the other's thoughts and they'd been arch-enemies since. Ronald Swindel had gotten royally pissed when he'd been the one assigned to work closely with Maxi on the science project.

"So, are you going to be my cabinmate for a week?" he asked, dismissing Ronald Swindel from his mind.

She crossed her arms over her chest. "I'll think about it."

"You may not have a choice."

"There's always Mya and Garrett."

"Three's a crowd."

Maxi tipped her head to one side and looked at him. "Why the change of heart? I got the distinct impression that you wanted to spend time on this cruise alone."

Christopher shrugged. He'd had that distinct impression himself. "You need a place to stay and I'm willing to make a sacrifice. For old times' sake."

"Fine. Great. You do whatever you want for old times' sake," she said poking him in the chest. "But you owe me an explanation about one thing that has bothered me for the last ten years."

Christopher picked up on the fact that Maxi's anger was brewing again. He took a step back just in case she got the urge to get violent once more. "What?"

"You left town without telling me goodbye. I deserved better."

Christopher's heart gave two hard knocks against his ribs. That had been the very reason he had left without telling her goodbye. Because he'd known she had deserved better, too, and that meant anyone other than him. Damn it, she should have been able to figure out that the reason he had left was because he had cared for her more than he should have. All it took was one look at her expression to know she evidently had not figured it out.

He dipped his hands in his pockets, not knowing what he could tell her and decided now was not the time to tell her the truth. "I had my reasons for doing things that way, Maxi."

After a few tense, silent moments she asked, "Is that all you're going to say about it?"

The hurt he heard in her voice got through to him. It was real and for the second time that day he'd been thrown for a loop. He took a deep intake of breath, feeling the need for another drink. "Yes, that's all I'm going to say about it."

He took her hand in his. "Let's drop it and go get something to drink."

CHAPTER TEN

Garrett Rivers drew in a deep fortifying breath as he stood over the bed and gazed down at his wife. After they had eaten dinner in their cabin, Mya had slipped into a sexy white lacy gown. Now she was in bed waiting for him and the sight of her pulled everything male about him to the forefront. Her breasts, firm and full, were veiled by embroidered lace. She was reclining on her back and the gown she wore had slits on both sides, exposing the smooth length of her long legs.

He removed his robe and slipped into bed beside her, drawing her into his arms. "Just me and you, baby, for seven days."

Mya chuckled softly as she was encompassed in her husband's warm embrace. Their sons were with their paternal grandparents and had plenty of cousins to keep them company. Like Garrett she was grateful for this time alone, just the two of them. The last six months had been hectic ones. It seemed one football season had barely ended before it was time to start training for another. And then her job with Monahan Investments had kept her pretty much on the go.

"I think we should make the most of our time alone, don't you?" she asked, seconds before leaning over and joining her mouth to his. He allowed her time to do things her way before seizing control. His lips became aggressive and took over, becoming hot, hungry, demanding.

Mya's body tingled in every place and blood rushed fast and rapidly through her veins, making her emotions whirl. Even after a lengthy courtship and the longevity of their marriage, Garrett could still make her want him with a need that went beyond anything rational. It was downright crazy. Whenever she was in his arms she enjoyed every single minute of the excruciating madness. He had the ability to give her the ultimate in sexual pleasure. He had a way of making her feel loved, wanted, and sexy.

She protested softly when his lips left hers to nibble at her earlobe before searing a path down her neck and shoulders. The touch of his mouth on her skin sent a shiver through every part of her body.

"Dinner was great," he whispered huskily as a smile hovered at the corners of his lips. He began removing her gown. "But now I want dessert."

Instant heat pooled in Mya's lower body and tempestuous steam simmered through her mind when Garrett began branding her entire body with his kisses. The pit of her stomach clenched with mindless, desire-driven passion and the toes of her feet actually curled from such demanding, sensuous assault. The flame that her husband could effortlessly ignite within her roared to blazing intensity. This is what she wanted. This is what she needed. This mind-blowing closeness, this hauntingly beautiful form of intimacy she had always been able to share with the man who had complete ownership of her heart.

All thoughts scattered to the wind when their bodies joined as one, the way their lives had been for what seemed like forever. Garrett established their pace, first fast, then slow, then fast again, repeating the process, feeding their need and fanning the fires blazing within them. Faster. Deeper. Harder.

Gasping for breath, before her world shattered into a zillion passionate pieces, Mya reached up and bracketed Garrett's face with her hands and stared deep into his eyes as he pumped his body into hers, the turgid length of him sensuously stroking her with relentless passion.

She whispered, "I love you," just moments before his strong, masculine body plunged deeper into hers, triggering every part of her into a delicious erogenous spin and sending her body, as well as his own, into a shattering climax that both of them wanted, needed, and treasured.

Mya listened to the sound of her husband's even, peaceful breathing and with a deep satiated sigh, she snuggled her body closer to his. Even in sleep his arm reached out and wrapped around her, bringing her closer.

She smiled upon remembering the first time she had met Garrett. She was in the ninth grade and his family had moved to Savannah from New York. The memory of that day was still so clear in her mind.

She had just walked out of her English class and had accidentally bumped into him. She'd been so embarrassed and to make matters worse he was with Elizabeth Standish, the prettiest and most popular girl at school. She'd known immediately that he was the guy all the girls had been whispering about lately. The good-looking, well-built brother with a northern accent who could play really good football. After mumbling her apology about being so clumsy she had quickly walked off. But later when school ended that day he had approached her at her locker.

"Hi, Mya," he said as he leaned against the locker next to hers. "You dropped this earlier."

She nodded and took the writing pad he was handing to her, wondering how he knew her name. "Thanks for returning it. My homework assignment for Ms. Bishop is in here. She can be a real pain if you don't turn in your homework."

"Really?" he asked smiling. "Then it's a good thing I ran into you today. I'm in Mrs. Bishop's third period class and English isn't my best subject. Maybe the two of us can get together and study after school sometime, whenever I don't have football practice." After a brief few moments he asked. "Do your parents let guys come over to visit you . . . to study?"

Mya's eyes blinked with surprise at what he was suggesting. "You want to come over to my house to study with me?"

"Yes. I would like to get to know you better."

She didn't say anything for a moment as she tried to give her frenzied mind time to catch up with her racing heart. "But what about Elizabeth Standish? I saw the two of you together today."

"Elizabeth has been nice enough to show me around since I got here."

Mya tried covering her chuckle with a cough wondering if he really believed that. Word was out around school that Elizabeth had dibs on him.

"So what about it, Mya? Will your parents allow me to come over and visit you?"

She shrugged. "I don't know. No guy has ever asked to come visit me before. My parents are deceased and I live with my grandmother. She probably wouldn't mind it if it were for us to study together. I'm only fifteen so she wouldn't let you come see me for any other reason."

He nodded. "Okay. Then I'll ask your grandmother if I can come visit you so we can study together."

And he'd done just that. That day he had walked her home from school and made it a point to meet her grandmother. Gramma Twila had been impressed with him the moment she'd met him, saying he was such a mannerable young man and gave him permission to come back and visit, but only when she was home.

That day began a courtship that carried them from junior high school, through senior high, and right on through college. They had celebrated the excitement of his first football game and winning touchdown, and had celebrated him achieving his dream when he'd signed up to play pro ball. He had kept the promise he'd made to her grandmother to always be good to her, take care of her and make her happy.

Everything about their marriage was good, both in and out of bed. They had two beautiful sons and she loved her husband as much today as she did the day she had married him. But a part of her felt a thin, slender thread was beginning to unravel. She knew he would not be happy with the news of her promotion since it meant more time away from home.

Mya sighed deeply, not wanting to think about that now. She was determined that they have their seven days of glorious bliss, and then when they returned to Dallas she would tell him. She leaned over and brushed her lips against Garrett's. She would let him sleep a while longer before waking him up to get dressed for the welcoming reception. She looked forward to seeing all her old friends again . . . especially Maxi.

This cruise would be the perfect time for her and Maxi to have a long talk and finally get to the root of the problem that had existed between them for quite a while. It was a bone of contention they had tiptoed around for years. A chasm had widened their relationship ever since the time they had left to attend separate colleges, causing a rift in their special friendship. It was time for them to sit down and talk about it. Although they had seen each other occasionally over the years whenever she had come to Savannah to visit her grandmother or Garrett's parents, things hadn't been the same, although they'd both tried pretending that they were. They had skirted around the issue for close to ten years. Now it was time to bring it out in the open and deal with it like two mature women and not two overwrought, emotional teenagers. More than anything she wanted to recapture that special friendship, that unique closeness and bond they had shared from day one when they had both been seven years old. And she believed it could be done. They had too much history together not to try. More than anything she wanted her best friend back.

CHAPTER ELEVEN

"So, Christopher, what have you been doing for the past ten years?"

Mentally running through an answer that he could give Maxi without deliberately lying gave Christopher pause. No matter what type of friendship they may have shared in the past, he wasn't quite ready to tell her everything just yet. "After I left Savannah I headed up north, to Detroit, and found work with a construction company there. Basically, I've been associated with the outfit ever since." He leaned back in his chair. What he'd just told her wasn't a total lie. It wasn't the complete truth either.

Maxi nodded, finding it amazingly easy to relax and enjoy Christopher's company, now that they had cleared the air between them earlier in the cabin. They had found a table in the back of one of the restaurants on board ship. Christopher had ordered a small glass of brandy and she had settled for a tropical drink. "So, what do you do at this construction company? Build things?"

He smiled over his glass at her thinking of all the upscale shopping malls and office parks that The Regency Corporation had built over parts of the United States within the last four years. The Landmark Project, their latest huge business venture, involved building several ski resorts, the first of which would be in Alaska.

"Yes, we build things." After taking a sip of his drink he asked. "What about you? Did you ever make it to Howard University?"

Maxi couldn't help noticing how the rays from the sun shining through a nearby window shone on Christopher, highlighting his sable brown coloring. She also noticed other things as well—like how his fingers, that appeared so innately strong, were curved gently around the bowl of his brandy glass. "Yes. I spent four years there, earning a degree in African-American studies. Then I returned home and got my graduate degree at Savannah State."

"Was it hard leaving Washington to return to Savannah?"

"What you should be asking me is if it was hard leaving Savannah and moving to Washington. My father died a couple of weeks before I was to report to Howard and that was hard on me. As you know, Dad and I were close."

Christopher nodded as he took another sip of his drink. He had liked and respected her father. The older man had made him feel welcome on the occasions that he had visited. "I'm sorry to hear about your father, Maxi." He'd known about Mr. Chandler's death from Mr. Thompson's updates. But at the time he had just gotten settled in his new life in Detroit and had been determined to put Maxi out of his mind.

"Thanks, Christopher." She looked down at her drink as she twirled the straw around in it. "What made matters worse was that Mya decided at the last minute not to go to Howard University with me. She followed Garrett to Texas Southern instead. That was something I hadn't counted on and the news nearly crushed me. Especially after all the plans the two of us had made." She released a long sigh as she remembered that time and the impact it had on her and Mya's friendship.

"Needless to say, I ventured to a new city and started a new phase of my life alone. Although it may not have been hard for some people, it was a big adjustment for me. I had grown up in Savannah all my life and felt comfortable with the people and my surroundings. Washington was totally different. The diversity in the culture as well as the attitudes of the people were totally overwhelming. It was hard for me to blend in at first."

Christopher studied her as he listened to what she was sharing with him. In a way he understood. When he had made it to Detroit he had found it overwhelming as well. But he had always been a loner and hadn't ever wanted to blend in and knew with Maxi it was different. By nature she was an outgoing person who made friends easily.

"I find it hard to believe you had trouble blending in, Maxi. You're the type of person who could blend in anywhere and with anyone. You have that air about you; that warm southern hospitality wherever you go," he said softly, the dimples in his cheeks extending into a smile.

"Well, I did have a hard time," she said dryly, remembering that time. "I got the roommate from hell; a spoiled brat whose father was a politician with clout. She decided I was a person no one should like and made sure no one did. For half a semester most of the people in the dorm wouldn't talk to me. Things got a lot better after my roommate popped up pregnant the second semester. Her father sent her out of the country for a while. I eventually moved off campus into an apartment and got a male roommate, a guy by the name of Wilson Harris. Wilson was smart as a whip, easygoing and fun to be around. He was also gay, which was something he wasn't ready to share with the rest of the world quite yet. And because he was so drop-dead gorgeous, no one had a clue. The two of us living together gave him the ruse he needed to keep his family in the dark for a while. It also gave me a chance to escape unwanted suitors since a lot of people assumed Wilson and I were an item. I discovered that a male roommate worked out better for me than a female. Wilson and I roomed together until we finished college. During those years we became good friends."

Christopher took another sip of his drink. No wonder she had found their co-ed sleeping arrangements on the cruise comfortable. "Do the two of you still stay in contact?"

"Yes, he writes to me often. He and his partner are living in Los Angeles and he's extremely happy."

"Did his family ever find out about his alternative lifestyle?"

"Yes. They gave him a hard time at first but eventually they came around. I'm glad they did. It had been hard for Wilson to deceive them for those three years."

"So what do you do now?" he asked smoothly, from genuine interest.

"I'm a college professor. I teach African-American history at Savannah State and totally love my job. It's very fulfilling and rewarding to educate students about things in our history that they didn't know about. This summer I'm teaching a special class on great African-American women."

"Sounds interesting." He checked his watch. "Are you planning to attend the function the class is having tonight?"

"Yes. You?"

"No. The only function I plan to attend is the reunion banquet the last night."

Maxi nodded. "I guess I better go back to the cabin and get dressed. Will you give me about thirty minutes alone to do that?"

"Yes."

"Thank you." She stood. "And thanks for buying me a drink." She turned and walked off.

For long moments after she left, Christopher continued sitting at the table alone, gazing out a nearby window, watching the blue-green waters of the Gulf of Mexico and going back over in his mind his conversation with Maxi. So much for his determination not to let her get under his skin. His intentions made little difference whenever he listened to her talk. Her voice was still soft and enticing. It could lead a man to all kind of irrational thoughts.

Doomed. He felt doomed.

CHAPTER TWELVE

Maxi had put the finishing touches on her hair and makeup and had slid into her dress when there was a soft knock on the cabin door. "Yes?"

"Are you decent?"

She smiled at Christopher's deep familiar voice. "Yes, just about. But come on in. You can help me with the zipper."

Christopher slowly opened the door and stepped inside, not sure what he would find. Again he was surprised but really should not have been. Maxi was a beauty. He had discovered that fact in the first grade. But what he hadn't counted on was her still being the most beautiful female he had ever seen twenty-two years later. But she was.

After leaving her face his gaze went first to her hair, liking the way she had combed it back away from her face with a beautiful white flower pinned to the side above her ear. In his mind the style made her look like an island princess. When she noticed where his attention had strayed, she said, "The welcome reception. It's a tropical theme. That's the reason for the flower."

A little smile touched his lips. "Oh."

He then moved his gaze down to her feet, which were encased in white open-toe sandals. She had pretty toes, he thought. They were polished a bright red. He'd never had a fetish for a woman's feet before but the sight of hers could definitely turn a man on. They seemed soft, cuddly, sexy.

His gaze then moved to take in her dress. It was a tropical print silk that looked as soft as a summer's breeze, and the way it swayed around her body clearly showed all her feminine curves. He took a step toward her, suddenly deciding he didn't want her going to the welcome reception without him.

"Are you going to stand there or are you going to come over here and zip me up?"

Maxi's question brought him back around. He crossed his arms over his chest as he looked at her intently. "I'm not Wilson Harris, Maxi."

She lifted a brow. "Meaning what?"

He took another look at her from head to toe. Slowly. Deliberately. He wanted her to feel his gaze touch her like an intimate caress. It worked. He saw the way her breathing went from even to uneven, the way the pupils in her eyes darkened and the way her lips parted when she released a breathless sigh.

"Meaning you can't feel as comfortable in sharing space with me like you did with him," Christopher said huskily. "Where he may not have been interested in you as a woman, that does not hold true for me. Fair warning."

Her gaze met his for a long moment. "Warning taken," she said before turning around and presenting her back to him. "Now zip me up, please."

He closed the distance between them, wanting to do more than zip up her dress. A few ideas came into his head but he forced them out. Standing this close he was getting the full effect of her perfume. Alluring. Seductive. Feminine. His hand trembled as he eased up the zipper, especially when he could tell she wasn't wearing a bra. He stepped back before he was tempted to do something stupid. "All done."

Maxi slowly turned around to face him. "Thanks." She then

noticed his attention had shifted to the beds. "They came and changed the sleeping arrangements. The bed had been two singles and they pulled them apart to make them up separately. I think the way they have them arranged now is sufficient, don't you? I'll take the one closest to the window. You can take the one closest to the door."

His gaze returned to her as the corners of his lips curved upward in a smile. The beds were not in close proximity to each other. They were separated in the middle by a long dresser and the bathroom. If she got the one by the window, there would not be a reason for him to cross into her area unless he had something on his mind. "Yes, I think the way they have them arranged is sufficient."

Maxi picked up her purse from the dresser. "I'm meeting Mya and Garrett a little early on the upper deck. I'll see you later."

Christopher gave the doorway Maxi walked through a disapproving glare. He then quickly moved into the bathroom to take a shower, deciding to make an appearance at the welcome reception after all.

CHAPTER THIRTEEN

Mya walked out on deck and was met by the scent of the ocean and the sight of Garrett looking out over the waters. As if he sensed her presence, he turned around. His gaze captured hers and he smiled, opening his arms to her. She automatically went into them.

"Sorry I kept you waiting."

He studied her outfit, a pair of white loose-fitting linen slacks and a matching white linen shell. "It was well worth the wait, sweetheart. You look gorgeous."

His compliment pleased her. "Thanks, Garrett." She glanced around. They were early. "Have you run into anyone we know yet?" she asked as they began strolling along the deck.

Garrett's face pinched into a frown. "I ran into Ronald Swindel. He was looking for Maxi. He claimed to have called her cabin and a man answered so he hung up. He figured there must have been some sort of mix-up."

Mya nodded thoughtfully. "I believe there was. Maxi mentioned it to me earlier. She must have gotten switched to another cabin or something."

"That explains it then, although I'm sure she would just as well not have gotten a call from Ronald. He hasn't changed at all. He still brags on himself and thinks he's all that. I have a feeling he's still interested in Maxi after all these years."

Mya shook her head smiling. "Well, Maxi was never interested in him. She only had eyes for one guy back then."

Garrett lifted a brow. "Who?"

"Christopher Chandler."

Garrett released a soft chuckle. "Too bad Chandler didn't know that."

"Why?"

"Because he only had eyes for Maxi."

Mya stopped walking and looked at her husband, surprised. "You're kidding, right?"

"No, I'm not kidding. All the guys knew it. That's why none of them bothered to hit on Maxi. Christopher was like a watchdog protecting her. And since he had started school late and was two years older than the rest of us—with a bad reputation for kicking butt, too—everyone took heed of his warnings. The only person who didn't was Ronald. That's why he and Christopher knocked heads so many times."

"Wow, I never knew. Neither did Maxi."

Garrett gave his wife a warm smile. "That's understandable. Back then Maxi had her eyes glued to the books and you had your eyes glued to me. Neither of you were very observant to other things going on around you."

Mya laughed. "I guess we weren't." She and Garrett began walking again. "We used to have some good times together, me and Maxi. They were the greatest."

"Yeah, everyone used to call the two of you M and M candy because you were so close."

"I remember. It was so good having a girlfriend who you could share things with. We used to tell each other everything."

"Yeah, I know," he said solemnly, taking her hands into his. "And that's the reason the two of you lost what you had. I convinced you not to tell her what was going on with us that summer and why you changed your plans about Howard University." He gazed down at his wife. "And to this day you never told her, have you?"

Mya shook her head. "No, I promised you that I wouldn't tell anyone."

"I think it's time you told her."

They stopped walking again. She looked up at Garrett. She wouldn't tell him that she had thought that very same thing. "Why?"

"Because it's time for the two of you to recapture what you once had. You and Maxi had a very special friendship, one few people can boast of sharing with another individual. You were closer than sisters. There was nothing she wouldn't do for you or you wouldn't do for her. I think this cruise provides the perfect opportunity for you and Maxi to patch things up."

He glanced over her shoulder. "Here she comes. After I say hello I'm going to leave the two of you alone. I'll catch up with you when it's time for the reception to begin. All right?"

Mya nodded. She then reached upward and kissed him on the lips. "Thanks for being the love of my life."

He smiled. "Thanks for being the love of mine."

They then moved forward to greet their old friend.

Garrett swept Maxi up into his arms, lifting her easily off her feet. "It's good seeing you again, Maxi-million," he said, calling her by the nickname he'd given her years ago. He kissed her on the cheek.

She curved her arms around him and hugged him. "Same here, Garrett. You still look good and although I still don't like football, I always tune in when I know you're playing."

He laughed as he released her. "That makes me feel special."

"You are." Maxi then turned to Mya and smiled. She was flooded with memories of the first day they had met. Even without all those braids, Mya practically looked the same. At twenty-eight her cute and adorable features had transformed into those of a beautiful woman with satiny brown skin, chocolate-colored eyes with a noticeable slant to them, huge dimples in both her cheeks, and a head of luxurious black hair that fanned around her shoulders. "Hi, Mya Ki'Shae."

Mya grinned. "Hi, yourself, Maxine Jeanae."

The two gave each other a warm embrace. "It's so good seeing you, Maxi," Mya said, holding back the tears in her eyes. "We have so much to catch up on, don't we?"

Maxi wiped the tears from her own eyes. "Yes, we do."

"I'll see you ladies later," Garrett said to them.

"Hey, you don't have to run off," Maxi said, smiling up at him.

Garrett returned her smile. "I'm not going far. I'll meet back up with you two at the reception." He turned to leave, then turned back around when he thought of something. He flashed Maxi a wide grin. "Oh, by the way, Maxi-million, Ronald Swindel was looking for you. Thought I'd give you fair warning."

"Thanks. I appreciate it." Maxi shook her head. That was the second fair warning she'd received that day.

Mya touched Maxi's arm, reclaiming her attention. "Come on."

Maxi lifted a brow. "Where are we going?"

Mya smiled softly. "Someplace where we can fix something that should never have gotten broken."

Maxi stared at Mya. "What?"

"Our friendship."

CHAPTER FOURTEEN

Maxi and Mya found an isolated spot in a restaurant located near one of the pools. Most people were either at dinner or savoring the nightlife since the ship offered a great variety of entertainment choices. They didn't call it the "Fun Ship" for nothing.

Sitting down at one of the tables they ordered a tropical drink for Maxi and a glass of white wine for Mya.

Maxi immediately picked up on Mya's nervousness. She reached across the table and firmly gripped her hand. "What's this about, Mya?"

A wry smile formed on Mya's lips as she studied their joined hands. She then met Maxi's gaze. "I owe you an explanation as to why I didn't go to Howard University with you."

Pulling her hand away Maxi slumped back in her chair. "No, you don't. It's in the past."

Mya shook her head. "No, it's not, Maxi, and we both know it."

Maxi stared at her for a long moment before saying. "Why now, Mya? Why do you want to tell me now after ten years? Why couldn't you have told me then?"

Mya shifted her gaze to an object on the other side of the room.

Moments later she returned her gaze to Maxi. "Because I couldn't. It was a secret Garrett and I couldn't share with anyone."

Maxi stared at Mya thoughtfully, wondering what it could have been. She and Mya had shared everything. There had never been any secrets between them. "And you can tell me now?"

Mya nodded. "Yes. Garrett and I think you should know. Hopefully you'll understand why I did what I did and find it in your heart to forgive me. I know changing my mind at the last minute about going to Howard messed things up for you in a lot of ways."

Mya waited for the waiter to place their drinks in front of them and leave before she began talking again, recalling that time right after they had graduated from high school. She met Maxi's gaze. "You know Garrett and I were sexually active."

Maxi nodded. "Yes." She'd known that Mya and Garrett had started sleeping together at the beginning of their senior year in high school.

"We'd always been careful but the night before he was to leave to began training at Texas Southern, we got kind of careless and he didn't use a condom."

Maxi raised a brow but said nothing.

"When I missed my period the next month I was fairly certain I was pregnant. You had gone on that trip with your parents to New York to visit your aunt and uncle, so I didn't have you around to talk to about it, and Garrett was in Texas. When he called one night I told him my suspicions, and he made up some excuse with his coach so he could come back home to see me."

Mya took a sip of her wine to relieve the sudden dryness in her throat before she continued. "Neither of us knew what to do so we went and talked to Coach Johns." Coach Johns had been Garrett's football coach and his mentor during high school. He had been instrumental in Garrett getting a full football scholarship to Texas Southern.

"Coach Johns explained to us that if Garrett married me because I was pregnant he would lose the scholarship. He suggested that I go somewhere and have an abortion."

A soft gasp escaped Maxi and she sat up straight in her chair. She should not have been surprised by what the older man had suggested. Mya had told her several times that Coach Johns thought Garrett's relationship to Mya was too serious and should take a back seat to his career in football. "Did you . . . get an abortion?"

Mya let out an audible sigh. "You know me better than that. And Garrett wouldn't hear of such a thing either. He got upset with Coach Johns for even suggesting it."

"So what did you do?"

"Garrett and I decided to get married anyway. Coach Johns wasn't happy about it but he helped us to make all the arrangements. Everything was done in secret. No one knew. Not my grandmother or his parents. Not anyone. Coach Johns said we had to keep it that way because if anyone found out, Garret would be stripped of his scholarship and get kicked out of college, destroying his dream of becoming a professional football player. The only persons who knew we were married were Coach Johns and the retired judge, a personal lady friend of his, who performed the ceremony but made sure it never became a part of public records."

Mya took another sip of her wine. "Needless to say it was a false alarm and a few weeks later I discovered that I wasn't pregnant after all. But it proved to me just how much Garrett loved me and just how much he was willing to give up for me. That made me love him just that much more, Maxi. We were glad I wasn't pregnant but since we were married he wanted me with him at Texas Southern, which was understandable."

She leaned back in her chair. "At first I had thought about telling him I couldn't go to Texas Southern, but Garrett had been under a lot of stress about making the team, and our marriage only escalated his worries. With me attending Howard, all he could visualize were skyrocketing phone bills between us and countless flights between campuses for us to be together whenever we could. He didn't want that because there was no way we could afford it. He wanted me with him and threatened to quit football altogether if I didn't attend Texas Southern with him."

Maxi nodded, fully understanding. She had always known how much Garrett loved Mya. But then she'd known that he had loved football too. In the end he'd been willing to give up his love of football for Mya. Anyone knowing Garrett Rivers knew that was some kind of love.

"I couldn't let him give up football for me, Maxi. I couldn't let him do that. But then I knew I couldn't tell anyone we were married. Not even you. It wasn't a question of me not trusting you with the information, it was a question of me keeping my promise to Garrett and not telling anyone what we'd done."

Mya held her head down for a second. When she lifted it up her eyes were filled with tears. "You don't know how much I wanted to tell you. How much I needed to tell you. I had felt so alone and confused. And that day when I had to tell you that I couldn't go to Howard with you, you got so upset because I didn't give you a reason why, I felt even worse. After that things began happening fast. In order to make the cheerleading squad at Southern, I had to leave right away and once I did things got too hectic to call and talk to you. By the time things slowed down you had left for Howard and I knew that, although we would always be friends, it wouldn't be the same. And it hasn't been."

Maxi stared at Mya until she lowered her gaze. She knew things had been hectic back then and her father's unexpected death had almost devastated her. It seemed both she and Mya had been going through their own personal crises that summer, and because they didn't have each other to lean on and confide in, they had suffered because of it.

"I just want you to know, Maxi, that I miss having you for my best friend. At times I would reach for the phone to call you to share things with you and then stop myself when I knew I couldn't because things weren't the same between us anymore. I wanted you there when the boys were born, and although you were at my wedding and at my granny's funeral, it was like you weren't really there—at least not for me. Not the way it should have been. You were supposed to be my maid of honor in my wedding, and you were supposed to be my sons' godmother. I was supposed to be your maid of honor but I didn't even know you were getting married until Gramma called to tell me your fiancé had gotten killed. It didn't seem fair after all we'd been through together."

Maxi nodded. "I know what you mean. I would cringe each time I got what I considered as one of your courtesy Christmas cards, one of your rare phone calls or whenever you would come back home for visits. Everything seemed so phony between us, so contrite, and you and I had never been anything but honest and genuine to each other. That's why I stopped calling or writing."

Mya reached across the table and captured Maxi's hand in hers. "I never meant to hurt you, Maxi, or to let you down. I had always wanted to be nothing more than your best friend for always." She inhaled a deep, long breath. "I know that rebuilding a torn friendship isn't easy. But I feel we'll be doing a disservice to each other if we don't try. We've always been there for each other, Maxi. I know there's no way we can go back and recapture all that's lost, but I believe what happens between us now is what's important."

Maxi nodded through her tears. She looked at Mya, seeing the same tears glaze her eyes. She reminded her so much of how she looked in the schoolyard that day so long ago. "Thanks for telling me everything. It explains a lot," she said quietly.

Mya wiped away a tear and smiled. "Like I said, Maxi. It was hard keeping things from you but I had to."

Maxi reached across and captured her other hand in Mya's.

She smiled. "Yes, you did and I understand now." She stood. "Come on, let's go to our class reunion welcome reception and see our other friends."

Moments later the two women walked off with their arms around each other.

Garrett nodded in visible satisfaction when he saw Maxi and Mya. He walked over to meet them, knowing all was well between them. "I thought I'd be the lucky guy who would escort two beautiful ladies inside the reception," he said smiling.

"That's not necessary, Rivers, I'm Maxi's escort tonight."

The three individuals turned at the sound of the deep, masculine voice.

"Christopher!" Maxi's face broke into a smile when she saw him. "You decided to come after all," she said, her smile widening when he walked up to them. He was dressed in a pair of tan linen slacks and a band-collar blue linen shirt.

"Yes, I decided to come."

Maxi turned to Garrett and Mya who were watching her and Christopher with keen interest. "You remember Christopher, don't you?"

Garrett nodded. He smiled as he extended his hand out to Christopher. "Good seeing you again, Chandler."

Christopher shook Garrett's hand. "Likewise, Rivers." Garrett had been one of the few guys that he'd gotten along with in school. During that time, the man had been too caught up in sports and Mya Ross to have time for much of anything else.

"Mya, how are you?" Christopher asked the woman at Garrett's side.

"I'm doing fine, Christopher." She looked from Maxi back to Christopher. There was a curious expression on her face. "The two of you have kept in touch over the years?"

Maxi chuckled. She knew Mya well enough to know exactly what she was thinking. "No. We hadn't seen each other since high school. There was a mix-up with the ship's computer and because we have the same last name, Christopher and I were given the same cabin, so we're cabinmates. Isn't that something?"

Mya smiled, remembering the conversation she'd had earlier with Garrett concerning Maxi and Christopher. "Yeah, that's really something."

Garrett shook his head grinning. "I see nothing's changed where Maxi is concerned. You still manage to protect what you consider yours, Chandler."

Christopher looked at Maxi and saw the look of surprise in her eyes at what Garrett said. He held her gaze and took her hand in his. "You're right, Rivers. Nothing has changed."

CHAPTER FIFTEEN

Maxi had learned over the years not to put much stock in some things, but she couldn't help her increased heart rate at the husky tone that had entered Christopher's voice when he'd spoken, the warm smile that played on his lips, and the feel of his hard, warm fingers tightening around hers.

She took a glance at him, then at Garrett and Mya. It seemed they were all privy to some kind of information that she should know. Why was Garrett making such a claim about Christopher having always protected her and considered her as his? And why was Christopher going along with such a claim when he'd barely noticed she was alive in school? At least not until that time they had worked together on the science project.

"It's about time you showed up, Maxi."

The four of them turned to the tall, muscular man walking toward them as he gulped down a big sip of whatever was in the glass he was holding in his hand. By most women's standards Ronald Swindel was good looking, but what cut him short was his "better than you" attitude about some people.

"I've been looking for you ever since this ship left dock. I hadn't seen you around and was beginning to worry," he said coming up to Maxi, showing his lack of manners by not acknowledging the others.

"Ronald, there was no need for you to worry about me. Like everyone else I was getting settled in my cabin," Maxi said, inhaling a deep, calming breath. Her tolerance for his impoliteness was at an all-time low. "I'm sure you know everyone."

It was only then that he seemed to have noticed the others. Especially the man standing close to her and who was holding her hand. It was obvious to everyone when recognition hit. Anger needled a thread of contempt through him when he recognized his old nemesis.

"Christopher Chandler! What the hell are you doing here? You're not welcome to be a part of this class reunion. And I see that you still forget your place in life."

"And I suppose you intend to remind me," Christopher said, his narrowed gaze soldering on a smooth smile.

Maxi's stomach clenched. Ronald was goading Christopher and she could feel something lethal radiating from within him. She moved closer to Christopher. "Ronald, Christopher *is* a member of our class and has every right to be here," she said angrily. "And I intend to make sure he has a good time."

Maxi knew the exact moment Christopher's gaze left Ronald to light on her . . . and linger. But she didn't dare look at him now.

"And so are we," Garrett piped in with annoyance in his voice as he backed up what Maxi had said. "I'd think after ten years your thinking on a lot of things would have changed, Swindel. After all, you are a police officer. With that position comes a bit of fairness and open-mindedness. Not to mention the fact that none of us were born with silver spoons in our mouths."

"So none of us have the right to think we're better than anyone else," Mya finished for her husband.

Ronald downed another gulp of his drink. It was obvious he hadn't liked being chastised by Maxi, Garrett, and Mya. Especially in front of Christopher. "We need to talk, Maxi. Privately," he said in a huff.

Maxi nodded slowly. "Yes, we do." It was time they talked. She was sick and tired of him acting like there was something between them other than friendship. "All right." She turned to the others. "Please excuse us for a moment."

Maxi took a deep breath as she watched Ronald pace back and forth in front of her for a full minute. He finally stopped his pacing. He looked at her quietly for a moment. She could tell he was still angry. Evidently the pacing hadn't helped.

"You, Garrett, and Mya had no right putting me down in front of Chandler. I can't believe you would associate yourself with him. Have you forgotten how much trouble he got into when we were in school? All those fights, suspensions, not to mention his bad-behind attitude."

"Ronald, that was over ten years ago. And have you ever stopped to think that maybe Christopher had a reason for acting the way he did? You and your friends were never nice to him."

"There was never a reason to be nice to him. He didn't fit. Hell, Maxi, he lived in the Vines," he said, speaking of the low-income housing project. "And everyone knew only cutthroats and hoodlums came from the Vines. It wouldn't surprise me if he hasn't spent the last ten years behind bars."

"Look, Ronald. Unlike you, I never thought I was better than the people who lived in the Vines. I got along with Christopher just fine, and have no qualms about spending time with him now."

Irritation flooded Ronald's features. "Don't you see what he's doing? He's only showing interest in you to aggravate me. Somebody must have told him about us and—"

"There isn't an *us*, Ronald. Why can't you accept that you and I are friends and nothing more? I've told you that countless times."

"I understand you're not over your fiancé yet, but—"

"Don't bring Jason into this. Accept the fact that I'm not interested in you other than as a friend."

"But you're interested in Chandler as more than a friend, is that it?" Ronald asked angrily.

Maxi sighed. "Christopher and I are just friends, too."

"He wants more. He's been hot to get inside your pants for years."

"That's not true!"

"Yes, it is. I've always known it and he broke my arm one time to prove it."

Maxi lifted a brow, remembering that day. "The two of you had been fighting over Lorraine Brown."

"Lorraine Brown? Who would fight over her? That just goes to show how little you knew about what was going on back then. That fight was about you! Chandler had this thing about you and got pissed when I told him that he didn't stand a chance with you, with you being the smartest person in school and him being the dumbest. Now, for whatever reason, he's decided to come on this cruise and cause problems. I wish the hell he would have stayed under whatever rock he crawled out from under."

Maxi's head was spinning with what Ronald had just said. Was it true? Had they been fighting about her and not Lorraine Brown that day? Surely he was mistaken. "Ronald, I think you—"

"Do me a favor and stay away from him, Maxi. He's nothing but trouble."

Irritation was evident in Maxi's voice when she said, "There's no way I can stay away from him since he and I are sharing the same cabin."

"What!"

"Yes, you heard me right. The cruise line thought we were married and assigned us to the same cabin by mistake. There aren't any more cabins left, so Christopher and I have decided to make the most of it."

"You can move into my cabin. Walter Casper can find some-where else to sleep. I won't have you sharing a cabin with Chan-dler. I want you out of there immediately."

Maxi's anger flared. "First of all, Ronald, I don't give a royal flip what you want. The sooner you realize that the better. Christopher is my friend just like you are, and I have all inten-tions of sharing his cabin for the rest of this cruise. It won't be the first time I've had a male roommate. I had one in college and it worked out just fine."

"Then share my cabin. You know you'll be safe with me."

"I have no reason not to think I won't be safe with Christo-pher."

"You don't know anything about him. I bet you don't even know what he's been doing for the past ten years. You're too damn trusting for your own good, Maxi. You're making a mis-take."

"And it's my mistake to make. I appreciate your concern but it's not needed." With those final words she walked off.

CHAPTER SIXTEEN

For some reaon Maxi was not surprised to find Christopher, Garrett, and Mya still standing in the same spot she had left them five minutes earlier.

She smiled faintly when Christopher left Garrett and Mya and began walking toward her. She thought about how good he looked and once again, instinctively, her senses picked up everything about him that was male, which was the last thing she needed. The purpose of this cruise was to relax and enjoy the company of friends, and not to rekindle the amorous feelings she'd had for one classmate in particular.

She may have thought those things but the minute he reached her, she knew she was still attracted to him as she had been ten years ago. The look in his gaze was filled with concern as he eyed her carefully.

"You okay?" he asked softly.

"Yes, I'm fine," she responded while noticing that his dark eyes hadn't left her for a moment. "Are you ready to go inside?"

He nodded. "Yes, I'm ready."

She took his hand in hers. "All right then, let's go and I guarantee you'll have a good time."

* * *

Over an hour or so later, Christopher grudgingly admitted that he was having a good time. Although a number of people here tonight had treated him as less than human when he'd attended school with them, now they appeared regretful over their youthful antics and were going out of their way to make him feel included and accepted. They were smiling and eager to converse with him. And he credited Maxi for it. Now he understood why she'd been so well liked and popular in school. She greeted just about everyone she saw with a hug and had remembered most of their names, where he had barely remembered their faces. She had easily brought him into the conversation like it was a natural thing for the two of them to be seen together ten years later at their class reunion. And for some reason those classmates they encountered didn't act like it was such a big deal.

Everyone except for Ronald Swindel. Whatever Maxi had said to him still had him fuming. Christopher saw the man cutting his eyes at him from across the room whenever he glanced his way.

"So, Christopher, what are you doing now?"

He turned toward Mya. The two of them had been left alone for a while. Garrett had gone to refill their drinks, and Maxi had decided to work the crowd. And she was indeed working it. He had noticed her movements around the room. They were graceful and deft, and every so often she would glance over at him and smile. He knew she was doing so as a reminder that she had not forgotten about him.

"I'm in construction." He decided to tell Mya the same thing he'd told everyone who had asked that night.

"Exactly what do you build?" Mya queried further.

Christopher inwardly smiled. No wonder Mya and Maxi had been friends for so long. Both of them liked to ask questions. However, where Maxi knew where to draw the line and not cross into an area that was considered as being nosy, it appeared Mya felt she had no such restrictions.

"I build a number of things, mainly commercial."

"What's the name of your business and where is it located?"

"The Regency Corporation and we are home based in Detroit." He met her gaze intently. "Is there a reason for all these questions?"

Mya's response was a series of chuckles followed by a quiet, no-nonsense look. "Just checking you out. You're sharing a cabin with Maxi and I want to make sure you're safe."

"Maxi's a big girl. Don't you think that should be her concern and not yours?" he asked coolly.

"No. Maxi never had a level head where you were concerned."

Christopher frowned. "What the hell are you talking about?" he asked in an irritated voice.

"Nothing. Just as long as you and I understand each other. I don't want to see Maxi hurt."

Christopher smoothed his lips into a flat line and met Mya's unwavering gaze. "I would never intentionally hurt Maxi." His voice was quiet but absolute.

Mya smiled, evidently satisfied with his response. "Good."

Their topic of conversation ended when Garrett returned with their drinks.

Christopher and Maxi made small talk as they walked down the long corridor to their cabin, partaking in chitchat about the surprises they had encountered that night.

"I can't believe Lee Jenkins is a minister. Ronald looked out of place without him as his sidekick."

Maxi nodded. She then met Christopher's gaze. "That just goes to show people do change and most of the time for the better." She had enjoyed seeing old friends again. Only a couple of people had asked her about Jason. Surprisingly, it didn't bother her as much as she thought it would when some had pulled out family pictures which reminded her of what she didn't have.

When they reached their cabin she stood aside while Christopher unlocked the door. Once they entered and turned on the lights she was suddenly made aware of how intimate their cabin was. That was something she had failed to take note of earlier that day.

"Are you going back out tonight?" Christopher asked, watching her survey the room like it was the first time she had seen it.

"Yes. Mya and I plan to do the midnight buffet. What about you?" she asked him as she tossed her purse on the dresser.

A smile creased his lips. "I've had my share of entertainment for one night. Especially since it had been my intent to just stay in my room tonight and chill. But now I'm glad I went." He studied Maxi intently before saying. "I need to pay a visit to the gift shop and buy a pair of pajamas."

Maxi lifted a dark brow. "You forgot to bring a pair?"

Christopher chuckled. "I don't own a pair. It wouldn't have mattered had I been in this cabin alone. But since I have a cabin-mate, I don't think you'd appreciate me walking around in the nude."

Oh, she would appreciate it, Maxi thought. She just didn't think she would be able to handle it. Around Christopher she was reminded, and not too subtly, that she was indeed still a woman.

"I'll see you later." He gave her a smooth smile before opening the door and closing it behind him.

CHAPTER SEVENTEEN

"If I eat another thing I'm liable to hurt myself," Mya said, pushing her plate back.

Maxi knew exactly what she meant. There was more than enough food at the midnight buffet to savor their every culinary delight and satisfy their every whim. And they had gotten a taste of just about everything.

"I'm too full to sleep," Mya groaned. "But I'm not too full to hear what's going on with you and Christopher Chandler."

Maxi smiled helplessly. She wasn't surprised that now that she and Mya had cleared the air about what had put a rift in their friendship ten years ago, it seemed natural for things to be back to normal with them. In a way they were somewhat better. They were older, mature, and they knew what they'd missed out on during the years they hadn't kept in touch. Neither wanted to go there again. True friendship was hard to find. And when two people had a history like they did, it was something you couldn't discount or throw away because of a misunderstanding. Restoring their friendship had been much more than just an effort. For the two of them it had been crucial. She hadn't realized just how much she had missed their girl talks until now. And there was so much she wanted to share with

Mya. Things she hadn't been able to share with anyone, not even her mom. Although she and her mother had a close relationship there were certain things you just couldn't share with your mom. Like this intense attraction she had for Christopher.

"What do you think is going on?" she finally asked.

"You tell me. Of all the people for you to get your cabin mixed up with, you get Christopher Chandler, Mister Bad Boy himself. He still looks good, you know," Mya said smiling.

"Yeah, I know," Maxi said grinning. "I would have to be blind not to know. And the reason for the mix-up is pretty logical when you think about it since we have the same last name. The computer goofed."

"Lucky you and Christopher."

Maxi shook her head. "There's nothing going on between us, Mya. Although he's made a few comments to let me know he's noticed me as a woman, there's nothing else there. It's like old times when he and I were friends. There's still a part of him he won't share with anyone. So I guess you can say in a way he's still a loner. I can tell that he still lives by his own rules and allows very few people to get close to him."

"Yeah, but you did get close to him once, Maxi. You got closer to him than anyone at school. And from the way he kept looking at you tonight, I believe you can do so again."

"But I don't want to get close to him. A lot of things are going on in my life, Mya. A man is the last thing I need right now." She inhaled deeply before continuing. "My doctor has informed me that I need surgery."

Mya sat up straight in her chair. "What kind of surgery?"

"A hysterectomy. The doctor discovered I had fibroid tumors several years ago and lately they've taken on a life of their own and have begun growing on me, literally."

Mya nodded. "Have you had a second opinion?"

"Yes, and additional tests were taken to see if there's any other way. So far there's not. So that means unless I get pregnant before the surgery, I'll never have a child."

Mya studied the dampness that appeared in Maxi's eyes. She of all people knew what having a family meant to Maxi and it didn't seem fair. First her fiancé had gotten killed and now this. She reached across the table and took Maxi's hand in hers. "I'm going to pray that things work out for you, Maxi. And for some reason I believe they will. You are too good a person not to have the family you've always wanted."

Maxi smiled through the light tears clouding her eyes. "Thanks and I appreciate that. And please do keep me in your prayers. I'm going to need them. I'm okay when I don't think about the trials and tribulations I'm going through, but when I do think about them they become almost overbearing and I ask myself, why me? Then I stop and think about all the other blessings I've had over the years and that makes it easier to bear," she said softly. "Like your grandmother always said, the Lord gives us strength to endure all things."

Mya smiled at the memory. "Amen, sistah." Tiny lines curved at the bottom of her mouth. "And there's always adoption. A couple that Garrett and I know adopted a little girl recently and she's the most adorable child you ever want to see. Anytime Garrett goes around her it reminds him of the daughter he's always wanted."

Maxi nodded. She remembered when they were in school together Garrett would say he wanted to one day have a daughter as beautiful as Mya. Maxi used to think that was the ultimate compliment a man could bestow upon the woman he loved, wanting her to be the mother of his child. "So the two of you plan to have another child?"

"Yes, but no time soon. Luckily Garrett hasn't brought the subject up lately and I'm hoping he doesn't. I just got my career where I want it to be and don't want to take time off to have another baby." She tossed off the uncomfortable feeling she'd always had whenever she talked about her job and how much she enjoyed it.

"And how does Garrett feel about you working? I thought it

was a long-standing rule in the Rivers family that the Rivers women don't work."

"It still is, trust me. None of his brothers' wives work. We've had a number of arguments about it. But what good is having a college degree if you don't ever use it? I wasn't one of those women who went to college looking for a husband. I already had one when I got there. You know how it is for me. I've always enjoyed keeping busy and raising the boys just isn't enough. I want to feel more useful than that."

Maxi smiled, nodding. "What will you do if Garrett brings up the subject of another baby?"

"I don't know. I recently got a promotion at work and haven't told him about it yet. I'm stalling because I know he's not going to like it if it means I'll have to travel more."

"And will you have to travel more?"

"Unfortunately, yes. The client I've been assigned to operates his business in Orlando."

"Orlando is a long way from Dallas."

"Yeah, tell me about it. I have to pick a good time to drop the bomb on Garrett."

"When do you start your new position?"

"Next month, which means I'll be going away quite a bit at the beginning of football season. That's going to be hard since I've never missed any of his games, both home and away. I really don't know how he'll handle that. I have a specific place where I sit in the stands and if he glances up, he'll expect to see me there."

Maxi nodded. "Things will work out for you and Garrett. The two of you have been together too long for it not to. I don't know of two other people more in love and dedicated to each other after all these years. You can still make him smile like you used to."

Mya chuckled as she remembered how she had him smiling earlier that day. "Yeah, I can make him smile," she agreed.

"Keep the intimate details to yourself," Maxi said jokingly. "Thinking about something like that is pure torture. I haven't been intimate with anyone since Jason."

"You're kidding."

"No, I'm not. Although I've dated occasionally, there hasn't been anyone who has interested me enough to take things to that level. I guess you can say Jason spoiled me for any other man. I don't want an affair with anyone where I'm just considered his possession. I want more. I want the same thing Jason offered me—a chance to have a lasting, loving, and fulfilling relationship with someone who loves me."

Mya studied Maxi for a long moment before asking. "What about this thing with Christopher? You can't convince me you're not attracted to him."

"Well, yeah, it would be hard for any woman not to be attracted to him. But what's new? I was attracted to him in school."

"But I bet you didn't know he was attracted to you as well. In fact it went beyond attraction. According to Garrett, Christopher pretty much warned all the guys away from you."

Maxi lifted a brow. Was that what Garrett had meant when he'd made that comment earlier that night? "Garrett told you that?"

"Yeah, can you believe it? And from the way Garrett talked, it had been going on for a long time and not just during our senior year of high school."

Maxi briskly pushed away the romantic thoughts that began swarming around in her head. "But he never said anything about it to me."

"Do you really think he would have back then? He probably saw himself as not worthy of your affections and decided not to pursue anything with you. But evidently he figured just because he wasn't going to pursue you didn't mean you were open game to anyone else. According to Garrett it was understood that you belonged to Christopher and he protected you from all those other guys. That's the reason he and Ronald never got along."

Maxi inhaled deeply. "Ronald said something to that effect tonight but I refused to believe him. I had no idea."

"And evidently Christopher wanted it that way." Mya lifted a curious brow. "Now that you know how he felt about you back then, what are you going to do about it?"

"Nothing. That was years ago, Mya. He probably hasn't given me a thought during the past ten years."

"But he's evidently giving you some thought now. While you were circulating around the room tonight he was watching you with enough intensity to make every single male at the reception know you're still off limits."

Maxi regarded Mya's statement thoughtfully for a moment, her mind recalling that night's event. Whenever she had looked up, she had noticed Christopher's eyes on her, his expression controlled, his gaze sharp, clear, piercing, as he regarded her with open . . . What? . . . Interest? Admiration? Lust? The thought that his full attention had been focused on her sent the blood racing through her veins.

Maxi released a deep sigh. "Even if there is interest on his part, Mya, the timing right now is lousy."

Mya sat back in her chair smiling. She had noted Christopher's interest in Maxi tonight, which had prompted her to ask him a few questions. "I happen to disagree, kiddo. I think it's perfect timing."

The light from the hall caught Christopher's attention when Maxi entered the cabin returning from the midnight buffet. "Enjoy yourself?" he whispered to her in the darkness.

"Oh, Christopher, I'm sorry, I didn't mean to wake you."

"You didn't. I wasn't asleep. Did you enjoy yourself?"

She turned on the lamp on the dresser, bringing light into the room. He lay in bed, flat on his back with his head propped up on the pillow and wearing pajamas just for her modesty. She met his eyes. Again the look in them was intense and almost took her breath away. "Yes, Mya and I almost ate ourselves silly. You should have joined us," she said softly, finally answering his question.

"I ran into Garrett in one of the casinos and hung out with him for a while, then decided to come back here and turn in." He tried not to notice her removing the flower from her hair, with such care and attention. A part of him imagined her touching him exactly that same way. He cleared his throat. "Will you be hanging out with the Rivers tomorrow?"

Tomorrow was deemed a "fun day at sea." A lot of different activities had been planned as the ship made its way toward the Cayman Islands. "No, Mya and Garrett will be doing their own thing. Although she invited me to join them, I didn't want to intrude on their time together. Why?"

"No reason. I think I'm going to just chill by the pool and read an interesting book I brought along."

She nodded. He was letting her know in a nice way that he didn't intend to spend any time with her tomorrow. "All right." Without saying another word she pulled her pajamas out of the dresser drawer and went into the bathroom, closing the door behind her.

A short while later Christopher watched Maxi come out of the bathroom wearing a pair of silk pajamas. They were red. His favorite color. And in his opinion she looked sexy as hell in them. Although she didn't look over in his direction his eyes stayed on her as she turned off the light.

"Goodnight, Christopher."

"Goodnight, Maxi."

He heard the sound of her knees touching the floor. She was saying her prayers, he concluded, and tried to recall the last time he'd said his. His body tightened moments later when he heard the sound of her pushing the covers back to slip into bed.

He lay awake for several long, tormented hours listening to the evenness of her breathing, letting him know she had drifted off to sleep. He shifted position in bed thinking just how deep Maxi was getting under his skin. Desire was a powerful emotion when it came to Maxine Chandler, and he was determined to be careful how he dealt with it.

CHAPTER EIGHTEEN

Christopher tried shutting off thoughts of Maxi as he picked up the telephone to call Gabe. He had gotten out of bed early that morning and had quickly dressed and left the cabin without waking her. He had spent his day lounging by the pool, reading. Only once had he seen her from a distance. She'd been with Connie Adams and Geri Hunter, two women from their group who had also come on the cruise as singles.

He tapped his hand against the phone as he waited for his call to connect. He was dialing Gabe's private number.

"This better be good, Chris," a rough voice snarled into the phone.

A smile lifted one corner of Christopher's mouth. "How did you know it was me?"

"This is my private number. I talked to the folks earlier so I figured it must be you. Why are you calling me? I thought you understood you were to enjoy yourself and not worry about things here."

A tiny frown flickered across Christopher's brow as he released a deep sigh. "I know, but it's hard."

"Then try making it easy. Go find a woman to spend time with. I'm sure there are quite a few on that ship. I understand that

more and more women are going on cruises alone looking for
Mr. Right, or Mr. Wrong, depending on the way you look at it."

"So there's nothing I need to know?"

"No, there's not. Everything's fine, so relax and enjoy yourself. And you better hope I don't tell Mama you called checking
up on things."

Christopher could feel his lips curving into an even deeper
smile than before. "Hey, I'm sure you have the good sense not
to. If I suffer, so do you, pal. Remember that."

"Yeah, yeah, just don't call back. We'll see you in a week. And
do like I said and find yourself a woman."

Christopher whirled around when he heard the sound of the
cabin door opening. His gaze immediately connected to Maxi.
He felt his muscles tense. He couldn't delude himself regarding his feelings for her any longer. Although he wasn't sure just
what the hell those feelings were, he knew he could not put distance between them any more than he could make this ship
turn around and go back to Tampa. No matter how much he'd
tried not to think about her today, he had. No matter how
much he'd tried getting into the book he was reading, she was
never far from his mind.

"Hey, Chris. You still there? Did you hear what I said? Find
yourself a woman."

Gabe's voice on the other end of the phone reminded Christopher that he was still talking to someone. "I already have," he
replied gruffly before hanging up the phone on his friend. "Hi,"
he greeted Maxi softly as he placed the phone back in the cradle.
He tried not to notice how good she looked in a pair of khaki
shorts and a polo shirt. He cleared his throat. "How was your day?"

He felt tension, the same tension he'd experienced earlier,
slowly ebb from Maxi as she entered the room and closed the
door, letting him know that he wasn't the only one uptight. She
continued to look at him as if he was a puzzle she didn't know
where to start putting together. "Fine, and yours?"

"It was fine, too," he said shifting to another foot, suddenly feeling shy and uncertain around her. The thought that he was behaving in such a manner with any woman was alarming. "Made any plans for dinner?"

She met his gaze. "No. Have you?"

He shook his head. "No. Would you join me for dinner?"

"Sure," she answered, meeting his gaze. "Do you want to keep our second dinner call or do you want me to change it to the first?"

"Second is fine since I want to go back by the pool and finish up the book I'm reading," he said, like he really thought that would be possible.

"Okay. I'm just going to lie down and take a nap for a while."

He smiled. "I'll catch you later."

Taking a deep breath he walked passed her as he left the cabin.

Later that evening, Christopher watched as Maxi nibbled on a succulent piece of shrimp. He was getting turned on—big time, literally, just watching how she was devouring the piece of seafood with her mouth. He'd never seen anything like it. His dark gaze followed every movement her mouth made. He inhaled deeply, wishing he could replace the shrimp with his tongue and let her nibble on that for a while. He changed position in his seat, trying to relieve the ache consuming the lower part of his body.

His sheer sexual magnetism toward her had increased ever since she had walked out of the bathroom dressed for dinner. Tonight was Captain's Night and he had chosen to wear a black tuxedo and she was wearing the most sexy-looking gown he'd ever seen on a woman's body. Just like her eating of the shrimp, the shoulderless tea-length white gown was a total turn-on. He wasn't sure how much longer he would last before the zipper on his pants burst at the seam. He was glad he was sitting down and hoped he would cool off before he had to stand. Exposing such arousal would be embarrassing.

Maxi looked up and flinched slightly at the impact of Christopher's piercing dark eyes. "Is something wrong?" she asked wondering why he was watching her so intently. Then she recalled her and Mya's conversation and swallowed the lump in her throat.

Almost reluctantly, Christopher shifted his gaze from her mouth to her eyes. "No, nothing's wrong. Why do you ask?"

"Because," she said, saying the single word softly under her breath. "Your eyes were glued to my mouth."

A few seconds ticked by before he responded. "Were they?"

"Yes."

"Umm . . . I was just wondering."

"About what?"

"Has anyone ever kissed you senseless?"

His statement sent a vivid picture to Maxi's sexually charged brain. "No."

"What about your fiancé?" he asked. His eyes seemed to harden and locked with hers. "Didn't the two of you ever do some heavy-duty kissing?"

A part of Maxi wanted to tell him what she and Jason had done was none of his business but she found herself answering anyway. "No, Jason knew how to control himself."

Christopher frowned, wondering what had been the man's secret because he had total lack of control where she was concerned. Her sensuality was so much a part of her, so natural, he doubted that she was even aware of it. At times it was so overpowering it literally took his breath away. "What would you like to do tonight?" he asked her.

She thought about his question and immediately knew what she would like. She would love to go dancing. When she had lived in Washington, Wilson took her out dancing all the time, but dancing was something Jason wasn't all that big on doing. "I'd like to go dancing."

Christopher's smile shone through his eyes. "All right, dancing it is."

CHAPTER NINETEEN

Mya and Garrett were lying side by side sharing one of those huge double loungers on their balcony. It was another beautiful evening at sea. A helpless smile formed on her lips, the glass of wine in her hand momentarily forgotten. "Lee Jenkins actually took you aside and said you needed prayer?"

Garrett's smile broke into a grin. "Yeah, it was the oddest thing. I was standing by the rail looking out at the ocean and he appeared by my side and said he had come to pray with me, and that he'd been led by the Almighty to do so."

Mya nodded. Lee Jenkins, who used to be a bully in school and one of Ronald's ace-boon-coons, was now a minister. "What did you say?"

"I told him that I thought Ronald needed his prayers more than I did but he said he was sent to pray with me."

"Did he say why?" Mya asked after a moment.

Garrett shrugged. "No, he just said he was told I needed it." He let out a smooth chuckle. "Maybe someone up there has told him I'm going to have a bad season or something. Or maybe after five years the Cowboys are going to cut me from the team. Hell, I don't know, Mya! All I know is that he said I needed prayer and I decided not to question it. The two of us went to the chapel and he prayed for me."

Mya took a sip of her wine. Like her, Garrett and been raised in the church. But over the years they had stopped going on a regular basis. In college they had attended services regularly because the grace of God and constant prayers had been the only thing that had sustained them through those turbulent years when no one knew they were married. She had to put up with the "hoochie momma man-hunters" who'd thought Garrett was open game although everyone around campus knew the two of them were an item. When they had moved to Dallas, they had joined a church not far from their home and the two of them had even joined a married couples group. But then the devil had intervened and chaos entered when it was discovered that the minister, a married man, had had an affair with one of the younger women at church. The church split. Half of the members wanted the preacher gone and the other half was willing to overlook his transgressions and keep him on as their leader. In the end the majority had ruled and Reverend Stonewall had gotten voted out. Those members who'd supported him had followed him and formed another church. One of those had been Garrett's best friend Hilton, and his wife, Alicia. Hilton's position of support for Reverend Stonewall was the only disagreement Garrett and Hilton had had during their years of friendship.

The entire incident had disheartened Garrett since he'd really liked and respected Reverend Stonewall. It seemed that after that he found one excuse after another not to attend church anywhere, saying if you couldn't trust a minister then who could you trust. Eventually Mya'd come to her own lackadaisical attitude about religion, but it wasn't as bad as Garrett's. She and the boys did go to church occasionally. And she was doing better since one of her New Year's resolutions had been to improve things in that department. She knew her grandmother, who'd been a devout religious woman, was probably up there in heaven frowning down at her and Garrett. And Garrett's parents, who were active in their church and who'd always been real southern Baptists like her grandmother, were also not pleased with the small amount of time she and Garrett were giving to God these days.

With great caution Mya broached the subject they had both avoided talking about for the past few years. "So, did his prayer help convince you to get back into the church, Garrett?"

"No, because I feel I am into the church. Just because I don't go to church doesn't mean I'm out of it. You know my Sunday schedule, Mya. I play a lot of my games on Sundays. I have you tape those church services off the television and I watch them whenever I can."

She decided not to point out that the Sundays he was unavailable because of football only lasted from September to January. Those other Sundays he'd been free to attend church if he really wanted to. She remembered all the videos she had taped of various church services that came on television on Sunday mornings for Garrett to watch later at a more convenient time. They were videos he hadn't gotten around to watching yet. What Garrett's mother had tried to drill into her son the last time they'd gone home for a visit was that watching church off television wasn't the same as being a part of a live congregation. She had preached to him that he needed to get over whatever sin Reverend Stonewall had committed and turn his life back over to God. Respectfully Garrett had listened to his mother and had even attended church service with her while there, but once he returned to Dallas he'd gotten back into his regular routine.

"Speaking of those tapes, Garrett, the box is full. When are you going to make time to watch them?"

"Don't push me, Mya. You know how busy I am these days. I'll get to them when I can."

She nodded. She'd been with Garrett long enough to know when to pull back and not push any longer. "I have an idea that I want to run by you," she said, deciding to change the subject.

"What?"

"Tomorrow, when we reach the Cayman Islands, I want to check out one of those nude beaches."

Garrett frowned. "Why would you be interested in seeing a bunch of naked people lying around in the sand?"

"Because it's something I've never seen before."

"And you won't anytime soon. The only naked male body you'll ever see is mine." Leaning toward her, he nipped her ear and whispered. "In fact I'd love to show it to you now. Are you game?" His voice was thick with desire.

Mya smiled. The effect of his warm breath in her ear and the seductive tone of his voice made intense heat settle in the lower part of her stomach. Just like he'd probably known it would. Her body held no secrets from her husband although at present, her mind did. She pushed that thought away and placed her wineglass on the table. "Yes, I'm game. I'm also putty in your hands and you very well know that, don't you?"

"Yes." Standing he reached his hand out to her. "Come on, Mrs. Rivers, let's go inside and get naked."

CHAPTER TWENTY

The lavishness of the cruise ship's Pinnacle Disco Club was enhanced even more by all the glittering lights reflecting off the golden columns and the ultra shiny parquet dance floor. A combination of music from the fifties through the present was being played, occasionally alternating with a live band.

Christopher pulled Maxi onto the dance floor the moment they entered, joining a group of people doing the electric slide. She laughed, enjoying the effect of moving her body to the music, keeping in graceful step with the others.

After a few more fast-paced songs where everyone turned to their partners and gave their bodies a good workout while boogying to the sounds of various artists the music then turned into a slow number. Without missing a beat Christopher pulled Maxi into his arms. "Now we take things slow," he whispered in her ear as they swayed to the sound of Brian McKnight. He tightened his arms around her.

Maxi fell into step with Christopher, feeling totally relaxed being held by him. "You dance often?" she asked, liking the feel of her hands resting on his shoulders.

He gave her a soft laugh as he tightened his arms around her waist. "No, can't you tell?"

"I think you're great. You seem to know all the modern stuff. I merely follow your lead."

"Trust me. It wasn't the modern stuff. It's the old stuff that's come back with a different name, and this is the first time I've been dancing in quite a while. My best friend and I used to hit all the hot spots in Detroit when we were younger. But that was years ago. Now I . . ." he stopped himself. He'd been about to tell her more than he'd intended to.

Maxi lifted a brow. "Now you what?" she asked.

The corner of his lips curved into a grin. Maxi had a way of getting a person off balance, totally off track. He quickly regrouped his thoughts. "Now I just manage to work hard and earn a good day's pay for a good day's worth of work. I have very little leisure time for myself." That much was true, he thought. Over the past five years he had driven himself to be successful, first with furthering his education, then with his business. That was one of the reasons Joella Blackwell had been so hard on him about taking a vacation. Everyone knew that Christopher Chandler was all work and no play. The only time he got to play was when he was in bed with a woman and lately even that had become scarce. He hadn't slept with a woman since that night he'd spent with Tori Smithfield.

"I know you aren't married or engaged, but are you serious about anyone?" Maxi asked, wanting desperately to know for some reason.

Her question made him smile. He was seriously into sex but not seriously into any particular woman. "I see a lot of women, but no one seriously. What about you? Have you gotten back into dating now that you're no longer engaged?"

"Not a whole lot. I've dated but nothing serious has developed. It took me a while to get over Jason's death."

"Are you over him now?"

Maxi thought that Christopher's voice was deep, with an edge of huskiness that any woman would find sexy. She took several steadying breaths before answering him until she was sure she had her voice, as well as herself, under control. Then she said quietly. "Yes, I'm over him."

"Are you sure?" The deep darkness of his gaze homed into hers.

"Yes, I'm sure."

He pulled her closer into his arms when the song ended and another slow number immediately started playing.

Silence descended upon them as they, as well as a number of other couples, slowly moved their bodies underneath the room's glittering prisms of lights. Maxi felt the strength in his hand on her lower back as he slowly moved, with her in his arms, to the slow tune being played. Her breasts suddenly felt tender, sensitive, as they pressed against the hardness of his chest. His thigh felt hard against hers and his hand gently stroked her back.

He broke the silence. "Your shoulders look creamy, like chocolate mousse," he said in a voice that was deeper than before and increasingly intimate. "It makes me want to taste you."

Before Maxi realized Christopher's intentions he dipped his head and with warm lips, kissed the curve of her bare shoulder. A shiver of desire, one she had never felt before, raced through every bone in her body. She would have melted in a heap right there on the floor had he not been doing a good job of holding her. She was thankful when his grip around her waist tightened. The music came to an end and she lifted her head and met his gaze. The look in his eyes was dark, seductive. And the fire that suddenly shot between them triggered something warm, sensuous, heated. Maxi couldn't begin to describe the emotion gripping her.

When a fast song began playing, a corner of Christopher's lips lifted into a smile. "Had enough or do we boogie some more?" he asked huskily.

She returned his smile. "I've had enough, what about you?"

He continued to hold her gaze. "Yeah, I've had enough. Would you like to go for a walk?"

She nodded slowly and let him lead her toward the door. Garrett and Mya were arriving as they were leaving.

"The two of you are leaving already?" Mya asked.

"Yes." Christopher answered. "We're going for a walk around the deck for a while."

Mya's eyes sharpened as her gaze moved from Christopher to Maxi. Christopher had the ability to school his emotions but that was not the case with Maxi. And from Maxi's flushed face Mya knew they would be doing a lot more than walking around on deck. She moved her gaze from Maxi to let it settle again on Christopher.

"We'll see you tomorrow," he said meeting Mya's stare.

"Are the two of you getting off the ship for the Cayman Islands in the morning?" Garrett asked.

Christopher's gaze moved from Mya to Garrett. "Yes."

"Then how about joining us on the tour?" Garrett invited.

"That's fine with me." Christopher looked at Maxi. "What about it?"

Maxi smiled and looked at Garrett. She refused to make eye contact with Mya again knowing Mya could read her like a book. "That will be fun. We'll see you in the morning."

Mya watched them walk away. "They're leaving early," she said thoughtfully to Garrett.

He pulled her closer to his side. He knew Mya had concerns as to where Maxi and Christopher's relationship was headed. "They're leaving early, or we're arriving late."

She smiled when she remembered the reason they were late. "True. Come on, let's dance the night away."

Christopher took Maxi's hand in his as they slowly strolled along the deck. The view of the ocean was beautiful and there were a number of couples out enjoying the sight.

"So, who is your best friend?" Maxi asked breaking into their moment of silence.

Christopher lifted a brow and looked at her. "Pardon?"

"Earlier, when we were dancing you mentioned that you and your best friend used to go out dancing a lot. Who's your best friend?"

When moments passed and Christopher didn't say anything, Maxi said swiftly. "I'm sorry, Christopher. I shouldn't have asked that. It's really none of my business, it's just that I was surprised to hear you say that. In all the years I've known you, I've never known you to get close enough to anyone for you to consider them your best friend. This person must be really special."

Christopher stopped walking and leaned against the rail. He thought about how his friendship with Gabe had started and how close they were now. "His name is Gabe Blackwell, and yes, he is special. His whole family is. Gabe and I work together." After a few moments he added, "And you don't have to apologize. The reason I didn't answer right away is because when you asked me the question I became caught up in memories of how Gabe and I became best friends. We started out as enemies."

Maxi lifted a brow. "Why?"

"Because of our stubbornness. We had worked together and discovered we did things differently and made a big issue out of those differences. It took a wise old man, who happened to be Gabe's father as well as my boss, to show the two of us that at times differences can be good, depending on how you work with them."

Maxi nodded. "I agree. I tell my students that all the time. Just think how boring things would be if everyone thought the same way or did the same things. Each of us is unique and no two people think or act alike. That's why we all have a right to our own opinions."

Christopher smiled. "It won't do me any good to ask if you'd always been this smart, because I know the answer since I was in most of your classes in school."

Maxi chuckled. "I'm not smart. I just like to analyze things and so do you. I found that out during those six weeks the two of us worked together on that science project. Remember?"

"Yes, I remember." Christopher didn't think he would ever forget. It had been a lifelong dream come true. It was as if someone up there had finally taken a liking to him. At the time he'd thought that being given the chance to spend time with Maxine Chandler for whatever reason, was the ultimate in a heavenly blessing. She'd been special to him ever since the first time he'd seen her when he'd arrived at school in the first grade, two years older than everybody else. His mother had grudgingly sent him looking raggedy, with no lunch, and no money. Instead of making fun of him like the other kids had done, Maxi had shared her lunch with him and for a number of days after that, until he began bringing his own lunch, she would always include a little extra something in her lunchbox for him. He doubted she even remembered that act of kindness but he had never forgotten it. Over the course of years following that first day, he'd been so smitten with her he couldn't think straight. He had fantasized about her for twelve long years, even during the time when he hadn't known or understood what fantasizing about a person was about. Her name had been carved on just about every tree in the housing project where he'd lived. To put it bluntly, he had been obsessed with Maxi and she hadn't known it, even when it was evident that he was wearing his heart on his sleeve. It wasn't that she had tried to deliberately snub him, she just hadn't had a clue. Now, ten years later and she could still make him get sweaty palms just being around her.

They stood quietly together, side by side, looking at the water. There was a full moon in the sky and its reflection made the water appear full of crystals. Christopher brought her closer to him and wrapped his arms around her waist. All evening it had been hard to keep his hands off her, so he decided not to try any longer. "Do you know why I wanted to be out here alone with you, Maxi?" he whispered huskily, his lips brushing her earlobe.

Maxi tried staying relaxed, although her pulse rate increased tenfold. "I think so, but tell me anyway."

"While we were dancing I had a mad urge to kiss you and didn't think I could wait a minute longer, but now . . ."

Maxi inhaled deeply as she met his gaze. "But now you've changed your mind?" she asked softly, the smallest of smiles curving her lips.

He returned her smile as he shook his head, "Not by a long shot. It's just that I don't think being out here in the open is an appropriate place for our first kiss. At least not the kind of kiss I want to give you." He decided not to add he'd waited quite a number of years for this opportunity and when he got started he didn't want to be interrupted until he had gotten his fill.

"Oh." Heat curled into Maxi's stomach and made her cheeks feel flushed as she thought of just what kind of kiss that might be. She had admitted to herself earlier that day that she was more conscious of Christopher than she had been of any man in a long time; especially since Jason's death. "Where do you suggest we go for privacy?" she asked although she knew the obvious. She hoped she wasn't sounding overly anxious.

"Our cabin. And I won't take things any farther than you want me to, but I've got to kiss you, Maxi."

She nodded. She knew the feeling. And it was slowly overtaking her in a deep sensuous way. "All right."

As soon as the words left her mouth, Christopher quickly ushered her toward the first elevator they came to.

As soon as Maxi and Christopher reached their cabin, he opened the door. Once inside and the door closed shut behind them, their gazes met. She watched his eyes darken as they slid dead center to her lips. She then felt a moment of caution that she was about to dive into unfamiliar waters.

"Say it," he murmured huskily, softly. "Say you want me to kiss you."

All sense of caution fled with his request. "I want you to kiss me, Christopher." She spoke quietly. The words, echoing softly in the cabin. The desire to taste her was there in his eyes. She saw it. He was making no attempt to hide it.

"I'm going to do more than just kiss you, Maxi," Christopher warned, speaking with fierce emotion storming through every part of him. "I'm going to make love to your mouth. I want to give you ultimate pleasure from my kiss." The grooves in his cheeks deepened and the huskiness in his voice increased. "Are you prepared for that?"

Maxi inhaled deeply, not sure she was prepared for anything, especially something of the magnitude he was alluding to. What would be so different about his kiss than the ones she'd shared with Jason? They had been enjoyable but . . . *ultimate pleasure?* She didn't have a clue what ultimate pleasure entailed but as she studied Christopher she had a feeling she was about to find out.

He took a few steps toward her. Her breath caught when his arms slid around her. "Are you prepared for that?" he repeated softly, bring her closer against him.

Maxi felt his heat and moved toward that heat. She wrapped her arms around his neck and met his hot fiery gaze. "Yes, I'm prepared for that," she responded softly.

He smiled. "Then hold on," he whispered roughly before leaning down and slanting his mouth across hers, forging them together.

She tasted his hunger, hot and sensuous, the moment their mouths met and the heat of it snared her, pulled her into sensations she'd never before experienced. His tongue filled her mouth completely, searching, exploring, as her mouth opened fully beneath his. He continued to probe the secret places of her mouth before capturing her tongue and mating it with his in a way she didn't think possible, slow, deep, intense. Blood rushed fast and furiously through her veins, heightening all her senses.

Maxi was fully aware she was kissing him back in a way that was downright greedy, scandalous. She could hear the sounds of his deep-gutted groans, which triggered soft little moans to quiver all the way in her throat, flooding desire through her bloodstream in a way that should have frightened her. The sound only blazed the fire within her that much hotter. She took in everything about him, the hardness of his body pressed against hers, the masculine scent of him, and the rich, hot taste of him that was making her tremble in his arms.

Then he touched her backside and pulled her closer to the fit of him. She felt hard evidence of how much wanting and desire their kiss was generating. His hand moved expertly over her body caressing her, slowly, gently, and sensuously and making heat pool in one spot between her legs. As he continued to kiss her that particular spot became hotter and hotter. She felt alive in a way she had never felt before and now acknowledged that not even Jason had ever aroused her so thoroughly, so deeply.

Breaking the kiss, Christopher lifted her and sat her on the dresser with her gown shoved up around her waist. His gaze met hers, gauging her response to what he'd just done, waiting for her to deny him the chance to continue, to take the intimacy of their kiss on a whole other level, letting her know the final decision was hers to make. And she made it when she leaned toward him, her lips inviting, welcoming. She placed her arms around his neck.

That was all the sign he needed. He clamped his mouth back down on hers, immediately deepening their kiss. She felt him nudge her legs apart to stand between them, angling his body intimately between hers. She felt his hand move from her back to her thighs, stroking a trail toward her center. The sound of her panty hose being ripped in the seat, sent an electrical charge all the way from the top of her head to the soles of her feet. And when mere seconds later she felt his fingers cup her through her satin and lace panties, and stroke his thumb over her, she raised her hips off the dresser, automatically drawn to his hand. Her legs instinctively widened. He swallowed her groan as he continued to kiss her as his finger stroked every sane thought from her mind. She tried pulling her mouth away from his when she felt herself wanting to scream but he wouldn't let her. It was as if their mouths were fused tight.

A few blistering seconds later, she couldn't take any more as smoldering heat overtook her. Her arms tightened around his neck when she felt her body explode in a thousand pieces. He absorbed into his mouth every moan of pleasure she made as his tongue continued to mate with hers, using the same rhythm his finger was using on her, draining her of everything.

It was only when her body went limp that he released her mouth. She slowly opened her eyes and stared breathless at him. Bewildered. Disoriented. Overwhelmed. She continued to stare at him. Her eyes felt heavy, her mouth felt bruised and the womanly core of her felt . . . wet.

The intense look Christopher was giving her did not try to mask the naked passion of desire still boiling inside him. He gently picked her up off the dresser and placed her on her feet and held her when he saw she had difficulty standing on her own. "You taste better than brandy," he said thickly. "I could drink you up all night and still would not get enough. You're one sexy woman, Maxine Chandler. You are well worth the wait."

Maxi blinked sluggishly, the sensations of what she'd felt still lingering. "The wait?"

He met her gaze. "Yes. I've wanted to kiss you ever since that first day in school when we were in the first grade." He smiled. "Not quite the way I just did since my mind hadn't matured that far. But every year as I got older my fantasies got wilder. What you just got was a good seventeen years worth of them."

Maxi blinked again. Finding it hard to do so. "Seventeen years?"

"Yes. Twelve years of school and five years after I left Savannah to rid you from my constant thoughts and heated dreams. It wasn't until Mr. Thompson wrote and told me you were getting married that I stopped thinking about you. It didn't seem right to continue having such intimate thoughts and dreams about another man's future wife."

"You knew I had gotten engaged to Jason?"

He hesitated briefly before answering. "Yes. Occasionally I would get a letter from Mr. Thompson. He kept me abreast of a number of things, especially about you. He knew how I felt about you."

Maxi's head began spinning with everything Christopher was telling her. "Mr. Thompson? Our science teacher?" At Christopher's nod she asked. "How?"

Christopher smiled. "You know Mr. Thompson. Nothing got past him and it didn't help matters when he found that letter."

"What letter?"

"The letter I had written to you one day in class. Somehow it had gotten mixed up with the work I had turned in to him. He gave it back to me the next day."

Maxi shook her head, trying to absorb everything Christopher was saying. "It's hard to believe that you thought about me after you left Savannah."

"I thought about you all the time, Maxi."

She inhaled deeply. "B-but you didn't even tell me goodbye when you left."

His hands moved up to cup her shoulders, bringing her closer to him. It was time to tell her why he hadn't told her goodbye when he'd left town ten years ago. A part of him wondered why he had made that decision. Maybe it was because he needed to hear it for himself, to fully understand why he had kissed her the way he had tonight. Why even now he wanted to kiss her again, and why she got to him like no other woman could. "Leaving you behind in Savannah was the hardest thing I'd ever had to do," he finally answered. "I couldn't bring myself to tell you goodbye, Maxi, but for my survival I had to. I had cared too much for you back then and I knew it was headed nowhere." He sighed. That kind of admission would be lethal in the hands of most of the women that he knew, but he wasn't dealing with most women. He was dealing with a woman who was in a class by herself.

For the longest time Maxi didn't say anything. The sane part of her mind was telling her to let it rest, but she couldn't. She had to let him know how she had felt back then, too. "And I probably cared just as much for you, and I thought it could go somewhere," she said quietly, looking away.

She gasped when Christopher immediately captured her chin in his hand and directed her eyes back to his. He looked stunned. "What are you saying?" he asked throatily, not taking his gaze off her. Emotions flashed in the hard set of his jaw and the darkness of his eyes as he looked at her.

Maxi swallowed, then gave in to a slow sigh. "I'm saying that I had cared deeply for you back then, too. The only person who knew how I felt was Mya."

"Mya?"

"Yes."

Christopher nodded, releasing her chin and dropping his hands to his side. No wonder the woman had tried getting all into his business last night. He then studied Maxi's face for the truth of her words. And he saw it, the naked truth shining in the softness of her brown eyes. "I didn't know," he finally whispered, slowly.

"Yeah, and I didn't know about how you felt either," she said. "I wonder if things would have been different had we known."

He slowly shook his head. "I'm sure we would have gotten around to kissing a whole hell of a lot sooner, but I still would have left Savannah, Maxi. Not even you could have kept me there." *Because I had nothing to offer you then,* he thought to himself.

"I would not have tried. But I would have wanted for us to stay in touch, Christopher. I had loved you just that much."

His gaze met hers, shocked, then touched by her words. During that time he'd felt no one had loved him and that no one had wanted him. At no time while living in Savannah had he ever felt a sense of belonging. And the scandal involving his mother had made things worse. It was only after he'd left and met the Blackwells that he'd fully felt a deep sense of belonging. They had opened up their hearts and home and had made him a part of their family.

He grazed Maxi's cheek with his finger and felt heat settle in his stomach when her lips quivered from his touch. He pulled his hand back as the full impact of what they had both admitted hit him. Ten years ago, just as he had loved her, this beautiful woman had loved him too. Loved him, Christopher Chandler, who hadn't had anything to offer her. A man who had been the town's bad boy, their holy terror. Ten years that neither of them would ever be able to recapture.

With supreme effort he took a step back. He needed to think. He needed to pull himself together. And he needed to curse the fate that had brought them together at the worst possible time, because things had changed. He had changed and so had his feelings. He wasn't madly in love with her as before. He wasn't madly in love with any woman. Those days were long gone. "I need to go out for a while." Without saying anything else he turned and quickly left the room.

For a few brief moments Maxi stood glued to the spot. She wondered how she and Christopher would handle things tomorrow now that they had stepped beyond what was normal behavior for cabinmates who weren't supposed to be involved.

Going into the bathroom, she undressed quickly, seeing evidence of the extent of what she and Christopher had shared when she removed her torn pantyhose and tossed them in the trash can. She sighed deeply. She had been on the cruise for only two days and already so much had happened to her. The thought that Christopher had cared something for her ten years ago had her entire body shivering. She inhaled deeply, determined to be in bed by the time he returned. She had a lot to think about but she didn't want to do it tonight. Otherwise she would be forced to remember his busy fingers, cocksure tongue, and "lock-you-in" mouth.

Less than thirty minutes later she was in bed feeling exhausted and feeling something she hadn't felt in a long time. Satiated. There could be a lot said about sexual release, she thought as she drifted into sleep.

Two hours later Christopher returned to find Maxi in bed asleep. He had walked the length of the entire ship, played the slot machines in the casino, and still hadn't come to terms with what had happened between them tonight. He had brought her to a climax while kissing and touching her. She had been so responsive, so passionate, so tasty, and so utterly Maxi. She was a person who was totally honest in her giving, so expressive in her feelings. And when she had told him that she once cared deeply for him, that had been too much for him to handle.

He looked across the cabin at her asleep in bed. It took every ounce of will power he had not to undress, cross the room, and slide into bed with her. He took a long, deep breath and rubbed at the tension knotting the back of his neck. It was his body's warning sign whenever he'd gotten himself into something way too deep; and all he had to do was to glance across the room at Maxi's angelic expression while she slept to know that he had. He forced his gaze away from her to take in the beauty of the ocean outside the porthole over her bed. He wasn't a long-term relationship kind of man. Hell, he wasn't a short-term relationship kind either. He was a hitter. He enjoyed scoring hits, then making it home. Alone. The last thing he wanted

or needed was to get seriously involved with a woman, even
Maxine Chandler. Emotionally, he didn't want it. Mentally, he
couldn't handle it. But physically, his body was aching for it.

Even after all these years, he still wanted to stamp his claim
all over her. He wanted her to be his in the most elemental and
primal way. He knew what he was feeling wasn't normal and
that it didn't make sense, but then he never had much sense
where Maxi was concerned. He'd always been ruled by a
deeper emotion than common sense.

CHAPTER TWENTY-ONE

"Hey, Mya, you got a minute?"

Mya looked up from the breakfast buffet table at Maxi and smiled. "Sure." She glanced around. "Where's Christopher?"

Maxi shrugged as she picked up a plate. "Beats me. He was gone when I woke up this morning."

Mya studied Maxi and smiled at the gloomy expression she wore. "What's wrong? Didn't he enjoy your walk around deck last night?" she teased.

"I have no idea what he enjoyed."

Mya studied Maxi some more. Concern then clouded her eyes. "You want to tell me what happened?"

Maxi reached over and filled her plate with pancakes, eggs, and bacon. "Trust me, you don't want to know."

"Oh, hell yes, I do!"

Mya and Maxi looked at each other and burst out laughing. It was just like old times. "Yeah, Mrs. Rivers, I suppose you do," Maxi said bringing her laughter under control. "It was foolish of me to forget just how nosy you are."

"And don't forget I'm a person who likes details."

"Another one of your faults." Maxi glanced around. "Where's Garrett?"

"A group of men recognized him and he's off somewhere signing autographs and talking football, so we'll have a chance to chat privately. And like I said, Maxine Jeanae, I want details."

"Wow, after listening to you the last thing I need is hot coffee in my system," Mya said, pushing her coffee cup aside. "What I need is something to cool me off. Just throw me in the ocean, will you? Girl, sounds like you might be headed for trouble."

They had found a table on the top deck to catch the morning breeze while they enjoyed breakfast overlooking the ocean. Maxi met Mya's gaze. She'd told Mya about her and Christopher's kiss but left out a lot of the details. It was something too private, too intimate to share even with Mya. "Trouble in what way?" she asked taking a sip of her coffee.

"Now that you know how Christopher felt about you back then and he knows how you felt about him, there's bound to be trouble."

Maxi raised her eyes heavenward. "You still haven't said in what way, Mya."

"In the way of history repeating itself. I heard that feelings never die. They just get tucked away until it's the perfect time for them to resurface."

"Well, you heard wrong. Christopher was ten years ago, Mya. He was before Jason and before Howard University."

"Umm, just be careful, Maxi. Kisses can lead to other things."

"Christopher would never force himself on me, Mya."

"No, but I wouldn't put it past you to force yourself on him."

"Mya!"

"Hey, wait, before you get your panties in a twist, just listen to what I'm saying. I've been doing the thang a lot longer than you have and it all started with kissing. You of all people know how it was for Garrett and me. We couldn't keep our hands off each other after our first kiss. Don't you remember how many times you had to cover for me with Gramma Twila? For you it will be a whole lot worse. Hell, Maxi, it's been four years since you've been with a man!"

"Trust me, you don't have to remind me, Mya."

"Okay then, you understand where I'm coming from, don't you?" Mya asked. She raised her brow when Maxi's attention was captured by something behind her back. Mya peered around to see what it was.

Christopher.

And he had seen them and was headed their way. Mya turned back to Maxi and watched as Maxi continued to looked at Christopher while unconsciously licking her bottom lip with her tongue. "You know what, Maxi?" Mya said breaking into Maxi's deep concentration.

Maxi broke eye contact with Christopher and looked at Mya. "What?"

"I hope you remember my warning."

"Good morning, ladies."

Maxi smiled nervously at him, remembering the intimacy of the kiss they'd shared last night and the response he had gotten out of her just from kissing her. She was still tingling in the area between her legs that his fingers had touched. "Good morning, Christopher."

Mya couldn't help but smother a grin. The sexual tension between Maxi and Christopher was so thick you could cut it with a knife. "Good morning, Christopher. You haven't run into my hubby have you?"

Christopher slowly shifted his gaze from Maxi to Mya. "Yes, in fact I did. He's on his way up and said to tell you that as soon as he can grab a bagel and a cup of coffee he'll be ready for us to go."

"You're still going with us?" Maxi asked surprised.

Christopher's gaze returned to hers. "Yes, I'm still invited to go along, aren't I?"

"Sure, I just thought you might have changed your mind."

There was a moment of dead silence before he spoke. "Do you prefer that I not go, Maxi?"

She shook her head. "Of course not."

Sensing that these two needed to be alone for a while, Mya cleared her throat and said, "I left my sunglasses in the cabin. Excuse me while I go back and get them."

Christopher took the seat Mya vacated. "Should we have told her that her sunglasses were sitting real pretty atop her head?" he asked Maxi, grinning.

Maxi chuckled. "No. She would have found another excuse to leave us alone for a while."

Christopher nodded. He then studied Maxi. It may have been his imagination but to his way of thinking she still had that thoroughly kissed look on her face. "Did you sleep well?" he asked.

"Yes. What about you?"

He started to tell her he had slept with a hard-on all night but decided that wouldn't be the proper thing to do. Instead he said, "Yes, I slept hard as a rock."

As soon as he said it, a fission of heat curled around in his stomach. He watched her pick up a piece of toast then opened her mouth to receive it. He wished it were his tongue going into her mouth instead of that piece of toast. She must have felt his eyes on her and she slanted him a glance that almost took his breath away and made him realize just how beautiful she was. It should be against the law for any woman to look this good in the morning, he thought, gazing across the table at her. She had her hair combed back under a Dallas Cowboys cap, with little pearl earrings in her ears. He could tell she had on barely any makeup but she had such a natural glow about her that he thought she really didn't need any.

"So, do you plan to shop the day away?" he asked, thinking steady conversation would ease the tension he felt pressing against his zipper.

"Yes, there's a few items I want to buy. I told Mama I would bring her something back."

He nodded. Then there was dead silence again. After a few moments he said, "Maxi, why are we so uncomfortable around each other this morning?"

Maxi took a sip of her coffee, ignoring the fact it had turned cold and said quietly. "I don't know. You tell me. You're the one who was gone when I woke up this morning."

"And you think I did it to avoid you?"

She stared at him. "Didn't you?"

There was dead silence again.

"Well, didn't you?" she asked again when the silence stretched on too long.

"Yes," he said truthfully after a few moments. "We talked about some pretty heavy stuff last night, Maxi."

"Yes, we did. Would you have preferred that we hadn't talked?"

"No, not as long as we both understand that all those feelings are in the past."

She looked at him from beneath her lashes. "And where else would they be, Christopher?" she asked quietly.

He looked at her, inwardly acknowledging that he was the uncertain one. Like he told her whatever feelings they'd once had for each other should remain in the past but a part of him wished to hell they were in the present, and that was what was bothering him more than anything. During the last few years, after hearing about her pending marriage, he hadn't thought about her . . . at least the majority of the time he hadn't. But he knew things wouldn't be that easy once he returned to Detroit; especially since he had kissed her, had touched her, and had tasted her. There was no doubt in his mind that she would be a torment he would have to find a way to deal with.

"And where else would they be, Christopher?" Maxi repeated when he had not given her an answer.

"Nowhere but in the past where they belong. What we felt for each other was then and this is now. I'm not looking for an involvement with anyone, Maxi."

"Neither am I."

He held her gaze for a moment then nodded, satisfied with her answer. "So things are back to normal and we're just friends again. No more kissing, no more touching, no more—"

"Looking at each other funny?"

He looked at her and she grinned. He shook his head and grinned back. Leave it to Maxi to make an uncomfortable situation comfortable. "Yeah, and no more looking at each other funny." He reached his hand out to her. "Come on, let's go find Garrett and Mya. I intend for us to enjoy ourselves in the Cayman Islands."

CHAPTER TWENTY-TWO

Three nights later at the class reunion banquet, Christopher sat at a table with Garrett, barely listening to what he was saying. His mind was all wrapped up in thoughts of Maxi. They had spent the remaining days of the cruise sticking to the agreement they had made. He wasn't supposed to think about kissing or touching her but that's all he'd been thinking about. And he wasn't supposed to look at her funny. But several times he had caught himself looking at her funny anyway and he knew that on more than one occasion she had noticed him looking. Hell. So much for breaking his own rules. To make things easier on them, he usually left the cabin early and came back late when he knew she would be asleep. He wasn't sure how she spent her days but they weren't with him. Other than the day they had spent together with the Rivers touring the Cayman Islands, they had basically gone their separate ways ever since.

"I don't like talking to myself, Chandler. If I'm boring you, just say so."

Garrett's words cut into Christopher's thoughts. He took a quick glance into the other man's face and smiled apologetically. "Sorry. My mind was elsewhere."

"Yeah, that was obvious. I see Maxi still keeps your mind in a spin."

Christopher lifted a brow. He wasn't sure he wanted to discuss Maxi with Garrett. After all, the man was married to Maxi's best friend and there was no doubt in Christopher's mind that anything he said to Garrett would probably get back to Mya. When two people had been together for as long as Garrett and Mya had, they usually shared everything. But still . . .

"What do you mean she still keeps my mind in a spin?"

Garrett chuckled. "That's just a figure of speech. What I mean is that it's nice to know Mya and I aren't the only two people in our high school class who're still into each other after ten years."

Christopher took a sip of his brandy. "Now that's where you're wrong, Rivers. Maxi and I aren't still into each other. Being on this cruise is the first time we've been together in over ten years."

"So, what's that supposed to mean? A lot could have happened in seven days."

Christopher frowned. "Trust me, it didn't."

Garrett took a huge swig of his beer before saying, "The cruise isn't over yet. This ship doesn't pull into port until tomorrow. And the way I see it, it's either you or Swindel and personally, I prefer seeing Maxi end up with you."

Christopher shot Garrett a disapproving glare. "What do you mean it's me or Swindel? Maxi isn't interested in him."

"No, but he's interested in her. Just like you, he always had a thing for Maxi. He's just been going about it the wrong way. One day I expect he'll wake up and realize he can't use the same approach with her that he uses with other women. She's not impressed by what possessions a person has or doesn't have."

Christopher nodded. He knew that much was true. "Swindel will be wasting his time."

"How can you be so sure of that?" Garrett asked. "Who knows

what might happen if Swindel turns over a new leaf? Remember he still lives in Savannah and you don't. That makes the playing field uneven, so to speak."

Christopher glared at Garrett. If the man was trying to get him angry, it was working. But still, he was determined to keep his cool. "There is no playing field, Rivers. Maxi and I are nothing more than friends. Whatever I felt for her ten years ago is dead and buried, and I intend for it to stay that way."

Garrett nodded slowly. "Okay, if that's the way you feel. Then it shouldn't bother you that Swindel and a few others have zeroed in on the fact that you've taken a step back."

Christopher frowned. "What the hell are you talking about?"

Garrett smiled. "What I'm talking about, Chandler, is that for years everyone knew there was an unspoken understanding of just who Maxi belonged to, even if Maxi never knew it herself. Now for the past few days you've been trying to make it obvious that you no longer have a thing for her, and that leaves it wide open to anyone who may have been interested but who'd always kept a safe distance for fear of your wrath. Now technically, you've given them your blessings. Take a look."

Christopher's gaze followed Garrett's across the room. Maxi had just walked in and immediately she was surrounded by a number of the single men from their class reunion group. But what irked Christopher more than anything was the fact that somehow Swindel had worked his way to her side and had his hand on her arm.

Christopher took a deep breath and swallowed his rising anger. "Your wife is also surrounded by them, Rivers," he decided to point out.

"Yeah, but they know Mya's taken. My name is stamped all over her. Make no mistake about it, although my woman looks good too, those men are there because of Maxi. For the first time you aren't her protector and they're taking full advantage of that fact. Things should be real interesting tonight, Chandler. Real interesting."

* * *

Christopher glanced around the table. Just as Garrett had predicted, things were real interesting. When Maxi and Mya had finally made it to their table, those men, including Swindel, had had the audacity to follow and each took a seat. And it didn't help matters that the outfit Maxi was wearing was enough to give a man cardiac arrest because it afforded everyone a glimpse of her lush cleavage every time she leaned forward. And you better believe that, other than Garrett, who was too caught up with how good his own wife was looking, every man's gaze at the table was centered on Maxi. Although Christopher knew she hadn't intentionally dressed provocatively, her outfit was provocative just the same. Hell, a plain flannel gown buttoned up to the neck would look provocative on Maxi.

He studied the faces at the table. It was crowded and it seemed everyone was speaking at once, all vying for Maxi's attention, but it was Colter Watson's deep, loud voice that eventually captured it.

"So, Maxi, I hear your church is one of the ones that protested the proposed tearing down of the houses in that old housing project off Vine Street."

Christopher's interest was immediately drawn to the conversation. He listened to Maxi's response. "Yes, the city plans to tear them down and rezone all that land for commercial use. The sad thing is that they have no plans to build more housing elsewhere for the people who live there. Literally, that will be putting them out on the streets."

"But think of the additional revenue the city will make if they sell the land to a developer," Ronald Swindel said before glancing across the table at Christopher. "It's my opinion that the people who live in the Vines will eventually find somewhere to live. I support the tearing down of that neighborhood. It has been an eyesore in Savannah for years. Nothing ever came from out of the Vines but trash."

Everyone got deathly quiet at Swindel's insult since it was a known fact that Christopher had lived in that particular housing project from the time he was born until the time he had moved away from Savannah.

Christopher put down the drink he was holding, deciding to knock the hell out of Swindel once and for all. But then, beneath the table he felt Maxi's hand lightly squeeze his thigh, a silent plea for him not to. He inhaled deeply to contain his anger as he met Swindel's glare. The man was just waiting for him to respond and he was more than willing to do so by putting a fist in his face. But Maxi's hand on his thigh stopped him. His fingers slipped beneath the table and tightened over her hand to assure her he was okay and that he wouldn't cause a scene.

"It doesn't surprise me that you would think that way, Ronald," said Maxi, who had been fuming ever since he'd made the slur and finally spoke up, breaking into the silence surrounding the table. "But I happen to disagree. More than just trash came out of the Vines. I can't help but admire people who can rise up above their less-than-desirable situation and make something of themselves. I would think all of us could appreciate that."

Ronald cleared his throat, clearly embarrassed by Maxi's statement. "What I meant is that I used to get more calls from that area of town than any other area. There was always something going on over there regarding drugs, prostitution, and domestic violence. You name it, the Vines had it."

"Yes, and fortunately that meant job security for you, didn't it?" Maxi asked in a curt tone. She had everyone's attention because it was evident that she was angry. And one thing everyone knew was that it wasn't easy to get Maxine Chandler angry but Ronald Swindel had succeeded. Ronald knew it, too, and was trying desperately to back-pedal into her good graces.

Christopher sighed when it occurred to him that Maxi's hand was still resting on his thigh and his hand was still covering hers. They were breaking one of their rules of not touching, but he didn't want to pull his hand away and it appeared neither did she.

He had watched her dance with just about every man at the table, including Garrett, and when another song, a slow one, started playing he knew it was now his time to dance with her. But before he could ask her, Swindel stood up and reached his hand across the table for hers, smiling.

"Finally a slow number. Come on, Maxi, let's dance."

Maxi couldn't believe that Ronald couldn't see how upset she was with him. She looked at his outstretched hand before saying softly. "Sorry, Ronald, I've promised this dance to Christopher." She then looked over at Christopher hoping he wouldn't make her into a liar.

He didn't.

He stood when Ronald had the common sense to sit down. Taking Maxi's hand in his, Christopher led the way from their table to the dance floor. Once there he pulled her in, wrapped his arms around her and with the music playing softly in the background he began moving slowly in place.

The moment their bodies touched, Christopher wondered why he had been avoiding the feel of this for the past three days? Why had he set himself up for such punishment? She felt wonderful in his arms and when she slipped her arms around his neck, he thought he had died and gone to heaven. The feel of her breasts on his chest was torture in one way and rapture in another. And the alluring scent of her perfume was something else he had to contend with. He pulled her closer when he realized the times she'd danced with others tonight had been fast numbers, including the one time she had danced with Swindel, but she had reserved this slow number just for him.

A part of him wanted to whisper to her that he had missed her these past three days. He had missed being around her, kissing her, touching her, and the freedom of looking at her funny. He had missed everything about her. And he had been miserable. He had felt alone. It was ironic that he felt that way since his main reason for coming on the cruise was to be alone and to rest. But once he had run into Maxi, that had changed. Like always, she had been like a magnet pulling him in, and he hadn't been able to resist. And he hadn't been resting at night knowing she was in the same room with him, just on the other side. So close, yet so far away. He had dreamed about her every night and flashes of those dreams were on his mind now. Vividly. He felt his body harden.

"A penny for your thoughts," Maxi said breaking the silence between them.

Christopher looked down at her. It would probably scare her to death if she knew he'd been thinking of the many ways and positions that he wanted to make love to her. Instead of answering her, he continued to stare at her and knew the exact moment she got an idea what he'd been thinking. He was sure his hard front pressing tight against her middle was a dead giveaway. He watched her quick intake of breath, then continued to watch as her bottom lip quivered nervously. He wanted so badly to take his tongue and calm those lips.

"It's not working is it, Christopher?"

He didn't pretend not to know what she was talking about. "No, it's not."

She let out a deep sigh. "I'm sure we can survive this one night since the cruise ends tomorrow."

This one night. It suddenly occurred to him that that's all they had. "I'm not so sure about that," he said huskily.

"Why?" she asked. He could tell she was confused. But then so was he. What they had felt for each other ten years ago shouldn't be coming back to toy with them, especially when those feelings had no place in either of their lives now. And especially when a relationship was the last thing he wanted with any woman, including Maxi.

Taking a deep breath, he decided to be completely honest with her. With Maxi he didn't know any other way. "I want you, Maxi. Although I know I shouldn't, I do." He looked down at her. "But I'm not interested in any long-term relationships. Do you understand what I'm trying to say?"

Maxi studied his features intently under the dim lighting overhead, then nodded slowly. "Yes." She now understood what Mya had meant by cravings. She had been craving Christopher's kisses for nearly three days now.

"Then what do you suggest we do?" he asked huskily.

She smiled up at him and he felt his gut clench in a thousand places. "Do you want to go to the cabin and talk about it?"

He wanted to go to the cabin, but talking was the last thing on his mind. "Yeah, let's go to the cabin and talk." Sliding his arm around her shoulder and tucking her under his arm he led them out of the dance club.

CHAPTER TWENTY-THREE

"What are we going to talk about?" Maxi asked the moment she walked into the cabin and watched Christopher close the door behind them. Taking a deep, slow breath, she tried to calm her jitters as well as the abundance of desire racing through her.

Stepping away from the closed door, Christopher stood in front of her with both hands in the pockets of his pants staring at her. As much as he wanted to forgo talking of any kind he knew that wouldn't be wise. He had to be sure he and Maxi were on the same page and that she wanted everything that he wanted tonight.

"We can talk about anything you want to talk about." He glanced around the room. "Would you like to sit down for a while?"

"Yes." Taking another deep breath she sat down in the love-seat in the room. He sat down next to her and placed his arms across the back of the sofa.

Maxi looked down nervously at her lap then back at him. "Well, what have you been doing the last few days?"

He didn't respond for a few seconds, then he answered. "Missing you."

Maxi inhaled sharply, quickly glancing up at him. "Be serious, Christopher."

He met her stare. "I am serious and I'm also being completely honest. I would deliberately leave before you got up in the mornings, then would intentionally stay away until I knew it was past your bedtime. During all that time I missed being around you, talking to you, seeing you, and—"

"Then why did you do it?" she interrupted.

"Because like I told you, I don't want to get involved with anyone, and I saw us on the verge of an involvement."

"If you still feel that way, then why are we here now, Christopher? Why are we alone in this room?"

Suddenly Christopher didn't know what he could tell her. How could he explain? "I really don't know," he finally said, feeling more unsure of himself where she was concerned than ever before. "All I know is that around you I look at things differently. I enjoy doing things that I normally don't like. Hell, I've even eaten broccoli and I hate the stuff." He frowned as he ran his gaze over her, taking time to analyze everything about her. "There's something about you that makes me forget the cruelties of this world. You are so full of goodness, so kind, it's a shame there aren't more people like you. You don't know the meaning of kicking someone to the curb. You're a crusader of good and noble causes and definitely not the type of woman I've been messing around with for the past ten years. There's not a self-centered bone in your body. Until I ran into you on this cruise, I was absolutely sure that a totally different type of woman appealed to me. You have proven me wrong. You're making my life rather complicated, Maxine Chandler."

She met his gaze and smiled warmly at all the compliments he'd given her, but noting the agitation in his voice. "I don't mean to, Christopher."

"I know you don't and it's not entirely your fault. The blame is mine for still letting you get next to me. And you do get next to me, Maxi. With you, old habits die hard. I can't stand the thought of anyone wanting you but me or, worse yet, anyone having you. I don't want to care."

Maxi took a deep breath as her heart hammered through her chest. She didn't want to become involved with him any more than he wanted to become involved with her. "Then don't care, Christopher. Let's not do anything we may regret later. Let's get out of here and go back to the Pinnacle Club. Tomorrow this ship will dock in Tampa and you'll go your way and I'll go mine, possibly never ever seeing each other again. Let's remember our friendship, let's cherish it but let's not destroy it by becoming involved tonight. It will only complicate matters and I feel complicated enough. I'm dealing with a pretty heavy issue in my life right now and the last thing I need is anything to complicate matters furthers. We're friends and we'll always be friends. Let's just keep it that way. Tonight, I thought I could go beyond mere friendship with you, but I was just fooling myself. I can't because I'm not into casual affairs. I can't sleep with a man just for the sake of doing so. It has to mean something more than assuaging overactive hormones."

Christopher leaned toward her. For some reason he wasn't surprised with her attitude toward sex in general. "What's this heavy issue you're dealing with?" he asked.

Feeling embarrassment spread up her back and neck, Maxi took her hand from him and looked away. Her medical condition was nothing a woman openly discussed with a man. "It's personal, Christopher."

Christopher was undaunted. "Whatever it is, it's bothering you and that makes it my concern, Maxi. Is there anything that I can do?"

"You've already helped, Christopher. Spending time with you on this cruise has helped tremendously. Around you I can remember days when I didn't have a worry in the world. They were days when my biggest challenge was acing one of Mrs. Potter's pop quizzes. Now, I have so much to deal with but when

I'm with you I put it to the back of my mind and don't even think about it."

He knew whatever it was, she was probably dealing with it alone. He had a feeling she wasn't the type to unload her burdens on anyone. He took her hand back in his. "I'd known you practically most of my life, but in those six weeks during our senior year, we established a very special friendship, Maxi, more special than most people can establish in six years. Do you know why?"

She shook her head truly not knowing. They had worked hard together to make that science project a success but they had also gotten to know each other, respect each other and care for each other. "No."

"Because without even knowing it, we cared something for each other and because we were honest with each other. I shared some things with you that I had never shared with another soul. You were someone I could talk to, unload myself on, and not feel I would be judged accordingly. You have that way with people."

Maxi smiled. "And so do you. I enjoyed spending time with you. Just being around you was special. You'll never know how much I would watch the clock waiting for you to show up at my house so we could get started on our science project. None of it was about me, but just being around you meant so much."

Christopher shook his head, still finding it hard to believe that she'd actually cared something for him back then and had eagerly looked forward to their time together as much as he had.

"Then why are we holding back, giving less than one hundred percent now? I'm still a good listener if you want to talk about what's bothering you. Like I told you a couple of days ago, I hadn't really thought about you in around five years, only because I thought you were happily married to someone else. I had convinced myself you were somewhere happy, enjoying the things you've always wanted, a husband, a house full of kids, and—"

He stopped talking when he suddenly noticed the tears that immediately sprang into her eyes. "What is it, Maxi? What's wrong? What did I say to upset you?"

Maxi tried pulling herself together but he had hit on the one thing she had always wanted out of life but now would never have. Children. "Please, let me have some time alone now. I—I need to be alone for a while."

Christopher looked at her as she wiped the tears from her eyes and knew he would do as she asked although he didn't want to. As much as he wanted to know what had gotten her upset, he would respect her right to the privacy she had requested of him.

He stood, crossed the room and walked out the door. The moment he had pulled it shut he heard her crying. It was a soft painful sob that touched him. In all the years he had known her, he had never seen her cry. Whatever was bothering her was hurting her down deep. Making a quick decision, he turned, pushed the door open and went back inside the cabin. She was still sitting in the same spot on the sofa with her face buried in her hands. He immediately crossed the room to her, sat down and gathered her into his arms. "It's okay, Maxi. Whatever it is, it will be okay."

"No, it won't," she said between sobs. "It won't be okay."

Christopher held her, helpless, not sure what he could do or say to calm her. "Tell me, Maxi. What is it? Maybe I can help."

"You can't."

"I'm a good listener and sometimes talking helps."

After a few brief moments Maxi's sobs turned into light sniffles as she tried pulling herself together. Moving out of his arms, she hung her head, feeling the weight of everything on her shoulders. She had placed everything about the surgery in the back of her mind and now, as the cruise was coming to an end, it was there lurking in the background, reminding her of decisions she was going to have to make and soon. Christopher was right. Talking did help and she knew from past experience he was a person she could talk to. Men had a tendency to look at things differently from women. And maybe at the moment that's what she needed.

"Although I have no reason not to believe I won't eventually marry one day, Christopher, in a few months I'll have to undergo surgery that will end any chances of me ever having children."

Christopher frowned, not believing what he was hearing. He of all people knew how much having children meant to Maxi. That's all she had talked about. Hell, she had even picked out names back then. Getting a college degree, getting married, and having a family had been her dream. It didn't seem fair that his dream had come true but not hers. "Are you sure?"

"Yes. I've undergone several tests. Unless I have a baby before the surgery, then that's it."

He shook his head, still not fully understanding when the answer to her problem seemed perfectly clear to him. "Then have a baby before the surgery."

She looked up at him and smiled . . . then shook her head. "Christopher, that's not possible. I'm not involved with anyone and even if I was, I couldn't ask a man to get me pregnant. What man would willingly give me his child? Men don't exactly go out of their way to get women pregnant, you know."

He nodded. He knew that was true when he inwardly examined his own situation. He made it a point to never have sex without wearing a condom since he had decided years ago never to father a child. His childhood had been a living hell and he refused to bring any child into the world to ever endure what he had gone through. His mother would never have earned a medal for displaying motherly affection. But a part of him knew if such a medal was given out, Maxi would. There was no doubt in his mind that she would make a child a perfect mother. Any man would be honored for her to be the mother of his child. Including him.

He sat up straight and his throat suddenly felt dry when he

realized something. She was wrong. There was a way he could help. He had the ability to give her what she wanted. He breathed in deeply, knowing he needed to think this one through. But then he knew there was nothing to really think about. If Maxi wanted a baby then he would give her one, it would be that simple. Hadn't she given him so much? Hadn't he been successful in life because of her faith and belief that he could and would make something of himself? For years he had cared more for her than he'd cared for any woman, and he knew he would be fooling himself if he believed he didn't still care something for her. When a man loved a woman for that long and that strong, it never completely died.

"I would, Maxi," he finally said softly.

She arched a brow at him. "You would what?"

"I would give you a child."

Maxi's breath caught in her throat. "Why?"

He looked at her. "Because I can't think of any woman more deserving to be a mother than you. The child would feel loved, wanted, and protected. I never planned on having children but I'm willing to rethink that decision for you."

Maxi was touched by his words. Truly touched. But she knew she couldn't take what he was offering. "Thank you, Christopher, but I can't let you do that."

"Why?"

"Things could get complicated."

"What's so complicated about one friend helping out another? What's so complicated about me giving you the gift of a child?" He sighed deeply. "I guess I don't see the big deal here. What if you needed a kidney or a liver and I was able to give you one? You would take it wouldn't you?"

"Yes, but—"

"There's no buts, Maxi. To me it all boils down to the same thing. You want something that I'm able to give you."

Maxi's head began spinning. "I don't know, Christopher, we're talking about another life."

"I know that, Maxi. It will be my gift of life to you. Like I said, I know of no other woman more deserving to be a mother, and I would feel honored if that child were mine."

Maxi nodded, remembering a conversation the two of them had had years ago. Being illegitimate had been hard on him because some people never let him forget he'd been born a child no man had wanted to claim. "Would you want to play a major role in your child's life?"

"No, but I don't ever want a child I fathered to doubt how I felt about him."

"And how would you feel, Christopher? You said earlier that you hadn't ever planned on fathering a child," she queried, trying to understand everything he was offering and making sure he understood it as well.

"Yes, and if it were any woman other than you, I still wouldn't." He looked at her for a long moment before saying calmly. "I think it's important that you understand something, Maxi. I couldn't help but love and want the child because we're not talking about just any child, Maxi. We're talking about a child that you and I would make together. It will be a child that will signify our very special friendship and our very unique bond. But the only relationship you and I will share is that of our child. No one has to know I'm the man who fathered your child. In fact, I think it will be for the best if no one knew. What I told you earlier this week still holds true. Marriage is not in my future plans. I'm a loner and I plan on staying that way. I am not into relationships of any kind and that includes being a family man. However, I will provide financial support for any child I make."

"Are you saying that you are willing to give me a child then just walk away, except for financial support?"

"Yes, that's what I'm offering. Do you understand?"

Maxi slowly nodded, understanding completely. He was letting her know he was willing to give her the gift of his child, but that was as far as things went between them. His life was his own and he would still continue to have one, apart from her and his child, to do what he pleased and with whom he pleased.

"I would not hide the fact from my child or anyone that you are the father."

"That will be your choice, Maxi."

She nodded. "There's a lot to think about and consider, Christopher."

"Yes, but you don't have to make a decision about anything tonight." He stood. "You want a child and I'm willing to give you one. Promise you'll at least think about my offer."

Maxi met his gaze. She hesitated a moment before saying, "I promise."

PART TWO

And forgive us our sins—for we have for-given those who sinned against us . . .

—Luke 11:4

CHAPTER TWENTY-FOUR

"It's so good to be home," Garrett said, standing in the doorway of his bedroom. He and Mya had just put their sons to bed. Both Daniel and David had been overly anxious to tell their parents about all the fun they'd had while spending time at their grandparents' home.

"Does that mean you didn't enjoy the time we spent away together?" Mya asked smiling as she got into bed.

Garrett chuckled as he walked across the room, removed his robe and slid into bed beside her and pulling her into his arms. "No, that means I'm glad to be able to walk on steady legs for a change. And I did miss the boys, and Dallas has never looked better to me."

"Yeah, I know what you mean." Although both of them had spent most of their childhood on the east coast, they had fallen in love with Texas. The two-story house they had built the year before the twins had been born was in the same upscale neighborhood where a number of other players lived. On occasion Garrett talked about moving farther out and buying a ranch with acres and acres of land and raising cattle when he retired from football.

"I think our time together on the cruise was special, don't you?"

Mya thought about the time they had spent together. "Yes, it was special."

She then thought of what Maxi had shared with them at breakfast on their last day on the cruise. Christopher had left the ship already so they hadn't had a chance to talk to him to say their goodbyes. "What do you think of Christopher's offer to father Maxi's child?"

Garrett shook his head. "Hell, I'm surprised. While on the ship, there was a moment when Christopher and I were hanging out together that I pulled out the boys' photo and showed it to him. He mentioned then that, because of his less than desirable childhood, he had no intentions of ever fathering a child. So for him to offer himself to Maxi like that comes as a shocker. Volunteering for stud service isn't something a brother normally does."

"So what do you think it means?"

"It means he's either stone crazy or he really cares a lot for her."

Mya nodded. "That's the same thing I've been thinking. What kind of information did you find out about him?"

"Mya, I didn't go snooping around in Chandler's business. Besides, he told us that he works for a construction company."

"Yeah, but did you take a good look at his watch? How many construction workers you know wear expensive watches like that?"

Garrett agreed but decided not to add fuel to the fire by telling Mya that. "Well, whatever Maxi decides to do is her business. I just hope she thinks things through. There are too many issues involved like child support and custody rights and there will always be a bond between her and Christopher because of the child."

"And that's why I think there's more to it than him being

grateful for the humane way she treated him all those years ago in school."

"Is that what Maxi thinks?"

"Yes."

"You're right," Garrett replied yawning. "There's probably more to it than that."

There was a moment of silence and Mya felt Garrett dozing off to sleep. "Garrett, before you go to sleep, there's something I need to tell you."

He yawned again and pulled her closer into his arms. "Can it hold until morning, baby? I'm beat tonight."

"Yes, it can hold but I prefer that it didn't." *I've been holding it too long already.*

Garrett stretched his body into a reclining pose and rested on an elbow. He looked down at Mya, confused at what she'd just said, and even more confused with the nervous tension expressed on her face. "Okay, what is it?"

She looked up at him, praying that he would take her news well. "I got a promotion at work."

As soon as her words registered, he smiled. "Honey, that's great! Does that mean you won't be doing any more traveling?"

She inhaled deeply. "No, it means I'll be doing a lot more traveling, Garrett."

He pulled away from her and settled back in the bed. "Sorry, but you can't do that."

Mya frowned. He had made the statement like it was the end of the discussion. "What do you mean I can't do that? I've already talked to Mrs. Butler and she's indicated that she can handle the extra hours of taking care of the boys so I don't—"

"Yeah, but who's going to take care of me, Mya? I don't like being here alone when you're gone."

"And I don't like being here alone when you're gone either, Garrett, but I've learned to deal with it. You act like it's okay for you to be gone when you have those out of town games but it's not okay that my job requires me to travel, too."

He glared at her. "It's not the same and you know it."

She glared back. "And why isn't it the same? They're both jobs, Garrett. I enjoy my job as much as you enjoy yours."

"Your job is taking care of me and my sons, Mya. My job is taking care of everything, including you and the boys, putting food on the table, and a decent roof over your heads. You know how I feel about you working. I never did like it, but to make you happy and to keep peace I put up with it. I don't like Mrs. Butler raising our boys. That's not her job. She's here to take care of them, not to raise them. But that's what she's been doing for the past year. It wouldn't surprise me in the least if they didn't start calling her momma."

Mya took a small breath. His words had hurt. "That's not fair, Garrett, and you know it. No matter how long I'm gone or how often I'm gone, I still spend quality time with you and the boys. I give you double because of the guilt I feel about leaving."

"Look, Mya, I don't want to talk about this anymore. You evidently took this promotion without talking to me about it first. You didn't give a damn how I would feel about it."

"Yes, I did!"

"Yeah, and you took the promotion anyway. To me that says a lot about how well you consider my feelings." He got out of bed. "I don't want to deal with this tonight."

"Where are you going?"

"In the guest bedroom."

Mya didn't say anything as she watched him snatch his robe off the bed and walk out of the bedroom, slamming the door behind him.

She threw the covers back and got out of bed, refusing to let him have the last word. She walked a few feet to the door before stopping. Her whole body began trembling in anger. There was too much anger in both of them for there to be any

type of productive conversation. They would only end up saying words they would regret later.

Mya went back to bed and slid beneath the covers. She wiped
tears from her eyes when she thought about the fact that this
was the first time during all the years of their marriage that she
and Garrett had not shared a bed when they had been under
the same roof for the night.

CHAPTER TWENTY-FIVE

Maxi released a pleasant sigh as she entered her home. Her first day back at the university had been hectic at best. Had she known the summer class she'd volunteered to teach that highlighted great African-American women would contain a collection of newly enrolled freshmen, she would have thought twice about doing it. It had been all but impossible to hold their attention. After one student kept saying it was too beautiful a summer day to be stuck in class talking about some dead comedienne they'd never heard of by the name of Jackie "Moms" Mabley, she couldn't help but agree with him and had dismissed the class early.

Half an hour later, showered, refreshed, and wearing a caftan she had purchased in the Cayman Islands, Maxi left the confines of her bedroom and headed toward the kitchen to prepare something for dinner. Looking around her she noticed her plants hadn't fared well without her personal attention during the week she'd been gone. Now she was back home and would take better care of them. It was business as usual.

Not quite.

There was no way things could be business as usual with Christopher's offer lurking in the back of her mind, always finding the perfect time to work its way to the forefront, like now. He had offered her the very thing her heart desired—a child of her own.

The only persons she had told about his offer had been Mya and Garrett. Neither had given her an indication of what they had thought, saying the decision would have to be hers and they would not influence it in any way.

The loud ringing of the telephone cut sharply into Maxi's thoughts. She glanced at the clock on the wall. It was too early for her mother's daily evening call. Crossing the room she picked up the phone. "Hello?"

"Maxi, how are you?"

Maxi smiled, recognizing the voice immediately. "I'm fine, Mya. What about you?"

"Don't ask."

Maxi lifted a brow. She could tell by Mya's gloomy response that something was wrong. It didn't take her long to guess what. "You've told Garrett about your promotion, haven't you?"

"Yes, and he's not happy about it."

"Well, you knew that he wouldn't be."

"Yes, but I had hoped he would try and understand my position and be supportive. He's not doing that. It's really affecting our relationship, Maxi."

Maxi hated hearing that. "Then the two of you should try and work things out. Mya. Just give him time, he'll probably come around."

"I'm not so sure. He's acting like my decision to take the job was an affront to his manhood or something."

"And maybe to him it is." Maxi paused briefly before saying, "Hear me out and let me play devil's advocate for just a moment. You've known Garrett a long time, and you've always known the Rivers men had a policy that their wives didn't work. His momma never worked outside of the home and when his older brothers got married, none of their wives worked. I'm sure at some point you knew Garrett would be no different."

"Yes, but I thought he would change."

"The die was cast early, Mya. I think it's a Rivers thing and you can't fault him for that when you knew about it in the beginning."

"Yes, I can fault him for not being fair to me, and for not being flexible to my wants and needs."

"Come on, Mya you need to be fair too. I've never known Garrett not to be flexible to your wants and needs. For as long as I can remember he's always catered to you, treated you like a queen. His queen."

"But that doesn't excuse how he's handling the situation with my working now, Maxi. Garrett is a wonderful husband, the best. He's also a wonderful father and a great provider for his family. What's wrong with me having another interest outside the home?"

"Nothing, other than the fact that Garrett may be feeling threatened by that interest."

"That's ridiculous and irrational."

"And who says men are rational? Just think about it. For years your life has been filled with Garrett. You've always made him your number one priority and now you're sharing that number one spot with a job. He's going through changes, Mya. Just be patient and understanding."

"I don't know how long I can. He's sleeping with his back to me every night in bed and he hasn't said more than two words to me in a week. We've never gone this long without communicating or bringing our feelings out in the open by discussing them."

"Then discuss them."

"We tried and all we did is end up screaming and yelling at each other. It wasn't a nice scene, Maxi."

"Then give it some time and try again. But don't give up. You have too much to lose if you do. Have you started your new job yet?"

"No, I don't start for another couple of weeks." Wanting to change the subject Mya asked. "Have you made a decision on Christopher's offer yet?"

"No, in fact I was just thinking about it."

"It's pretty tempting isn't it?"

"Very."

"How do you feel about being a single mom?"

Mya's question was one she had asked herself a thousand times since Christopher's proposal. "The thought of being a single mom doesn't bother me, although I believe a child should have both parents. That's the kind of family structure I'm used to. I'm surprised that he doesn't want to be a part of his child's life since his own father was never around either while he was growing up."

"Maybe he doesn't think he'll know how to be a father or even a good one."

"But I think he would make a wonderful father if he gave himself a chance. But all he wants is to get me pregnant and step out of the picture."

"And how do you feel about that?"

"I guess it's no different from using an anonymous sperm donor. But in this situation I'll know the identity of the man who fathers my child."

Mya thought about her words. "If you decide to go through with it, how will you get pregnant? Will you do artificial insemination or will you sleep with Christopher?"

Maxi sighed. That was something else she had thought a lot about. "I get cold chills at the thought of being impregnated on some table at a clinic. That's not how I envisioned my child to be created. But then on that same note, I don't know if I'm ready to share a bed with him for the sole purpose of getting pregnant. When Jason and I slept together it was for love." There was no doubt in Maxi's mind that she would enjoy sleeping with Christopher, love or no love, since she had already gotten a taste of ecstasy in his arms from a mere kiss. But still, she wanted more between them than a night filled with orgasms . . . although the thought of that was pretty tempting.

"I've only made out with someone I love too, so I can understand you there, girl," Mya was saying. "I can't imagine sharing a bed with someone I don't love, although there are women who do it all the time. You and I are different, Maxi."

Maxi smiled. "Yeah, we're different. I'm going to think about Christopher's offer some more before making a final decision."

"When is he expecting you to call him?"

"He didn't give me a time frame, although I'm sure he doesn't expect me to drag things out forever." Maxi reached across the table and picked up the business card Christopher had given her on their last day on the cruise. After studying the card, she hadn't been surprised to discover that he was one of the CEOs of the company. On the cruise he had led everyone to believe he was employed as a construction worker, which wasn't a total lie but still, he had intentionally left out a number of details; like the fact that his company, the Regency Corporation, was nationally known and financially successful. She smiled. She was proud of his accomplishments and had always known he would succeed in life. "I'm going to pray about it some more."

"And while you're praying, how about remembering me and Garrett?"

"I will, but I know the two of you will work things out. You have too much history behind you and too much of a wonderful future ahead of you."

"I hope you're right."

"I am right."

Mya sighed. "It's so good having you to talk to, Maxi. It's like old times. You don't know how good it feels having you back in my life. I missed the friendship and the closeness of being able to share things with another woman I can trust. Although I'm friends with the wives of the guys on Garrett's team, I'm not real close to any of them. There are too many differences in

personalities and attitudes, not to mention jealousy and petti-
ness to deal with at times. But our relationship has always been
genuine, right from the beginning."

Maxi smiled, remembering that day in the schoolyard. "Yes,
it was. I love you, girl."

"And I love you. Now let me hang up this phone before I
find another thing to cry about."

"OK, you take care."

"You, too."

After Maxi hung up the phone she couldn't help but think
that both she and Mya had big issues to deal with and wondered how they would go about handling them. She decided to
do just what she told Mya she would do.

Pray.

CHAPTER TWENTY-SIX

As far as Christopher was concerned, this had to be the longest week of his life. After being out of the office for the past seven days, he was too deep in correspondence he needed to answer, phone calls needing to be returned, and faxes needing to be read, to have his mind on anything but business. Yet Maxi and the offer he had made to her were never far from his thoughts.

That night after he'd made the offer, they had left the cabin. Deciding not to rejoin the others at the banquet, they had walked along the deck holding hands, enjoying the beauty of the moon-kissed ocean. They had sat at a table in a restaurant and over a cup of cappuccino, they had talked about a lot of things—other than the offer he'd made earlier. It had been close to three in the morning before they'd finally left the restaurant to return to the cabin. He had gone back on deck to visit the casinos to give her the private time she needed to prepare for bed. He had deliberately stayed away, not returning until he'd known she'd be asleep. And just as deliberately, he had purposely been packed and gone when she had awakened the next morning, leaving her a note that simply said, "The decision is yours," along with his business card on how to reach him.

Christopher pushed away from the conference table and walked to the window when the other four men in the room began an intense debate about something he couldn't remember. He was in the middle of an important board meeting, yet his mind wasn't focused on the business at hand.

"So what do you think about that proposal, Mr. Chandler?"

He slanted a thoughtful glance across the room at the man who had asked him a question. "What proposal, Crawford?" He didn't miss the looks that passed between the men. There had never been a time they'd not had his absolute attention when discussing business. Even Gabe was looking at him strangely.

"He was asking about the land that might interest you at the North Pole, Chris," Gabe said, amazingly straight-faced.

But still, Christopher caught on, especially when the other three men at the table tried hiding their smiles. "How about if we meet on this again in the morning? It's been a rather long day," he said, glaring at Gabe.

Less than five minutes later the room had cleared of everyone except Gabe. At first Christopher tried ignoring his presence, but after a few annoying minutes he turned his head toward his best friend and caught him staring at him with those dark, curious eyes of his. "Is there a problem, Blackwell?"

"Evidently there is, Chandler. Do you want to tell me about it?"

"No."

Gabe glanced down at his watch. "All right." But he remained sitting at the table and watched as Christopher threw items into his briefcase. He stared at him for what seemed like ages, when in fact it had only been a few seconds when Christopher gave in—just like Gabe knew he eventually would. Christopher was not one to let anything interfere with business. Yet today he had. In fact, Gabe had noticed him being rather preoccupied since returning from the cruise. He had encouraged him to go on the cruise to relax, not to come back dense.

Christopher's gaze, which had been staring blankly at a document he'd picked up off the table, shifted abruptly to Gabe's. "I saw her on the cruise."

Gabe wasn't sure who he meant, although it was obvious Christopher thought he should. "Who did you see?"

"Maxi."

Gabe lifted a brow. "Your Maxi?"

Christopher smiled. He remembered the time when he and Gabe had first met and become close friends that he'd told him all about Maxi. "Yeah, my Maxi."

"Was her husband with her?"

There was a lifting of Christopher's eyebrows before he also remembered he'd mentioned to Gabe a while back, after he'd received the news from Mr. Thompson, that Maxi was getting married. "No, she never married. Her fiancé was killed in a car accident the week before the wedding."

"How tragic."

"Yes, it was."

Gabe waited a beat for Christopher to go on. When he didn't, he took the initiative and asked. "So, did the two of you spend any time together?" He watched as Christopher smiled. It was a slow smile and as far as Gabe was concerned a dead giveaway.

"Yeah, you could say that. Due to a computer glitch, we got assigned to the same cabin. Since there weren't any other available cabins, we were cabinmates for a week."

Now it was Gabe's time to smile, a slow smile, as a vivid picture entered his mind, given Christopher's reputation with women. "Must have been interesting," he drawled. "Real cozy, too."

Christopher frowned. "Not the way you think, so wipe that stupid-looking grin off your face, Blackwell."

"Losing your touch, Chandler?"

Christopher's gaze narrowed. "No. You know how I feel about Maxi."

Gabe shook his head. "I know how you used to feel about her but that's been over five years ago."

"I still think she's a very special lady."

Gabe gave Christopher a smirky grin across the space of the long walnut table. "Should I tell Mama to get out her best dress because there might be a wedding in the near future?" he asked jokingly.

Christopher frowned. "No, that's not a possibility." He leaned back in his chair to watch Gabe's reaction to his next words. "However, she may want to get out your old pair of booties since I did offer to be the father of Maxi's child."

CHAPTER TWENTY-SEVEN

"Hi, Garrett."

Garrett smiled at the woman who had spoken to him. "Hi, Paige. I see you've survived your first week of practice."

She returned his smile. "So have you, although I'm sure yours have been a lot more rigorous than mine." She glanced down at the car keys in his hand. "Going home already?"

"Yes. I always go home directly after practice. If I don't, then I'd never get to see my sons since they're still sleep when I leave in the mornings and are in bed by eight o'clock every night."

"I heard you had two darling twin boys. I'd like to meet them one day."

"I'm sure you will. Mya brings them to practice every once in a while."

Paige's lips curved slowly. "And how is Mya? I understand she has a job that requires her to travel quite a bit. That must be exciting." She didn't miss the frown that appeared in Garrett's features. It was a frown he discarded but not quick enough.

"Mya is doing fine and yes, she does travel a lot for now but hopefully that will be changing soon," he said as if convincing himself that would be the case.

Paige nodded. "Every once in a while some of the other

cheerleaders and I whip up a good home cooked meal for any of the players who want to come over and join us. You're welcome to join in anytime."

Garrett chuckled. "Thanks, I'll keep that in mind." As she walked off Garrett couldn't help but admire the skimpy shorts and tank top she was wearing. His last thought as he headed out toward the parking lot was that she looked pretty damn good in them.

Mya looked across the dinner table at Garrett. He was in the same mood he'd been in for the past three weeks and she'd just about had it. Things had never been this tense between them and she was having a hard time handling it.

The boys had eaten earlier and were now in bed. Garrett had come home from practice, taken a shower and had spent time with them. *At least he'd been in a real good mood for Daniel and David,* she thought to herself. "Garrett, can we talk?" she asked quietly.

He lifted his face from his meal and looked at her. "What do you want to talk about?"

"Us."

"What about us?"

It took Mya a long time to get the words out. The lump felt deep in her throat. "Do you still want there to be an *us*?"

She could tell by the expression on his face that her question had startled him. "What kind of foolish question is that, Mya?"

"It's one a wife would ask her husband who'd been totally ignoring her for the past several weeks. And it's not fair, Garrett. You have been unfair to me."

"And do you think you've been fair to me? What about the boys? Does your job mean that much to you?"

"Yes, it means a lot to me, but you and the boys mean more. Do you want me to choose, Garrett? Is that it? Well, if you do, then fine, I'll choose, if that will make you happy." She stood. "I'll call Mr. Lee now and tell him that I quit because there's no competition when it comes to what's first in my life. You and my sons have always been it." She turned to leave the room.

"Mya!"

She turned back around. Garrett stood and came around the table. He walked over to her.

"No, I don't want you to quit your job. I know I haven't been the easiest person to live with the past couple of weeks but I'm trying. I'm trying to deal with a lot of things right now. It's not just your job, it's my job as well."

Mya pulled back out of his arms. "What about your job?"

Garrett sighed. "You know how things are this time of the year. A lot of players are getting cut from the team, and I can't help but have that on my mind now."

"But you're good and they know it, Garrett," she said reassuringly. "You're a good player and the team can't afford to lose you. You did a super job last year."

"Yeah, but this is another year and with it, I'm also a year older. There're always younger and better players out there. There's no one who can't be replaced."

Mya nodded. Although she knew that was true, she really didn't think Garrett had anything to worry about. The Cowboys, although they hadn't made it to the Super Bowl in the past few years, had had a rather good season last year. They had made it to the playoffs. And Garrett had been cited in the papers as being one of the key players who had helped to get them there.

"I don't like it when we're at odds with each other, Garrett, and not getting along for any reason. You and the boys are my life, you have to believe that."

"And I do, Mya. I know I can be an ass sometimes, but you and the boys are my life, too. Just give me some time to deal with some things, okay?"

She looked up at him, knowing her job was one of the things he was still trying hard to deal with. "Okay." He leaned down and kissed her and she hadn't known how much she'd missed the intimate contact until his mouth met hers. The kiss was everything she wanted and needed. She almost melted in the knees with the way his tongue was mating with hers. It was evident that he had missed her as much as she had missed him this way. She couldn't wait until they made it to the bedroom. He had slept too many nights with his back to her and was glad that tonight he would pull her into his arms and make love to her.

They reluctantly pulled apart when the phone rang. "I guess one of us should answer that before it wakes the boys," he whispered close to her moist lips after breaking off the kiss.

"Yeah, I guess one of us should," she said, removing her arms from around his neck. She walked over to the phone. "Yes?"

A surprised expression covered her features. "Yes, Mr. Lee, this is Mya." After a few moments she said, while glancing over at Garrett. "No sir, that shouldn't be a problem. I'll make all the necessary arrangements. All right. Goodnight." She then hung up the phone and looked across the room at Garrett. "That was my boss, Mr. Lee."

Garrett frowned. "I gathered as much. What did he want?"

Mya could tell that Garrett was angry about the call and what she had to tell him might make him angrier. "He was wondering if I could leave for Orlando a week earlier than planned. Our client's schedule has changed and he's leaving the country in two weeks."

"And of course you told him it wouldn't be a problem to go a week earlier," he said glaring at her.

"Well, yes, I didn't see a reason why I couldn't."

"Evidently you didn't," Garrett said harshly. He crossed the room heading for the door.

"Where are you going?"

"Out."

Mya lifted a surprised brow. Once Garrett came in from practice he never went back out, especially if he had to get up early the next morning for practice. "Out?"

"Yes, Mya, out. I'll be back later," he said, slamming the door behind him.

Mya sank into a nearby chair and closed her eyes. So much for her attempt at repairing what was wrong with their marriage.

"I see you twice in one day, I don't believe it."

Garrett glanced up from looking into his drink while sitting at a bar that was a popular hangout for the players. "You're out late aren't you, Paige?"

She slid onto the stool beside him, making sure the skirt she wore showed an ample amount of her thigh. She inwardly smiled when she saw him looking at the smooth creamy flesh. "I couldn't sleep and thought I'd drop by for a beer. How about buying me one?"

"Sure." He then motioned to the bartender to bring her a beer.

"Thanks."

"You're welcome."

She studied his features. "You're out pretty late yourself. Don't you have practice before five in the morning?"

"Yeah, but I'm used to getting up early. There won't be a problem."

Paige nodded. "So, do you think you'll get a Super Bowl ring this season?"

"We're going to try our best."

"I've watched you practice a few times. Boy, you're awesome." She knew every man liked his ego stroked.

"Thanks."

"And that play you did today at practice; that pass you made to Mayhews was great."

Garrett smiled, pleased with himself. "Yeah, the coach thought so too." He looked over at Paige and again thought she was a good-looking woman who fitted her clothes nicely. "I didn't know you were at practice today."

"Yeah, I go sometimes and stand on the sidelines and watch the team practice. I'm always amazed at how much energy you all have. I especially like to see you make your moves. They're always slick, smooth, and easy. You are one confident man on the field. You're a man who knows what he wants and doesn't hesitate going after it."

Garrett thought about her words. She was so right. He was a man who liked getting results. As he studied her further he felt a tightening in his gut when she took the tip of her tongue and licked beer suds from her lips. He sucked in a deep breath and couldn't help imagining . . .

He suddenly knew he had to leave. "I guess I'd best be going," he said sliding off the stool.

"Are you sure you don't want to hang around and have another beer and keep me company?"

"Nah, I better be going. I'll see you later."

"All right, Garrett, see ya." She smiled as she sipped her beer. Her body felt hot. A few more chance meetings and he would be eating out of her hand and then sliding between her legs in no time.

Mya awoke when she heard the sound of Garrett returning. She glanced at the clock on the nightstand next to the bed. It was past midnight. She remained awake while he went into the bathroom to shower. Later, when he came to bed, just like the nights before, he turned his back to her, a clear indication he was still angry.

The next day since she didn't have much to do at work, Mya decided to take the day off and go to the football field and watch the Cowboys practice. She hadn't done that in quite a while, at least not since her job had begun taking up most of her time.

"Mya, long time no see, girl!"

Mya smiled as she hugged Danielle Hughes. Like Garrett,

Danielle's husband Mark was a member of the team, and he and Garrett were good friends. Mya sat down next to Danielle on the bleachers. "How's the girls?" she asked. Danielle and Mark had two daughters, ages six and eight.

"You mean how are the women? Those two are something else and keep me pretty busy. And Mark had the nerve to tell me the other night that he wants another child. I looked at him like he was out of his friggin' mind. Rachel and Michelle are enough for me."

Mya smiled. Danielle's statement reminded her that Garrett wanted another child as well. "Boy, time flies. I remember when Mark first joined the Cowboys, Michelle was only five."

"Yeah, it's been three years," Danielle said smiling. "It's hard to believe it's been that long." She chuckled. "I can't believe Mark has played on the same team for that length of time. With Mark three years is usually the max. That's usually all the time a coach can handle him and his attitude."

Mya nodded. She knew from listening to Garrett that, although Mark was an excellent player, he was also something of a hothead. Last season he had cost the team a number of penalties for taking out his frustrations on members of the opposing team. "So, how do they look?" she asked glancing out at the men on the field.

"Umm, they look okay but I wouldn't count on that Super Bowl ring just yet. I've seen too many fumbles and interceptions today. They still have a lot of work to do before the season starts."

"Garrett mentioned a number of players have gotten cut already."

"Yes, which makes everyone antsy. But I don't think Mark and Garrett have anything to worry about."

Mya smiled. "Neither do I." She then moved her eyes over to the sidelines where a group of other women were standing. Mya immediately recognized the woman she had met at the party a few months back by the name of Paige Duvall. Usually the cheerleaders didn't make it a habit to come out and watch the guys practice. She wondered if Paige was dating someone on the team. She started to ask Danielle, then decided not to.

It was a good hour or so later before Garrett looked up and saw her sitting in the stands. As soon as the coach gave them a break he jogged her way. Excusing herself from Danielle and a few other wives who'd joined them, Mya walked down the bleachers to meet him. She could tell from Garrett's smile that he was glad to see her. He had already left for practice when she had awakened that morning and she'd hoped he wasn't still angry that she would be leaving town sooner than expected.

"Hi. This is a pleasant surprise."

Mya studied the features of the man she loved with all her heart. "I wanted to see you practice. I hadn't been out in a while and thought it would be nice."

"It is nice. How long do you plan on staying?"

"For another hour or so. Why?"

"Do you want to grab something to eat with me later?"

Mya tilted her head to the side and gazed up at him. Sweat was pouring off him from all the physical activity of his practice, but she thought sweat or no sweat, Garrett Rivers was a total turn-on. "I'd love to, but I thought you had a long practice session today."

"No, practice will be short today. In another couple of hours we'll shower and leave."

Mya smiled. "Okay, I'll wait until practice is over."

He smiled and gave her a quick kiss before jogging back to rejoin his teammates. Mya turned to rejoin Danielle and the others. She glanced over to where she had seen Paige Duvall earlier. The woman was still there and for some reason she was staring at her with an odd, unreadable expression on her face.

Later, at the café when they went to get something to eat, Mya asked, "That new cheerleader, Paige Duvall, is she dating someone on the team?"

Garrett lifted a brow as he took a sip of his soda. "I don't think so, why do you ask?"

"Because she was there, at your practice session. Isn't that unusual?"

He shrugged. "What's so unusual about it? Anyone can come watch us practice."

"I know but . . ."

"But what?"

She said nothing for a moment, wondering why he seemed so defensive, or was it her imagination. "But nothing," she finally said.

He looked over at her. "Are you sure?"

She nodded. "Yes, I'm sure."

CHAPTER TWENTY-EIGHT

"So, you and Mya finally got things straightened out?" Gwen Chandler asked her daughter.

Maxi glanced over at her mother. It was a Saturday morning and they were on their knees in the backyard working in her mother's beautiful flower garden. "Yes. It was just a big misunderstanding."

Gwen nodded. "Those things do happen to friends, even the very best of friends. I'm just glad the two of you were finally able to sit down and talk about it. I can remember the first time you brought Mya home with you from school."

Maxi smiled. "Yes, I can remember, too." She looked over at her mother. At forty-eight Gwen Chandler was still a good-looking woman but since Maxi's father's death ten years ago, her mother had dated only one man, a widower by the name of Jim Hudson. Gwen and Jim spent a lot of time together and had done so for a number of years. However, as of yet her mother had never mentioned marriage. "Mom, can I ask you something?"

Gwen stopped what she was doing long enough to look up. "Sure, honey, what is it?"

"Why don't you and Jim get married?"

Maxi could tell her mother was taken aback by her question and had to take a moment to collect herself before answering. "I think you know the answer to that, Maxine."

Maxi nodded. "Because of Dad?"

"Yes. I loved your father very much."

Maxi had known her parents had had a very close and loving relationship. "You loved Dad too much to ever love another man?"

Gwen sat back on her haunches. She studied her daughter. "Jim and I enjoy each other's company but he loved his wife just as much as I loved your father. In our own way Jim and I do care deeply for each other but we're not ready to make a commitment yet."

Maxi knew it was more her mother resisting the idea of marriage than Jim. He would marry Gwen Chandler in a heartbeat if she ever gave the word. "So are you saying that I can't truly love another man now that Jason is gone?"

"No, honey, that's not what I'm saying at all. Your father and I were married for twenty years and Jim and his wife were married for twenty-two years. When people have been married that long sometimes it's hard letting go. But you're young. You and Jason had dated only two years before he was killed. I know it's hard on you sometimes but you have to get on with your life. There's someone out there for you, Maxi. You have to give yourself a chance for happiness."

"I feel like my time is running out."

"Because of the surgery?"

"Yes."

Gwen paused a moment before asking. "What happened to you and that doctor Bessie was all excited about?"

Maxi thought about Reginald Tanner. "He's still hung up on his ex-wife." Gwen shook her head as she resumed working with her roses. "It happens that way at times, unfortunately."

After a few moments Maxi asked. "Mom, do you remember Christopher Chandler?"

"Is that Cousin Albert's boy?"

"No, Mom, Christopher isn't related to us. We just have the same last name. He and I went to school together and—"

"Oh, *that* Chandler. Yes, I remember him. And I also remember the scandal involving his mother and the mayor, Will Potter. If I recall she ended up committing suicide behind that mess, which surprised a lot of people. She'd been sleeping with married men for years so she must have cared a lot for Potter."

Maxi nodded, remembering hearing bits and pieces of the story back then. "Well, I ran into Christopher on the class reunion cruise." She decided not to tell her mother that the two of them had shared a cabin."

"How is he doing?" Gwen asked.

"He's doing fine. He owns this big construction company in Detroit."

"Then you must be proud of him."

Maxi raised her brow. "Why would you say that?"

Gwen smiled. "Because if I remember correctly, you were one of the few friends he had. Also, I recall on a couple of occasions that you made an extra sandwich and put it in your lunch box just for him, because you were concerned about him not having his own lunch. That's when your father used to tease you about not feeding anyone not living under his roof."

Maxi chuckled, remembering those times. Her father had been the greatest.

"Then when you got older you had this huge crush on him."

Maxi lifted a brow. "You remember that too?"

"Yes." Gwen glanced over at her daughter. "I also remember when he left town, swearing he wasn't ever coming back." After a few moments she asked softly. "Is that about to change?"

Maxi shrugged knowing her mother was studying her intently. "I don't know. It might."

"And if it does, would you have anything to do with it?"

Again Maxi didn't know how to answer her mother's question. "I'm not sure what his future plans are, Mom. He and I are just friends."

"Friends who are interested in each other?"

Friends who might be sharing a baby is more like it, Maxi thought. Her mother had always been very perceptive where she was concerned but Maxi would bet a million dollars her mother would never suspect anything close to Christopher's offer to get her pregnant. "That's hard to say, Mom. We only spent seven days together but I did enjoy his company, and I want to think he enjoyed mine."

"Well, make sure I'm one of the first to know if he ever decides to come back to Savannah."

"Why?"

"So I can prepare a nice welcome home dinner for him."

Touched by her mother's kind offer Maxi leaned over and hugged her. "Thanks, Mom. You're the greatest."

Later than evening Maxi was in deep thought as she walked outside her home. She had purchased the house three years ago and the one thing that had drawn her to it were the numerous magnolia trees in the backyard. Jim had built her a gazebo and for privacy purposes, he had also installed a fence around her entire back yard. She enjoyed siting under the gazebo in the late afternoons while sipping a cup of hot herbal tea.

She also enjoyed coming out here to think about things that concerned her. Her period had started that day and with it came the painful cramps that reminded her of the surgery she would eventually have to have. Remembering the surgery only made her remember Christopher's offer. It had been nearly three weeks since he'd made it.

She had thought about it, prayed about it, and had even dreamed about it. Now she knew her mind was finally made up about what she would do. She just needed to make sure Christopher still wanted to go through with it. She would let him know of her decision and discuss how best to proceed.

CHAPTER TWENTY-NINE

The buzzer sounding on Christopher's desk caught him by surprise. He had instructed his secretary to hold his calls because he hadn't wanted to be disturbed. "Yes, Mary, what is it?"

"You indicated you wanted any call put through from a Ms. Maxine Chandler."

Christopher straightened in his chair. "Yes, is she on the line?"

"No, sir, she's here to see you."

Christopher blinked, thinking he hadn't heard his secretary correctly. "Could you repeat that?"

"Yes, sir. I said there's a Maxine Chandler here to see you."

"Maxine Chandler is here? In Detroit?"

"Yes, sir. Do you want me to send her in?"

"Yes."

"Thank you, sir."

Christopher tossed the huge envelope he was just about to open aside, then stood to face the woman who had been plaguing his thoughts relentlessly for the past four weeks. Several questions began flooding his mind. Why was she here? Had she made a decision on his offer? Why hadn't she called?

His door swung open and he placed a tense smile on his lips as Mary escorted Maxi into his office. "Thanks for showing Ms. Chandler in. That will be all for now." He saw Mary look at him and Maxi curiously. Since she knew he didn't have any relatives, it was apparent she was trying to figure out what Maxi's relationship was to him, given they had the same last name. Was she a long-lost relative or was she an ex-wife he'd never bothered mentioning he had? "That will be all for now, Mary," he repeated. "And make sure I'm not disturbed."

"Yes, sir." Mary then gave him a wry smile before leaving, closing the door behind her.

His attention was then immediately drawn to Maxi. She looked just the way he last remembered seeing her. Beautiful. "I didn't know you were coming to Detroit." If she hadn't planned to take him up on his offer, she could have easily made a phone call to let him know it. Since she was here that could mean only one thing.

At first Maxi couldn't find the words to say anything. She had seen him in a business suit before during one of those times they'd had to dress for dinner on the cruise. However, she found that seeing him again dressed in a starched white dress shirt and a pair of tailored navy blue trousers that emphasized his long muscled thighs, legs, and hips was unnerving and was making her lose the ability to think clearly. "I didn't know myself until a few days ago. I thought it would be best to come see you face to face, and I didn't think you'd want to come to Savannah. I need to ask you something."

There was a brief pause before he asked. "What do you want to ask me?"

Maxi stared into his intense gaze and felt the floor feel unsteady under her feet. She swallowed the lump in her throat and somehow found her voice. "I want to know if your offer still stands? If you're still interested in doing what you said you would do?"

"To give you a baby?"

Maxi's breath caught on his words. She had heard the huski-ness in his voice. The sound of it had run all the way up her spine. "Yes."

He nodded. "The offer still stands, Maxi."

She studied his features. "And you're absolutely sure about this?"

"Yes, I'm absolutely sure." He watched her shoulders relax. "And are you accepting my offer?"

She nodded. "Yes. We need to talk about it and make some necessary plans. I'm here for the weekend and will be staying at the Marriott Hotel."

"You're welcome to stay with me. In fact that arrangement would probably work better since we have a lot to discuss, and the Marriott is on the other side of town from where I live. You being at my place will be more convenient."

"I wouldn't want to intrude."

He smiled, remembering she hadn't wanted to intrude on the cruise either. "You won't be. I have a large apartment."

"Thanks."

Christopher looked at his watch. He then glanced at the huge envelope on his desk that he'd been about to open before she'd arrived. His plans to stay and work late immediately changed. "Come on, let me take you to my apartment and get you settled in. You must be exhausted after your flight."

"Oh," Maxi said entering Christopher's apartment and glancing around. "This place is humongous." He'd said he had a large apartment but she hadn't visualized it as being this big. It was nearly the size of her house.

"I like a lot of space," he said smiling, upon seeing the ex-pression on her face. "All my years while growing up and living in the Vines, I always dreamed of having a spacious place to call my own."

"And you've succeeded," she said, watching him place her luggage down by his feet.

"Yes, I've succeeded."

She was tempted to ask what else he'd made up for having now that he had gotten successful but decided not to.

"Come on, let me show you to the guest bedroom and then I'll show you around."

After taking a tour of his home she was more than impressed. His kitchen was to die for. It was spacious and all his appliances were totally modern. The entire décor of his apartment had a distinct masculine touch, even the guest bedroom.

"You can rest up while I prepare dinner."

She lifted a brow. "You cook?"

He smiled. "Of course. I've been fending for myself all my life and that also included cooking for myself."

She nodded suddenly remembering how at one time he'd told her if he didn't make his own meals he wouldn't get fed. His mother had had other things to do with her time than seeing about her only child's well-being. "So, what do you plan to prepare tonight?" she asked following him into the kitchen.

"I thought I'd throw a couple of steaks on the grill and make a salad."

"Can I help?"

"Are you sure you don't want to lie down for a while and rest?"

"I'm sure. I'm not tired."

"All right then. I can grill the steaks and you can prepare the salad. Will that work?"

She smiled at him. "Yes, that will work."

"Umm, this steak is melt-in-your-mouth tender, Christopher," Maxi said savoring the piece of meat she'd just eaten.

"Yeah, and this salad is pretty good, too. I'd never thought about adding raisins and almonds to my salad before. I like it."

"I wasn't sure if you would. That's why I had placed them on the side."

The corners of his mouth twitched. "I admit I'm kind of

picky when it comes to certain foods but I think this is delicious."

Maxi smiled. "I'm glad to know that you're not hard to please."

Ten minutes later they had finished their meal after engaging in light conversation. He had told her more about Gabe and also about Gabe's parents and how close he was to them.

"What time do you fly out on Sunday?" he asked Maxi as they began clearing off the table.

"That morning around seven. Why?"

He thought about inviting her to have dinner with him and the Blackwells but didn't think that would be a good idea. He'd already explained to Gabe what the real deal was between him and Maxi, but had decided not to divulge that kind of information to the older couple. If he took Maxi to the Blackwells on Sunday for dinner, Joella Blackwell would hear wedding bells since he'd never brought a woman to dinner before. And he didn't want to put any ideas into the older woman's head; especially ideas that were definitely not true.

He suddenly came up with his own idea. "Would it be a lot of trouble to get your flight time changed to later? I'd love for the two of us to have breakfast together."

Maxi was touched by his invitation. "Changing my flight time shouldn't be a problem. In fact, I'll check with the airlines now."

He nodded. "When you come back you can join me in the den where we can talk about things."

Maxi bit her lip, beginning to feel somewhat nervous about what they would be discussing. "All right."

Maxi found Christopher in his den where several original paintings by black artists lined the wall. He was sitting on the sofa and had settled in the seat, drinking a glass of wine. He looked up when she entered.

"Would you like something to drink? In addition to wine there is fruit punch, tea, and ginger ale in the fridge."

"No, I'm fine," she said, taking a seat in the wing chair across from where he sat. "There wasn't a problem changing my flight time. I don't leave until noon."

He nodded. "Thanks for changing it." He then sat up straighter in his seat and watched as she nervously looked at everything in the room but at him. "So, how do you propose for us to handle your having my baby?" he asked, deciding the best way to start off the discussion was to be direct.

Maxi glanced quickly at him and was caught by the deep dark brown of his eyes. They were eyes watching her intently. Her gaze then shifted to his mouth and her heart began to beat a little faster. She tried not to remember the one and only time they had kissed. She nervously began rubbing her hands together. "I know you gave me the option of artificial insemination or the traditional way, and if it's all right with you, I prefer the traditional. I don't want to get impregnated on some table in a clinic. But if you have a problem with it, then I'll understand."

He looked at her wondering if she really thought he would have a problem making love to her? "No, I don't have a problem with it. Then I guess my next question is how soon do you want to do it?"

"I want to get pregnant right away."

He chuckled. "Is this weekend soon enough?"

Maxi shook her head, and he noted she'd suddenly turned shy. "No, this weekend is too soon. I—I didn't come prepared to do anything like that."

He shrugged wondering what was there to get prepared for. "Okay. Will next weekend work? We can fly somewhere for the weekend to be in a more relaxed setting. How about Las Vegas?"

Maxi's brows bunched thinking next weekend was too soon, too, but she did want to get pregnant right away. "What if nothing happens after next week?"

"Then we'll keep trying until we finally get it right."

Maxi nodded as she released a sigh. She was glad his offer wasn't a one time only deal. "Becoming involved with me won't interfere with your social life will it?"

Christopher smiled. "No, I plan to give you my absolute attention until you're pregnant." He paused before continuing. "Just as long as you understand I'll be assuming my usual lifestyle after the deed is done. I'm not the marrying kind nor do I ever plan on being the marrying kind. The only thing you'll get out of this is a baby."

Maxi met his gaze. "And that's all I want."

CHAPTER THIRTY

The next day Maxi got the chance to meet Gabe when he joined them for breakfast. She liked him immediately and could tell his and Christopher's relationship was a rather close one.

After breakfast Christopher took her on a tour of the city after telling him it was her first visit to Detroit. He also pulled a lot of strings to get tickets to a Brian McKnight concert for that evening. She had mentioned to him on the cruise that she was a big fan of the popular singer.

Maxi was still humming one of Brian McKnight's songs when they returned to Christopher's apartment after the concert. "Wasn't he just wonderful, Christopher?"

"Yes, I guess," Christopher responded dryly, leaning against the closed door watching her. To say she was on cloud nine was an understatement. A part of him was glad he was responsible for her happiness, but then another part of him was slightly peeved that she was carrying on this way about a man who wouldn't know her if he passed her in the streets. He shook his head and walked into the room. "It's still early. Do you want to watch a video with me?"

"Umm, what you got?"

"Probably everything you've already seen at the movies. I prefer waiting until they come out on video."

Maxi looked at him thoughtfully. "You don't take your dates to the movies?"

"No."

She lifted an arched brow. "Then where do you usually take them?"

He met her gaze wondering if she really wanted to know. He didn't think she would appreciate knowing his bedroom was the usual place. "It depends. Do you want to watch the video or not?"

She smiled, wondering if she had put him on the spot. "Sure. I'll be back after I change into something more comfortable."

When she returned moments later after changing into a lounging outfit she had purchased while on the cruise, she found Christopher on the floor in the den, stretched out in front of a big screen television. He smiled when he saw her.

"You're just in time to select a movie for us to watch," he said handing several to her.

She joined him on the floor frowning when she noted they were all action-packed movies. "Don't you have anything that Steven Seagal doesn't star in?"

He thought for a moment. "No."

Maxi raised eyes to the ceiling. "You mean you don't have any movies with Taye Diggs, Denzel Washington, or Morris Chestnut?"

"No."

She shook her head. "Okay, then, any of these will work. I'm not usually into action-packed movies but I guess I'll suffer through it." She stretched out beside him.

"What type of movies do you watch?" he asked curiously.

She chuckled. "Usually anything with a lot of black folks, like *Two Can Play This Game, Soul Food, The Wood, The Best Man, Love and Basketball, The Brothers* . . . that sort of movie."

He gazed at her thoughtfully. "None of those had any action in it."

"My point exactly. My taste in movies is evidently quite different from yours."

Christopher slipped a video into the VCR, thinking how comfortable it felt having Maxi here with him like this. "Would you like me to get you anything before the movie starts?" he asked her.

She glanced over at him. "Anything like what?"

"There's some microwave popcorn in the kitchen, and if you're thirsty I can fix you something to drink."

"No, I'm fine."

The movie began playing and they both got quiet. A good twenty minutes later, Maxi, Christopher soon realized, was all into the movie with her eyes and ears glued to the television screen. For someone who claimed she didn't enjoy action-packed movies, she sure was all into this one, he thought. She seemed to enjoy watching Steven Seagal kick butt. She was into the movie so much that she didn't notice when he stood to turn off all the lights, making the room dark except for the light from the television. Nor did she notice that he had scooted closer to her on the floor. And when a scene came on with Steven Seagal kissing the leading lady, her eyes stayed pinned to the screen the entire while.

"That's all fake you know," he decided to tell her.

"Umm," she responded without taking her eyes off the television. "You think so?"

"Yes, you can tell there isn't any tongue interaction going on. What good is a kiss without tongue?"

The room got silent. The only sound was that from the movie of the two people on the screen sucking face. "Christopher?"

He glanced over and met Maxi's gaze. "Yes?"

"I enjoyed kissing you that time on the ship."

He smiled a seductive little smile, pleased that she had. "Did you?"

"Yes." No sooner had that single word left her mouth Maxi discovered Christopher had moved closer to her on the floor, almost hovering over her.

"What exactly did you like about it?" he asked as he continued to look at her. He thought about all the tongue interaction they had shared that night.

"Probably everything." She couldn't quite help herself when she smiled at the memories of that night. "I'd never done anything like that before."

He knew what she was alluding to but wanted to hear her say it. He wanted to hear her explain. "You'd been kissed before."

"Yes, but never like that and never to the point where I . . ." She released her gaze from his and tried her best to turn her attention back to the movie, deciding she had said enough. Probably too much. When she glanced over at Christopher moments later, he was still staring at her with dark penetrating eyes. She inhaled a deep, quick breath when the room went pitch black. He had used the remote control to switch off the television and VCR, plunging the room into total darkness.

When he reached out and pulled her into his arms, she couldn't help herself, and went willingly. And when he covered her mouth with his, she knew she was lost. For the second time in four years, fire was being ignited in every part of her body as once again he made her remember just what it felt like to be a woman.

He kissed her with the same hunger that he had that night on the cruise, making scandalous love to her mouth, eliciting groans from deep within her body as she latched onto his tongue and held on. But he was having none of that and a duel began. He released her mouth only when they needed to breathe and then they were back at it again. A surge of hot, frenzied excitement raced through Maxi and she recalled what

Mya had told her on the cruise. Kissing led to other things and when she felt Christopher's hands at the waist of her pants, tugging them down she knew she had to stop him. They had plans to do this next week, and that would be soon enough for what their bodies craved.

But she wanted him *now.*

He pulled back and looked at her, as though expecting her to say something that would put an end to what they were doing. But she didn't. Because she couldn't.

"Christopher." His name left her lips, a seductive plea of unadulterated wanting and desire.

He heard the sound of her voice and knew its meaning. Without wasting any time he continued to remove her pants then tossed them aside. He then gave all of his attention to removing her top, which he managed to execute without much trouble. He sat back on his haunches and looked down at her, dressed in bra and panties.

Maxi knew he was giving her a second chance to stop him. "Do we do it now or do we wait till next week . . . until you are ready?" he asked her in a quiet, husky voice.

The first thing that came into Maxi's mind was that she could be dead by next week, and her body was more than ready. She wanted him and she needed him and if she got pregnant tonight, then it would be all right.

"Say something, for heaven's sake!"

Christopher's outburst made her realize he was waiting for a response. Deciding she could show him better than she could tell him, she slanted him a rueful smile as she reached up to remove her bra. He watched her every moment with deep, dark eyes. After finishing the task she tossed the bra aside and went to remove her panties while Christopher was pensively quiet as he continued to watch her. Maxi kind of liked the thought of him watching her close and she deliberately made it worth his while.

"You're getting quite a kick out of teasing me, aren't you?" he asked her hoarsely, moments later.

Her smile was slightly sheepish when she responded honestly, after tossing her panties aside. "Yes."

Christopher moved his gaze down the full length of her body, appreciating everything he saw, every single inch of her.

"So, are you going to stay dressed?" she asked, trying to sound casual when she felt anything but casual.

Shaking his head, he began removing his shirt. A few moments later he tossed it over to where her bra and panties were. He stood to remove his pants. Maxi bit her bottom lip as he watched him. Her gaze didn't waver. Not even when he stepped out of his pants and reached for the waist of silk boxer shorts. Her eyes glittered with passion when he peeled the pair of shorts down his legs. "Like what you see, Maxine Chandler?"

She blinked remembering those same words he had spoken one day in school during physical ed. when she had seen him wearing a pair of gym shorts, and he'd caught her staring just like she was doing now. "Yes, I like what I see," she admitted unashamedly.

He smiled. "Then that makes two of us. I definitely like what I see."

Maxi swallowed. The physical attraction radiating between them was stronger than it had ever been. The heat, the passion, the desire completely filled the air in the room. He slowly came back down to her, kissing her again in a deep, drowning kiss that rocked her entire body. When he released her mouth, his name sounded from her lips. "Christopher."

Instead of answering her, he stood with her in his arms and carried her into his bedroom. He stopped before placing her on the bed, remembering the women he had shared this same bed with. He didn't want Maxi to be just another woman who slept with him. She meant more to him than that. She would be the one and only woman to ever have his baby.

Maxi moaned softly, deep in her throat when he placed her on the bed in the guest room she had slept in the night before. He then joined her there, pulling her into his arms and once again she melted into his kiss. He broke off the kiss to trail his mouth along her neck and throat, while his fingers found their mark in the haven between her legs, touching the sensitized area there.

Her body automatically responded to his touch, his intimate caress and something clenched tight within her. She sucked in her breath when she felt his mouth capture a nipple between his teeth and gently began bathing it with his tongue. She wasn't sure how much of this she could take. How much longer she would last. "Now," she whispered huskily, when fragments of sensations started passing through her.

Breathing hard, Christopher made a low guttural sound when he placed his body directly over hers, between her legs, placing the tip of his manhood to the opening of her femininity. Eyes locked with hers, he slowly began filling her, breathing even harder when she lifted her hips to take him all the way in. The first thought that entered his mind was, damn, she felt hot. And the second was that he could get addicted to this. When he didn't think he could go any further inside her, he lowered his head to her.

Maxi raised her head to meet him halfway, wanting another kiss as much as he did. And the second their lips touched and she had wrapped her arms tightly around his neck, the hardness of his thighs held her in place when he thrust deeply into her. Her moan was captured in his mouth as he continued kissing and began pumping his hips with urgent intent into her, stroking every part of her body, increasing his rhythm as he thrust in and out of her.

For the first time while making love to a woman, Christopher let his every emotion escape as he reveled in the sensations that being inside her were bringing him. Making love to her this way left him bare, vulnerable, crazed. His entire body shook with the need to possess her, totally, completely. And when he felt the waves of pleasure right there, within both of their reach, he increased his rhythm, rapidly, at a fast pace, thinking he didn't ever want to stop.

He broke off their kiss, intent on working his body into hers any way he could to give both of them maximum satisfaction. He slipped his hand beneath her hips, lifting her to him to go deeper. And as much as he didn't want it to happen just yet, an orgasm shook him, sending thick, liquid warmth shooting right into her womb, so much so that he could actually feel it happening. He thrust into her one final time, enjoying the feel of his heated release exploding inside her. He held her in place as his body continued to fill her to capacity, giving her a part of him no other woman had claimed. And when he felt her body reach the pinnacles of sexual delight, he came again—a second time—automatically, unabashedly inside her.

When it was over, he collapsed on top of her, being careful not to press his full weight onto her. Barely able to catch his breath he lay still, completely drained from the force of his release—two orgasms back to back. That had never happened to him before.

"Christopher—"

"Umm," he responded as his hand continued to rub the slippery soap over her body with one hand while his other hand was caressing her breast under the steady stream of water from the shower. Maxi's heart was pounding against his hand, and the heat between her legs had sensations flowing all over her body. They were sensations the water from the shower couldn't drown out.

Christopher had backed her against the shower wall with her legs wrapped around his waist. Water cascaded over them when his mouth crushed down on hers with a hunger that had her melting under him. She gripped his shoulders to hold on for the ride she knew he would give her.

When he drove into her, her inner muscles were ready, clenching at him for dear life, holding him tight inside her. But he was having none of that. And he pulled out only to thrust back in again, fast, deep. Over and over again.

Maxi screamed out her release when she felt him explode inside her, coating her insides with his semen, signifying his own climax as he held her body in place with his. She deliberately squeezed her inner muscles around him, milking him dry.

He released her mouth and stared at her as water ran over both of their faces, knowing what she was making her body do to his, feeling exhilarated that she wanted his seed planted deep within her. He found joy in the fact that Maxine Chandler wanted all of him, especially this, the very thing he had withheld from every other woman. And he was determined to give her as much of him as he could. He grabbed her hips and thrust again, pushing as deeply inside her as possible. He watched her gasp, and her eyes widened when she felt him getting hard inside her all over again.

And then he was starting over.

Thrusting in and out, making love to the woman he had once considered his. A woman he'd thought he wasn't worthy of ever having. He tried to remember how many times he had dreamed of being inside her like this. Making love to her over and over again, touching her in ways that only a lover could.

She came again, screaming his name and with a loud grunt he gave one last thrust when an orgasm hit him hard.

Moments later, barely able to breathe, barely able to stand, his gaze met hers and he leaned toward her and kissed her in a sweet and tender exchange that was different from any kisses they'd shared. When he released her mouth, he relinquished his hold on her and she shimmied downward off his wet body.

He began lathering her all over again, then let her lather him. Moments later, they rinsed off. Emerging from the shower they toweled each other dry, then he picked her up and took her into the guest bedroom.

Christopher placed her on the bed and joined her there, gathering her into his arms. Closing his eyes as a serene peace settled within him and holding her securely in his arms, they both slept.

Christopher walked Maxi to the gate after she had checked her bags at the terminal. A part of him regretted her leaving. After an entire night of making love they had awakened that morning, eaten the breakfast he had made, and had gone back to bed to make love again. "I enjoyed my weekend with you, Christopher."

"And I enjoyed my weekend with you as well," he responded, tightening his hold on her hand. "I'll call you later in the week after I've finalized the plans for Las Vegas, all right?"

She nodded, then looked around at the people coming and going. She wished they were alone again so she could kiss him the way she wanted to.

"I know what you're thinking, Maxi," Christopher said huskily, putting his hands on her shoulders and then running them down her arms.

She looked up at him, trembling from his touch. "Do you?"

"Yes. It's the same thing I'm thinking, too."

Maxi sighed. She could believe that. She knew from his actions this weekend that he enjoyed kissing her, especially when he initiated a lot of tongue interaction. "Are you looking forward to this weekend?" she asked, moments later.

"Most definitely."

She nodded. A few minutes later the airline receptionist called for passengers to begin boarding the plane. "I guess I had better go." She stretched up and placed a light kiss on his lips. "I'll see you this weekend." Without waiting for him to respond she turned and walked away.

She had gotten in line to board the plane when she made

the mistake of looking back. Christopher was still standing in the same spot watching her. Without any thought to what she was doing, she pushed through the crowd of people trying to board the plane and ran back to him. He captured her in his arms and kissed her the way she wanted to be kissed. Long, hard, deep.

"Bye, Christopher," she whispered when he released her. Without looking back she ran to board her plane.

CHAPTER THIRTY-ONE

Mya keyed information into her laptop, grateful that her secretary had been able to book her a flight straight to Orlando. The plane would be landing in another hour or so.

She glanced around the cabin at the other passengers, thinking she wasn't the only one who was using a laptop. She then turned her attention back to the information she had pulled up on the screen. After she was satisfied with the figures she had worked up, she turned her attention to reading the information she had gathered on her newest client, Robert Noble, the thirty-five-year-old male wonder.

Noble had graduated with a bachelor's degree in business administration from Howard University and a master's degree from MIT, at the top of his class. After working a couple of years for Microsoft, he had formed his own company, Noble Technology, becoming the largest black-owned computer software company in the United States. For years, the company she worked for, Monahan Investments, had tried wooing him away from Skylark Financial Services, and he hadn't budged. Then, he had contacted Monahan unexpectedly one day and inquired about their services. It seemed that he and Skylark were parting ways. Of course, Mr. Lee had jumped at the chance to do business with the wealthy entrepreneur. And because of her expertise in high-technology as well as her in-depth knowledge of her company's many financial services, she had been not only selected, but had gotten promoted into the position of being Robert Noble's financial adviser.

The plane landed in Orlando a little past noon and, as planned, Mr. Noble had sent a car to meet her at the airport that would take her to the hotel. Their meeting was set for three-thirty.

Once she had gotten settled in her hotel room she called home, speaking briefly with Mrs. Butler making sure everything was okay and leaving her number for Garrett. She was about to remove her jacket when the phone rang.

"Hello?"

"Ms. Rivers?"

"Yes."

"This is Robert Noble. I'm just calling to make sure you arrived okay and that you like the accommodations that were made for you."

Mya lifted a brow. She hadn't expected him to call to check on such matters himself. Usually businessmen of his caliber left that task to their secretaries. "Yes, everything is fine, Mr. Noble, and thanks for sending a car for me at the airport."

"You're welcome, and I look forward to our meeting, however, I'm sorry to say there will be a slight delay. I'm still tied up in a meeting that should have ended hours ago and it seems there's no end in sight, at least not before our three-thirty appointment. Is there anyway we can change our meeting time to later?"

"That will be fine," she replied, keeping the disappointment out of her voice. She had hoped they would cover as much business as they could beginning today, then possibly she could fly home a day earlier than planned.

"I appreciate your flexibility. How about if I pick you up at the hotel at five? I'm sure we'll both be hungry by then. Let's plan on a business dinner."

"All right."

"I'll meet you in the hotel lobby at five."

After they hung up the phone she took off her jacket and tossed it across the back of a chair. She then opened her laptop to e-mail Garrett, knowing he would get online after putting the boys to bed. Things were still pretty tense between them and knew when she returned to Dallas, they would need to sit down and resolve the problems plaguing their marriage.

"Hi, it will be late when I call tonight. Meeting time was changed to later. I hope practice went okay today. Love, Mya."

Shutting her laptop down she then decided to undress and lie across the bed and rest. Her last thought before closing her eyes was that Robert Noble had a nice sounding voice.

Impeccably dressed, wearing a navy blue linen business suit, matching navy pumps, pearl earrings, and carrying her leather briefcase, Mya arrived in the hotel lobby a few minutes before five. She didn't wait long before the man she recognized from photographs as Robert Noble walked through the revolving doors. Dressed in what she saw to be a very expensive business suit, there was something about him that demanded attention.

And he was getting it.

She noticed a number of people's gazes, especially females, turned his way and she could see why. He had a walk of a man who was self-assured, comfortable with his surroundings and with anything else he came into contact with. He was tall, well built, and handsome. She mentally compared him with Garrett and decided where her good-looking husband had an athletic air about him, Robert Noble seemed to be all about business.

She was glad for that, because so was she.

"Ms. Rivers?" he asked extending his hand to her as a broad smile touched his lips and male appreciation shone in his eyes.

She smiled. He may be all about business but she could tell that the man in him had noticed her as a woman. She didn't have a problem with that since she had definitely noticed him as a man. There was nothing wrong with appreciating the opposite sex as long as it went no further than mere appreciation. She couldn't help but note he had walked directly over to her like he'd known just who she was although the two of them had never met. "Yes, Mr. Noble, it's nice meeting you and I'm looking forward to working with you."

"Likewise," he said easily. "I suggest we leave now. Traffic this time of the day is crazy, but I promise to get you to the restaurant in one piece."

She laughed. "Thanks, I would appreciate that."

During the drive to the restaurant, they talked about where her company wanted to take him and precisely just where he wanted to go. He made sure she understood that, although he enjoyed working, he wanted to retire before he reached fifty.

She chuckled. "Trust me, Mr. Noble. I'll have you retired long before then."

"It's Robert," he said, once again giving her a mega-watt smile that was sexy as sin. "I still think of Mr. Noble as my father. And I hope you don't mind if I call you Mya."

She shook her head. "No, not at all."

"Good."

Dinner was pleasant and she was able to cover a lot of information with him that he seemed receptive to. It was quite obvious that he was highly intelligent and knew just what questions to ask.

"I'm sure you're aware that I'm thinking about taking my company public," he said smoothly, after the remains of their dinner had been taken away and they were enjoying coffee.

"Yes, I'm aware of that."

"That's the reason I need you to spend the next two days here, working closely with my vice president, Simon Prentice. He has a lot of concerns. He wasn't too happy when I severed my ties with Skylark."

Mya nodded. She wasn't clear on the details of what had ended the relationship. "Well, I hope to convince him that you made the right decision in coming to us."

After dinner he had taken her back to the hotel. Letting the valet park his car he walked her into the lobby. "After studying the information I gave you tonight, call me if you have any questions. I'll be up rather late going over items for my meeting tomorrow with Mr. Prentice," she said.

"I hope you don't plan to be up too late. I don't want to be the cause of your exhaustion tomorrow."

She chuckled. "Trust me, I'll be very alert tomorrow. For some reason I think I'll have to be, with Mr. Prentice."

He laughed good-naturedly. "Don't let Simon intimidate you, which I'm warning you he will try to do. Just be as thorough with him as you were with me tonight and he'll buy into anything you say." His eyes turned a darker shade of brown when he added. "You're a very persuasive woman, Mya, and definitely an asset to Monahan Investments."

"Thank you, Robert. I'm glad you think so. Will you also be at tomorrow's meeting?" she inquired politely.

"Unfortunately, no. I have an important meeting in Miami tomorrow. I'm flying out in the morning but will return before you leave on Thursday. Let's get together again on Wednesday evening when I return and you can bring me up to date."

"That will be fine," she said quietly. It didn't look like she would make it back home early after all.

"Thanks again for coming," he said shaking her hand again.

"And thank you for doing business with my company." She then watched as he left, walking back through the revolving doors.

As soon as she was back in her hotel room she placed a call to Garrett. She was surprised when Mrs. Butler answered. "Mrs. Butler? Is Garrett available?"

"No, Ms. Rivers. He called earlier and said he would be delayed and to go ahead and feed the boys and put them in bed." Mya could tell by the sound of Mrs. Butler's voice that she was as surprised as she was. Garret always made it a point to come straight home from practice each day, no matter what. "The boys are okay?"

"Yes, ma'am, they are fine. Of course they miss you."

Mya nodded. Her first day away was usually the hardest on the boys. "And I miss them too. Well, I had better go. Don't forget to let Garrett know that I called."

"Yes, ma'am.

"Goodnight, Mrs. Butler."

"Goodnight, Ms. Rivers."

After ending her conversation with Mrs. Butler, Mya went into the bathroom to take a shower. Afterwards, she sat at the desk in the room and worked, preparing for her meeting with Simon Prentice tomorrow. It was close to eleven when her phone rang. Thinking it was Garrett she picked up on the first ring. "Hi, sweetheart."

There was a chuckle on the other end. Then a deep voice said, "I've been called a number of things lately, but sweetheart isn't one of them."

Mya smiled in embarrassment when she realized the caller wasn't Garrett but was Robert Noble. "Sorry, Mr. Noble, I thought you were my husband. I was expecting his call."

"Then I won't hold you. I was wondering if you could look over some papers that I'm leaving with Simon. They're a summary of all the services I had with Skylark. I just want you to review them to make sure we're on target with your company."

"Yes, I'll be glad to look at them."

"Good. Well, goodnight, and I'll see you Wednesday."

"Yes. Goodnight."

Mya yawned after hanging up the phone. She was about to shut down her laptop for the night when the phone rang again. Deciding not to take any chances as to who the caller might be, she answered in her professional voice. "Mya Rivers."

"Mya?"

She relaxed when she recognized Garrett's voice. "Garrett, hi, I thought you had forgotten me."

"No, I didn't forget you. I hung out at Mark's house tonight. I guess you heard, since it's been all over the news, that he got cut from the team."

Mya's heart jumped. "No, I hadn't heard. I haven't been watching television." She sat down in the desk chair remembering her conversation with Mark's wife, Danielle, two weeks ago. "How is he taking it?"

"Not good. So some of the guys and I went over there after practice."

"I'm sure he appreciates everyone's support."

"Yeah, he would prefer having his job back but we all know that isn't going to happen."

Mya nodded. "Has any other team called him yet?" Sometime a player would get a call within hours of being cut from a team.

"No. You know Mark's temper. Some coaches see him as a liability."

"You can't blame them with the number of penalties he usually gets each season."

"But still, he was a damn good player."

Mya heard the irritation in Garrett's voice and knew he was upset. "How are you handling things?" she asked. He and Mark shared a close friendship.

"Okay, I guess. A lot of us are still in shock. Mark did a hell of a job on the team—penalties or no penalties." After a slight pause he asked, "Will you be coming home early?"

"I had hoped so but now it doesn't seem like I'll be able to."

"Oh."

Even with that single word, she heard the disappointment in his voice. "But I hope to be back early on Thursday hopefully before lunch."

"It would be nice to come home and find you here."

Mya flinched, knowing he hadn't meant it as a compliment but was being sarcastic. "I'll call you tomorrow," she said quietly, not wanting to fight with him tonight.

"Yeah, right. Goodnight, Mya."

"Goodnight, Garrett. I love you."

They hung up then. Mya was a little hurt that Garrett hadn't taken the time to tell her that he loved her, too, before hanging up but she decided not to let it bother her.

Her thoughts moved to Danielle and Mark. She wanted to call Danielle but it was too late to do so tonight and made a mental note to do so first thing in the morning. Shutting down her laptop she called the front desk for a wake-up call in the morning. Moments later she got into bed wondering what Mark and Danielle would do now that Mark didn't have a job, and from what Garrett had said, he didn't have any prospects. A short while later after saying a prayer for the Hughes family, Mya dozed off to sleep.

CHAPTER THIRTY-TWO

"Are you feeling better, Mr. Chandler?" Christopher's secretary asked when he walked past her desk as he headed for his office.

"I wasn't sick, Mary," he said with an answering smile.

"Oh, I just assumed you were, sir. I've never known you to miss a day from work, especially on a Monday."

"There's a first time for everything," he responded in a light-hearted mood. "Has Gabe arrived yet?"

"Yes, sir, he came in thirty minutes ago."

Christopher nodded. "Ask him to come see me when he gets the chance."

"Yes, sir."

Christopher entered his office and closed the door. Placing his briefcase on the desk he opened it and began removing the files he had come by his office to pick up on Sunday afternoon after taking Maxi to the airport. He had intended to work on them but had found he'd been too keyed up after her visit to concentrate on anything.

And yesterday instead of coming into the office, he had spent most of the day relaxing and making airline and hotel reservations for their trip to Las Vegas, something he was looking forward to. If anyone had told him he would be this anxious to get a woman pregnant he would not have believed them.

Goose bumps broke out on his arms when he thought of making love to Maxi again. He had had sex with a number of women but he had never actually made love to any of them. In the past all his focus had been on seeking pleasure in a hot feminine body but with Maxi it had been more than that. Never before had he experienced anything so beautiful, so wholesome, so sensuous, and above all, so pure. Nothing had ever felt so right. She had taken him into the very essence of her body and had satisfied him more than any woman he'd ever had, because everything Maxine Chandler did, she did from her heart and a part of him knew that also included making love to him. And he had given her a part of him that he had never wanted to share with any other woman. Yet he had given it to her without any reservations or misgivings because in his heart Maxi was deserving of anything and everything he had.

"So you decided to remember you need to earn a paycheck?"

Christopher glanced up. Gabe had entered his office, closed the door behind him and was leaning against it with his hands shoved deep into his pants pockets. "I take it you missed me yesterday, Blackwell."

Gabe smiled. "Envious of you is probably a better word. I figured you had talked Maxi into staying over until Monday and that was the reason you played hooky."

Christopher chuckled. "No, she left as planned on Sunday but now that you mention it, that would not have been a bad idea. Too bad I didn't think of it."

Gabe walked over and stood in front of Christopher's desk. "So what was the reason you didn't come in? Not that I'm complaining, mind you. I think you spend too much time in this place anyway."

"The reason I didn't come in was because I just wanted to

stay home and chill . . . and to remember." He met Gabe's gaze. "I enjoyed having Maxi here this weekend."

"Yeah, I'm sure you did. I like her, Christopher."

A low chuckle rumbled in Christopher's chest. "Yeah, and she mentioned that she likes you, too."

"You're going ahead with your plans to get her pregnant?"

"Yes, that's what this is all about."

Gabe lifted a brow. "You sure about that?"

"Yes."

"Yet you claim she means a lot to you."

"She does. Maxi has always been able to make me feel something I usually don't feel around other woman."

"What?"

"Special. Even when I was young and was going through my worst moments, she never made me feel like a charity case. She always made me feel special and without a whole lot of effort in doing so. She has that knack."

"Yet, you won't consider marrying her."

"No, because as much as I care for Maxi, I'm not in love with her. I've outgrown those feelings I once had for her. I don't think I'm capable of loving a woman. I like a lot of women but I don't love any of them. It's just that simple."

Gabe nodded, wondering if Christopher really believed that. He glanced at the pile of mail that had accumulated on Christopher's desk. "Well, it seems you definitely have a lot to do today, so I'll leave and let you get to it. What did you want to see me about?"

"Just to let you know that I'll be out of the office a couple of days next week. Maxi and I are flying to Las Vegas for the weekend and will probably stay through Monday."

Gabe nodded. "Okay. Will she be coming back here?"

"Why would she? After she gets pregnant I probably won't be seeing her any more until probably after the baby is born."

"And she has agreed to that?"

Christopher met Gabe's gaze. "Yes. I offered Maxi a baby, Gabe, not my life. She understands that once she gets pregnant it's business and pleasure as usual for me."

"In other words you go back to screwing anything in a skirt and reinstate your philosophy that 'there's nothing like getting between a great pair of legs.'"

"Whatever works."

Gabe shook his head. "You know whatever you do, you have my full support. But I don't think you're thinking straight with this thing involving Maxi."

"Meaning what?"

"Meaning any man in his right mind can see she's the marrying kind."

"Yeah, and she's also the mothering kind. All she wants is a baby and that suits me just fine because that is all I'm prepared to give her."

"Well, you better hope Mom never meets her because she'd do anything to get us married off. And if she ever finds out you plan to get Maxi pregnant without marrying her, you may as well—"

"What the hell!" Christopher's loud voice cut into Gabe's words.

Gabe frowned. "What's wrong?"

Christopher handed him the large photograph he had just taken out of the envelope. "Take a look at this."

Gabe did. He smiled. "Good looking woman from what I can see. However, it's hard to do so with your mouth planted so firmly on hers. Who is she and what is this about?"

"That's Tori Smithfield." Christopher knew that was all he needed to say. Although Gabe had never met Tori, he knew about Christopher's occasional affair with the journalist who worked for CNN. "She came to Detroit on business a month before I went on the cruise."

"Who took the picture and why was it taken?"

"The hell if I know. I don't recall anyone around with a camera that night and even so, Tori and I don't have to sneak around since we're two consenting adults. We're both single, so this photograph doesn't make sense."

Gabe nodded. "It seems that someone wants you to know that they are aware of the two of you together."

"Yes, but who and why?"

Gabe didn't say anything for a moment as he studied the photograph of the scantily dressed woman locked in Christopher's arms. He then looked up and met Christopher's gaze. "And you're sure she isn't married? The only reason a person would send a photo like this is because they feel it could in some way be damaging to either one of you."

Christopher shook his head. "When I met Tori three years ago she was single and as far as I know she's still single."

"If I were you I would make sure, Christopher. There's a reason someone sent you this photograph. Since we know for a fact that you're single and this picture won't have a damaging effect on you, that won't be true for Tori Smithfield if she's married."

"I don't mess around with married women, Gabe," Christopher said curtly.

"Not if you know they are married. What if she was married all along and just didn't tell you?"

Christopher drew a long steadying breath, not liking the feel of things. He couldn't believe Tori would deceive him that way. They had been open in their relationship, which had been one based on sexual need, nothing more. Now with what Gabe was saying, Christopher couldn't help but recall just what he did know about Tori. He had never wanted to get into her business like he had never wanted her to get into his. But he was fairly certain that she hadn't been married when they had first started seeing each other. She had told him that straight out. Had she gotten married but hadn't told him and intended to keep things between them as they had been before?

"It's not uncommon for some married women to take lovers, Christopher."

"I don't like being used that way, Gabe, and I'm going to find out what the hell is going on."

"What are you going to do?"

"Try contacting her. I don't know her home number but I'm sure I'll be able to track her down through her employer." He took the photograph back from Gabe. "I plan to get to the bottom of this immediately."

CHAPTER THIRTY-THREE

"Getting upset won't do you much good at this point, Christopher. Calm down and let's analyze the situation to see what we're up against. It may not be as bad as it seems," Gabe said encouragingly.

"I disagree, Gabe. It *is* as bad as it seems. I slept with another man's wife," Christopher said with barely contained anger. According to the person he had spoken to at CNN, Victoria Smithfield had decided to become a freelance journalist since her marriage eight months ago. "Dammit, she should have told me."

"But the fact of the matter is that she didn't, so you didn't know. Stop kicking your own butt for it. What we should be doing is trying to figure out what's motivating the person who sent that picture to you. Chances are Tori Smithfield received a copy of that photograph as well. And if she really is married, she has more to lose than you. Maybe her husband suspected she's been cheating and hired a private detective to prove it."

And that was what Christopher was afraid of. Just how far would this suspecting husband go to prove his wife's unfaithfulness? For reasons Christopher had never shared with Gabe, the last thing he wanted was to become involved in any sort of scandal. Because of his mother, he had been part of a scandal before and the depth of it had had a lasting effect on him. No one knew how he'd felt being a part of such negative publicity. He had made a pact with himself to never do anything that would put him in that sort of situation. For the past ten years he had worked hard to establish decency and honor to the Chandler name, something his mother had never thought of doing.

For nineteen years he had witnessed a good number of the married men in Savannah being constant visitors to his mother's bedroom. He had sworn he would not be like those men who did not respect the marriage vows they had taken. He had also gone a step further and decided never to marry.

It had been hard for him to watch those men sneak into their house at night, then see them in the daylight with their wives and children. Such was the case of Mayor Potter who somehow had gotten exclusive rights to his mother's bed during the beginning of Christopher's junior year of high school. It had been an affair that had lasted two years. During that time Christopher would go to school every day and sit in Mrs. Potter's class remembering the sounds of her husband screwing his mother's brains out the night before. And the sad thing was that Deborah Chandler had fallen hopelessly in love with Will Potter and had believed his lie that he would one day divorce his wife and marry her. How his mother had been so gullible, Christopher didn't know. All he knew was that when the scandal broke out, in an effort to save face with the community and with his family, Potter had further trampled his mother's already tarnished name as well as her heart. One night after having drunk an entire bottle of Johnny Walker Red, she had gotten the nerve to ingest an entire bottle of Valium while Christopher slept in the other room. He had been the one to find her the next morning, lying on the sofa with the most peaceful look on her face. At first he had thought her merely sleeping, until he had found the letter she had written to Potter.

"Christopher, are you okay?"

Gabe's question reeled Christopher's thoughts back to the present. "Yeah, I'm fine. I was lost in my thoughts for just a moment."

At that moment Mary sounded the buzzer on Christopher's desk. "Yes, Mary, what is it?"

"Tori Smithfield is on the line, sir."

Christopher released a deep sigh. He watched as Gabe silently excused himself and left his office, closing the door behind him. "Put her through, Mary."

As soon as he heard Tori's voice on the phone, he lit into her. "Why didn't you tell me you had gotten married, Tori?"

Tori bit her bottom lip. She could feel Christopher's anger all the way through the phone lines. She wondered how he had found out about her marriage. "I had planned to tell you that night, Christopher, but then, later, afterward, I didn't think it was important."

"Evidently your husband doesn't feel that way since he's having you followed."

Tori's breath caught. Panic seized her. "I don't understand. What do you mean? My husband is not having me followed."

"If you're so sure it's not him, then it's someone else. Somebody sent me a photograph of the two of us together. It was taken the last time we saw each other as we stood in the open doorway of your hotel room, kissing. "I take it that you haven't gotten your copy of the photo yet."

"No, but I just got back in town and haven't gone through my mail."

"Then I suggest you do so. And what makes you so sure your husband didn't send it?"

She paused for a moment before replying. "He trusts me."

"If he does then he has a case of bad judgment."

Although he had spoken the truth, Christopher's words hurt

nonetheless and she reacted. "What makes you think that photograph came from someone that *I* know? It could be from one of your former girlfriends who has a jealous streak, especially since I didn't get a copy. I would think if I was the intended target I would have gotten a copy before you did. How do you know it isn't someone trying to hurt *you*?"

Christopher didn't say anything for the longest moment. She did have a point. A man couldn't make it to the top of his profession without making some enemies, and he would be the first to admit that he had made a number of them. But still, he couldn't see any of them going to this extreme to ruin him with this sort of scandal. "Who did you marry, Tori?"

"I'd rather not say."

Christopher balled his hand into a fist at his side. "Look, Tori, this isn't getting us anywhere. I can find out the information if I want to, so you may as well go ahead and tell me. Unfortunate as it may seem, we're in this mess together and it's going to take the two of us cooperating to get to the bottom of it."

"He's not behind this, Christopher," she said with strong conviction.

"Well, somebody is and whether that person intends to damage your reputation or mine is the issue right now and my main concern."

Sighing defeatedly, she said, "All right. I'll contact you again."

"When?"

"The first of next week. Will I be able to contact you at this same number then?"

Tori's question made Christopher realize that he had planned to be off the first couple of days during the beginning of the week. "Yes, you can contact me this time next week. If I'm not here my secretary can forward your call to me."

"All right. Goodbye." She then hung up the phone.

* * *

A short while later Gabe entered Christopher's office. "I was able to get that information that you wanted, Christopher. Tori Smithfield is married to Adam Benedict."

Christopher turned from where he had been standing, looking out the window for the past half hour or so. "Adam Benedict?"

"Yes, *the* Adam Benedict, retired senator from California. I'm surprised Tori Smithfield wasn't more discreet."

Christopher shook his head. "I can only assume she thought me coming to her hotel room was being discreet enough."

"Not when she's married to Adam Benedict. I'm surprised you didn't recognize her face on television when they first got married. It made news since he's so much older than she is."

If that was eight months ago it was during the time I went on that monthlong cruise to Alaska, remember, trying to get that Landmark Deal."

Gabe nodded. "Yeah, it was about that same time and by the time you returned all the sensation about their marriage had died down. The media had turned its attention to the September 11 tragedy. Well, at least you know the photograph wasn't taken by anyone in the media. With the senator's long history in Washington, news of his wife having an affair would have been plastered in all the tabloids."

Christopher inhaled deeply. "It still might. We still don't know who we're dealing with here."

"And she doesn't think it's the senator who's having her investigated?"

"No, she doesn't think that it's him. She even suggested it may be someone I know."

Gabe gave that some thought. "In that case, have you considered Pamela Carlyle?"

"Pamela?"

"Yes, she is a photographer and you did piss her off that time you came home and found her naked in your bed."

Christopher nodded, remembering that day and Gabe was

right. Pamela had left pretty mad at him, and he hadn't seen or heard from her since that night. She was a freelance photographer who worked for a number of major magazines. Her profession would place her in the company of a number of high-profile individuals. And he knew for a fact that she had worked exclusively in the California area a year ago. Had she seen him and Tori together and had remembered Tori as being the senator's wife and this was her way of getting back at him?

Christopher sighed deeply. "I need a few days off to make a trip to Savannah."

"To see Maxi?"

"Yes. She deserves to know what's going on."

"Why? This has nothing to do with her."

"Yes, it has, especially since she has indicated that she plans to let others know that I'm the father of her child. Just think of the major mess if a copy of that photo is sent to the press. I learned the hard way that any sort of a scandal has far-reaching effects on people, and I don't want Maxi affected by any of this."

Gabe shook his head. "It's not like you've assassinated the president or slept with the First Lady."

"No, still, I refuse to place Maxi in an embarrassing situation."

CHAPTER THIRTY-FOUR

Mya slipped into a pair of jeans and pulled a tank top over her head, grateful to be home a day earlier than planned. She was to have remained in Orlando to meet with Robert Noble today but he had called and left word with Simon Prentice that his trip from Miami would be delayed. He suggested that Mya return home, then make plans to meet with him again in Orlando in a few weeks. Although she didn't relish the thought of having to return to Orlando any time soon, she was glad to be home.

She had arrived just before the boys' nap and they had been happy to see her. Since Garrett had already left for practice when Mr. Prentice had gotten word to her that she could leave, she had no way of letting Garrett know she was returning home a day early. She hoped he would be happy to see her. She knew he was going through a bad time about Mark being cut from the team and regretted she had not been here for him.

She checked her appearance in the mirror. She was going to surprise Garrett and show up at practice hoping to catch at least the last two hours of it. Then maybe later they could go someplace to eat like they'd done the other time. She was determined to resolve the problems they were having in their marriage, not sure how much more she could take of his attitude regarding her job.

Less than thirty minutes later Mya was pulling her Lexus SUV into a parking space. She quickly grabbed her purse and got out. She met Nathan Phelps, one of Garrett's teammates, coming toward her to get into his own vehicle that was parked nearby.

"Hey, Nat, practice over already?" she asked smiling at him.

"Yeah, the coach let us out earlier than expected and I'm glad. Today was one grueling day. If you're looking for Garrett, he's still in the locker room but should be heading out in a few shakes."

"Thanks."

Mya walked toward the vicinity of the locker rooms and stopped at a distance when she saw Paige Duvall standing in front of the doors as if she was waiting for someone. Mya couldn't forget the fact she had seen her openly make a pass at Garrett that time at the party. So instead of joining Paige in her wait for whomever it was she was waiting for, Mya decided to hang back near the trees and wait for Garrett to come out. That way she wouldn't have to make phony conversation with the woman.

Moments later Mya smiled when Garrett walked out. A frown then covered her face when it was apparent that Garrett had been the person Paige Duvall had been waiting for, too. Mya watched as the woman smiled radiantly at him before reaching out and grabbing him around the waist, getting all in his face. Mya then watched as Garrett walked the woman to the side of the building, away from prying eyes, and stood there talking to her. She blinked back tears as she turned and headed back to the parking lot. Before starting her vehicle she ran a trembling hand down her cheek to wipe away her tears. If she hadn't seen it with her own eyes she would not have believed it. Garrett was cheating on her.

* * *

"Mya, please calm down. You may have misread what you saw." Maxi's soft voice tried to coax Mya into calming down. She had called her, crying and upset, and had told her about the incident she had witnessed at the stadium.

"I know what I saw, Maxi. How could he do this to us?" Mya asked fighting back more tears. She felt so hurt her body felt numb. She had barely made it home without having an accident, she'd been crying so hard. Once she had let herself inside the house she was grateful that Mrs. Butler had taken the boys to the park. She would not have wanted anyone to see her in such a pitiful state.

"Just give him a chance to explain, Mya. You may have jumped to the wrong conclusions. Garrett loves you, you know that. Please give him a chance to explain."

"There's nothing to explain. I know what I saw. Look, Maxi, I'll talk to you tomorrow."

"Mya, what are you going to do? Where are the boys?"

"The boys are fine. They're spending the night at Mrs. Butler's house. I told her I wanted to spend the evening alone with Garrett." Mya smiled to blink back more tears. "She thinks I've planned this romantic evening for just the two of us. Boy, is she wrong."

"Promise you'll call me later, Mya, no matter what. Promise me."

"I promise. I got to go. I want to have myself together when Garrett gets here."

After ending her conversation with Maxi, Mya just sat there for a long moment before she rose wearily from the chair and went into the bathroom to wash her face and reapply her makeup. She then went back and sat in her favorite chair in their bedroom to wait. By her estimation he was an hour late in coming home already.

No sooner than she thought that, she heard the sound of his

key rattling in the door. She heard him call her name but she refused to answer him. Then suddenly he appeared in the doorway.

"Mya, I didn't know you were coming back today. Welcome home."

She lifted her eyes and looked at him and she felt a sharpness cutting at her heart. She loved him so much and he had trampled her pride. She wondered if anyone else had seen him and Paige together the way she had. Just how long had it been going on? "You're late," she said softly as she continued to look at him.

Her statement seemed to take him aback since she had never in all the years they'd been married kept tabs on his comings and goings before. The smile on his face wavered somewhat. "Yes, I stopped by Mark's place to see how he's doing." After a few moments when it became apparent she didn't have a comment to what he said, he asked. "Where are the boys?"

"They're with Mrs. Butler. They're going to stay overnight."

Garrett lifted a brow. "Really? Why?"

When Mya didn't say anything Garrett continued to look at her. He walked closer into the room. He had known her long enough to know when something was wrong. "What is it, Mya? Something is going on here. You're not yourself."

She made herself respond to the question in his eyes and the question that had come from his lips. "No, I'm not myself, Garrett." She then stood and crossed the room to stand in front of him. "I arrived back early today and thought I'd surprise you and show up at practice again."

She watched his brow lift. "Really, I didn't see you."

"But I did see you, Garrett. I saw you and Paige Duvall together."

He looked at for a few brief moments then asked in a low voice. "What are you accusing me of, Mya?"

"You tell me, Garrett. Should I be accusing you of anything?"

"No, and if you're insinuating that I've slept with the woman, you're wrong. I've told you countless times not to pay attention to women who come on to me. You're the only woman I love and want."

"And I have always believed you all those countless times. And no, I'm not accusing you of sleeping with her, although I may be wrong about that, but I do know something is going on between the two of you."

"You don't know anything, Mya."

"Yes, I do. Trust me, Garrett, a woman knows. And I know what I saw. She was all over you, all in your face. And she touched you in a way that she felt comfortable with doing. She touched you, *my* man, in a way that only I should touch you. In a way that only I have a right to. But you let her do it, Garrett. You let her get into *my* space. Space that should belong only to me, your wife, the mother of your sons, your former girlfriend, your best friend. And whether you admit it or not, Garrett, there is a reason she felt that comfortable with you, and it's more than you sending out some pretty strong signals that you may be interested in her. It's more than that, Garrett, admit it."

Mya's words echoed loudly between the walls of their bedroom. Garrett looked at her as a bout of guilt tore into him. He reached out for her and his heart ripped in two when she took a step back as if his touch was poisonous. "It's not what you think, Mya. It meant nothing."

She swallowed the thick lump in her throat and asked softly. "What meant nothing?" She watched Garrett and knew from the look on his face, the regret lining his eyes, that she hadn't misread what she had seen that afternoon. Her heart began to ache.

"It was the night all of us went over to Mark's place to console him after being cut from the team. Paige was there, too. She didn't have a way back home and asked me to drop her off at her apartment and I did. She wanted me to walk her to the door since it was late and I did that too. I was in a bad way that night, Mya. What had happened to Mark had me pretty uptight and when she invited me in for a drink I accepted." He held her gaze for a while before adding, "I was kind of lonely that night and you weren't here."

"So going into her apartment and getting all cozy with her was my fault? Is that what you're saying, Garrett?" she asked hurt and betrayed.

"I wasn't inside her place but a few minutes."

"But something happened in those few minutes, didn't it, Garrett?" She watched him battle with his inner self, with the knowledge that what he was about to say would undoubtedly hurt her.

"Yes, we kissed. But that's all we did, Mya. And I knew it had been a mistake as soon as it happened. I felt bad about it, baby. But try to understand that I was lonely that night," he implored, trying to keep his voice calm. "I was missing you. A lot has been happening between us since we came back from the cruise. Your work became all that mattered to you and this thing with all the players getting cut had me in a bad way. I made a mistake that night, Mya. I know it was a bad mistake but it meant nothing. The kiss meant nothing. And what you saw tonight was me telling Paige that it meant nothing so she wouldn't get any ideas that I would be coming back for more, because there won't be anymore. You and the boys are my life, Mya. Please believe that and please forgive me for a moment of weakness."

Tears filled Mya's eyes. "I can't forgive you, Garrett, and the reason being is that I was lonely that night as well. I had missed you. But I wasn't that lonely that I turned to my client, Robert Noble, who is a very handsome man, I might add, to ease my loneliness. I didn't invite him to my hotel room nor did I let him kiss me. I behaved in a manner that was befitting your wife. And the reason for doing so is because everything about me, everything on me belongs to you and no other man. Just like everything about you and everything on you belongs to me. But you let Paige Duvall violate what was mine, Garrett. You

gave her that right. She put her tongue in a mouth that belonged only to me. She put her arms around a body that was
supposed to be mine. Only mine."

"Mya, please—"

"No, Garrett. You broke your marriage vow to love and
honor me as your wife."

"No, honey, I do love you and I do honor you."

She shook her head as she wiped her tears away. "No, what
you did was let another woman disrespect me and I'm not sure
I'll ever be able to forgive you for that."

"Please, Mya, we can work through this. We love each other.
Our love is strong. We've had some pretty tough times before."

"But never like this, Garrett. There has never been an issue
of trust between us."

"Yes, but we can still work through this. You're my life. I love
you so much, Mya, you've got to believe that."

"I don't know what I believe anymore. I used to believe that I
was all the woman you needed, now I see that's not true. You've
hurt me, Garrett. You have hurt me so much."

"For heaven's sake! I didn't sleep with her. It was just a kiss,
Mya. You are all the woman I need. Surely, you're not going to
throw away what we have because I had a moment of weakness
and kissed another woman! Can't you find it in your heart to
forgive me over a kiss?"

"No, at the moment I can't. I can't erase the picture from my
mind of seeing the two of you together today, with her all in
your face, all in my space. My mind is too filled with that."

"Okay, then we'll give it some time, Mya. We'll work through
this. All you need is time."

"What I need is for you to leave."

"What?" he said with wide eyes focused on her.

"I want you to leave. I don't want to spend a single night
under the same roof with you."

"Mya, surely you don't mean that. I—"

"No, I want you gone, Garrett. I can't handle the pain of see-

ing you every day. You can make arrangements to come by and
see the boys when I'm not here but I don't want you here."

"And just where am I supposed to go?"

"Back to your girlfriend."

"Mya, you are being irrational about this. Paige is not my girlfriend. I explained how things happened. It was just that one
night and that one kiss. A night and kiss I will regret for the rest
of my life. Surely you're not making me leave my home for
that."

"No, not just for that, Garrett, but also for the lack of respect
and the violation of vows."

"Mya, please—"

"No!" She said, crossing her arms in front of her. "Either you
leave or the boys and I will. I will not sleep under the same roof
as you so please pack your things and go." She then walked
around him to leave the room. Grabbing her car keys off the
kitchen table she went outside and got into her SUV. She
needed to take a drive around town to relax her nerves and she
hoped that by the time she returned Garrett would be gone.

Garrett's hands shook as he placed the last piece of clothing
into the luggage, not believing what was happening. It was evident from the way Mya was handling things that he had hurt
her deeply. His heart ached at the thought that he had put that
look of pain in her eyes.

He took a deep breath, wondering where he could go. He
decided to call Mark and Danielle to see if he could at least
crash on their couch for the night, then tomorrow he would
have to look into finding more permanent housing.

He shook his head. No, he needed temporary housing. His
permanent house was here with Mya and his sons. Hopefully in
time she would see that, and hopefully in time she would forgive him for his transgression with Paige. He loved Mya with all
his heart and admitted that he had made a mistake. A huge
mistake. It was one that was costing him his family.

Going into the living room he picked up the phone to call his coach. A few minutes later he was hanging up the phone after telling the man that he needed to miss practice tomorrow for personal reasons.

Garrett walked out the door, locking it behind him. The vision of Mya standing in their bedroom crying tore at his heart and he knew he would feel just as betrayed if he had found out that she had kissed another man. So in a way, he understood her hurt but still, she should have let him stay with her to work things out. She had no right to throw away what they had together.

When he got inside his Mercedes he leaned over the steering wheel as emotions tore into him. He felt ashamed for what he had done and he felt angry for being such a weak person and allowing it to happen. Inhaling deeply he leaned back and picked up the cellular phone next to him. He needed to hear his father's voice. He needed to tell someone what a fool he was.

"Hello."

"Dad? It's me, Garrett."

"Garrett, how are you, son? Is everything okay. How are Mya and the boys?"

"Not good, " he said choking out the words. "I screwed up, Dad. I've really screwed up. It involves another woman and Mya wants me to leave. She doesn't want to be with me anymore. I've hurt her. I've hurt her bad."

There was a long silence and David Rivers didn't say anything. Garrett could hear his mother in the background asking what was wrong. Finally, his father spoke.

"Look, Garrett, I'm not going to ask for any details but I will give you some good advice. You and Mya have been together too long to throw anything away. What I want you to do is pray and seek counseling from your minister."

"I don't have a minister, Dad."

"Then find one. What about that minister you used to have?"

"Reverend Stonewall? The one who committed adultery? Just what can he tell me?"

"For starters, something about forgiveness. Before Mya can forgive you, you must seek forgiveness for yourself. If you ask me, the best person to talk about something like this to is someone who's been there."

Moments later after pulling out of the driveway, Garrett had to concede that his father did have a point about Reverend Stonewall. Sister Stonewall had forgiven her husband for his indiscretion—which was worse than what he'd done—and they were still together.

After checking his watch Garrett made a quick decision. He headed toward the subdivision where he knew the reverend lived. It was Wednesday, prayer meeting night, and he hoped he would be quick enough to catch Reverend Stonewall before he left for church.

CHAPTER THIRTY-FIVE

As Maxi paced the floor, worry was evident in her face. She wondered where Mya was. She had tried calling her a few moments ago and she still wasn't home. Taking a deep breath she glanced down at her watch. It was past ten o'clock. She had left several messages on Mya's answering machine asking that she return her call but she hadn't heard from her.

Mya had called her from her cell phone around five o'clock and told her she had just left Garrett at the house packing. She had not gone into the details of their conversations but she did say he had admitted to kissing another woman.

Maxi jumped when she heard the phone ring and raced over to it. "Yes?"

"Maxi, it's me."

"Girl, where have you been? You had me worried. I've been trying for hours to reach you."

"I know. I can tell by the number of messages you left. First I drove around town a while then stopped at a café and got something to eat. When my cell phone rang I thought it was Garrett and started not to answer it. Then I realized it could have been Mrs. Butler concerning the boys. But it was Garrett's mom."

"Oh. Did she know about you and Garrett?"

"Yes, he had called them earlier. From what I understand he didn't go into a lot of details but he did tell them we were having problems and were separating for a while."

"How did Mrs. Rivers handle that?"

"Well, you know Ma Rivers. Garrett may be her baby boy but she never takes sides and I've always appreciated it. She just wanted me to know that the family would be praying for us and that she hoped things worked out. She also told me that she was still my mother as well as Garrett's and if I needed to come home for a while to do so. I've always been so blessed having her for a mother-in-law."

"Yes, you have. But you still haven't said where you've been for the past five hours."

"Mrs. Rivers suggested that I go talk to my minister. Since the one we have at the church I'm attending is fairly new, and I haven't been going often enough to know him that well, I decided to go to Reverend Stonewall's new church."

"Reverend Stonewall?"

"Yes, he was the minister of my church before he left to start another church elsewhere." Mya didn't want to get into a deep discussion as to why Reverend Stonewall had left.

"Well, did you? Did you go to Reverend Stonewall's church tonight?"

"Yes, they were having prayer meeting and I joined in on that. Afterwards, I talked with him a while in his study. He told me that Garrett had dropped by his house to see him earlier tonight."

"And how do you feel about that?"

"Right now I'm still incapable of feeling, Maxi."

"That's understandable, Mya. You're probably still in shock."

"Probably. Right now I'm feeling more hurt than anything. It was easier to talk to Reverend Stonewall than I thought. And he did tell me that Garrett sought God's forgiveness tonight and that I should find it in my heart to forgive him as well. The problem, Maxi, is that I don't know if I can forgive Garrett.

Even though he didn't sleep with that woman, I still feel betrayed just the same."

Maxi nodded. She could understand why. Mya had always felt secure in her relationship with Garrett. During all the years she had known Garrett, he had never shown any interest in another woman. Of course there had been girls at school who had shown interest in him but it had meant nothing to him. Mya had been wrapped around his heart pretty tight. Mya and football were all he had ever cared about. "Do me a favor."

"What?"

"Take a shower, go to bed, and get a good night's sleep. Do you have to go to work tomorrow?"

"No, I'm going to take the day off and spend time with the boys. I have to get them prepared for the fact that Garrett won't be coming home to them every day like he used to. Daniel and David are crazy about their daddy."

"And he's crazy about them, Mya. You know Garrett will still come to see them, even if the two of you are separated. I hope you don't plan to stop him from doing that."

"No, of course I won't. I won't make my sons suffer because of what is happening between me and Garrett."

"Good. Now do like I ask and take a shower and go to bed. I'll call you tomorrow to make sure you're okay."

"Thanks. Are you and Christopher still planning on going to Las Vegas this weekend?"

"Yes. I haven't spoken to him in a couple of days. He called Monday night to say he had made all the necessary arrangements. I'm to meet him in Atlanta on Friday evening, and then we'll catch a plane to Nevada together."

"I'm so happy for you, Maxi."

"I'm happy for me, too. I'm glad I went to Detroit to see him."

"I'm glad you went, too. You deserve happiness, Maxi. I love you."

"And I love you, too, Mya. And I believe that things will work out for you and Garrett."

"We'll see. Goodnight."

"Goodnight."

Maxi hung up the phone then bowed her head and said a silent prayer for her two friends. She had just lifted her head when she heard the sound of her doorbell. She wondered who would be paying her a visit at this late hour. Crossing the room she squinted her eyes when she glanced through the peephole in her door.

Her heart jumped and she brought a hand and held it to her chest. It was Christopher. She quickly unlocked the door. "Christopher?"

Christopher stood under the porch light looking at Maxi. For a moment he couldn't form words to say anything. He just wanted to absorb her beauty, her presence, the essence of everything that had ever been right in his life.

"Christopher? Aren't you going to come in?" She looked at him closely, shocked to see him. "What is it?"

He continued not to say anything and she took a step back when he came inside.

Maxi closed the door behind him. She wondered what had brought him to Savannah, a town he'd sworn he would not return to. She noticed he did not glance around the room. His eyes stayed glued to her. She reached out and touched his hand. "Christopher, please tell me what's wrong?"

He captured her hand in his, then said, "I'm going to have to withdraw my offer to give you a baby unless you agree not to let anyone know I'm the father."

CHAPTER THIRTY-SIX

Maxi didn't say anything. Neither did she withdraw her hand from his. In fact she did the opposite. She tightened her hand around Christopher's. She remembered their weekend. She also remembered his phone call to her Monday night. He had sounded excited, as if he was looking forward to their weekend together in Las Vegas. So what had happened since then? She watched as he looked down at their joined hands and felt tension radiating from him. "Are you going to tell me why?" she finally asked quietly, meeting his gaze.

He lifted his head and met her gaze. "It will be for the best."

"Shouldn't I be the one to decide that, Christopher?"

"Yes," he agreed, still looking at her. "You should and you probably will agree with me once I tell you why."

"All right, let's hear it."

He glanced around the room for the first time, liking what he saw. The décor of her home reflected her, soft and warm. "Is there someplace where we can sit and talk?"

"Yes." She led him through her living room and into her kitchen. "I was just about to have a cup of coffee. Do you want one?"

He shook his head as he sat down at the table. "No, thanks. Isn't it kind of late to be drinking coffee?"

"Not if you have papers to grade." She sat in the chair across from him. "Okay, Christopher, let's hear it."

He reached across the table and enfolded her hands in his, feeling a need to touch her and be connected to her in some way. He gently stroked the back of her knuckles, liking the way her hands felt in his. "Although I haven't lived a celibate life, I've always been selective. I made sure any woman I slept with understood that sleeping with me was just what it was—a good time in bed and nothing more. Well, it seems that one of the women I've been involved with off and on for the past three years got married and didn't tell me. The last time she came to town, two months ago, we were seen together. Someone, for whatever reason, took a picture of us kissing. The photograph was sent to me."

Maxi shrugged. "So what's that got to do with me? I know you hadn't lived a celibate life."

"No, but don't you see the implications of someone taking that picture and sending it to me? As far as I can tell it could very well be some sort of scandal in the making, Maxi. Since I'm single and she's the one who's married, I can only assume that someone wants to expose her extramarital activities and will use me to do it, although I didn't know she had gotten married when I slept with her this last time."

Maxi nodded. "I still don't understand what that has to do with me."

Christopher lifted a brow. He knew Maxi was too smart to be dense. Either she was deliberately playing dumb or she really didn't understand. "I'm talking about a possible scandal, Maxi. People in this town who know enough about my past will think you're crazy for having my baby, and I won't put you in the position of defending yourself in the wake of this new possible scandal. Nor do I ever want a child of mine to grow up embarrassed that I am its father. The only way I'll agree to get you pregnant now is if you promise to tell no one—and I mean no one—that I'm the child's father. A person's name and reputation mean everything. I've been involved in a scandal before so it will be old hat for me. But I won't let you get involved in one because of me. I can't and I won't."

Maxi looked across the table at Christopher for a long time. She then shook her head feeling more love for him at that very moment then at any time in her entire life.

Here he sat, trying to protect her. She had learned during the cruise how he had protected her and looked out for her in school when she hadn't even been aware he was doing so. Now it was her time to look out for him and to protect him. "No deal."

"Excuse me?"

She met his leveled gaze. "I said no deal. I intend to have your name on my child's birth certificate and anyone who asks—and I'm sure many people will—I'll proudly tell them that you're my baby's daddy. And my baby will grow up proud that you are its father."

"Maxi, listen—"

"No. I don't give a royal damn what people say or think. Besides, it's too late."

He glared at her, not understanding why she was being difficult. "What's too late?"

"It's too late for you to back out. I slept with you last weekend without protection. I could be pregnant now, as we speak," she said, although she knew chances were she wasn't since she had been on her period the week before going to Detroit. But as far as she was concerned he didn't have to know that. However, she did know for a fact that this coming weekend her womb would be a good time for her to get pregnant if her calculations were accurate.

"Are you?" he asked softly.

She shrugged. "Too soon to tell. But if I am, everybody in Savannah will know you're the baby's father because I refuse to keep it a secret."

"Why? Why do you have to tell anyone?"

"Because I will be proud of the fact that you cared enough for me to father my child. And I've never been ashamed of you and I won't start being ashamed of you now, so don't ask me to."

He sat there, remaining silent as he looked at her. She looked back at him, refusing to back down.

"Haven't you heard anything I've said?" he asked tersely.

"Yes, I've heard everything you said but it doesn't matter. Besides, nothing may come of it. You may be getting worked up for nothing."

He sat up in his chair. "And what if something does come of it? There are some who'll believe I make sleeping with married women a habit."

Maxi sighed. "Let them believe whatever they want. I'll know differently."

He met her gaze, challenging her. "Will you?"

"Of course." She reached across the table and took his hands in hers. "I know, Christopher. I know how you feel about married people breaking their vows. Have you forgotten that I also know why? And I also know why you don't want to get caught up in a scandal. I know just how you feel about that, too."

Christopher frowned. "I shared too damn much with you during the time we were in school together, Maxi."

"No," she said with a reminiscent smile. "You didn't share enough. You didn't let me know how you felt about me during that time."

"I had my reasons," he said huskily.

"Yes, just like I'm sure you have your reasons for wanting to protect me now but it won't work."

He glared at her. "Tell me something," he said in a low, furious voice. "Why are you being so damn stubborn about this?"

She smiled wryly. "Oh, that's an easy answer. Because I love you."

"Maxi, I don't—"

She quickly pressed her finger to his lips to silence him. "I know you don't love me back and I understand. It's enough to know how much you care. If you didn't care you wouldn't be willing to give me such a precious gift. I may not have you but I will have your child and for me that will be enough."

He nodded, knowing he did care for her more than any woman he knew. He had done things with her that he had never done to other women. But he didn't want her to love him. She needed to love someone who would love her back.

"May I ask who is this woman?"

"Mrs. Adam Benedict." He watched her expression when he gave her the name. She didn't seem too surprised. Maybe it was because Tori was married to a much older man or something. "Until I find out who sent that photograph and the reason it was sent, things may be unpredictable."

"Let things be unpredictable. I can handle pregnancy and unpredictability. Now will you take me in your arms and kiss me?"

He didn't have to be asked twice. He stood and walked around the table to her, pulled her up into his arms and gave her the kiss he had wanted to give her when she had first opened the door.

When he finally ended the kiss she smiled up at him. "Where are your bags?"

"Outside in the rental car. I had planned on checking into a hotel tonight. I have to fly back out in the morning."

Maxi nodded. "Stay here with me tonight."

He smiled at her invitation. "Umm, I think I will."

In every possible way, their lovemaking had been beautiful. Afterwards, they talked and laughed and made all kinds of plans for the weekend. It was during that time Maxi told Christopher about Mya and Garrett and the problems they were having. And like Maxi, Christopher hoped things worked out for the couple because he knew just how much in love they were.

"So are you as excited as I am about this weekend?" Maxi asked smiling up at him while lying naked in his arms.

"Yes, although according to you, this weekend may not be necessary."

"Maybe. But I want it anyway."

He pulled her into his arms. "So do I, baby. So do I!"

CHAPTER THIRTY-SEVEN

Holding both of her sons' hands firmly in hers, Mya entered the sanctuary of the Evergreen Baptist Church and was immediately greeted by an usher. Reverend Stonewall had invited her to Sunday service when she had spoken with him on Wednesday night.

The usher was leading them down the aisle when David's hand anxiously pulled from Mya's. He ran toward a pew ahead of them. She then saw why. Garrett was sitting at the end of the pew and David, having seen his father, was running straight to him. In the minute it took Mya to recover from the surprise of seeing Garrett, Daniel's loud, happy greeting of "Daddy!" filled the sanctuary. He then snatched his hand from hers and, like his twin, he took off for his father as well. Although Mya preferred not sitting with Garrett, she quickly concluded that other than making a scene, her sons had left her no choice. They were glad to see their father and hadn't cared if the entire congregation knew it.

Thinking she could try and at least tolerate Garrett's presence while they were in God's house, she walked to the pew where Garrett held their sons in his arms. He automatically slid over to make room for her to sit next to him and the boys.

Without giving him any type of greeting, she reached for the hymnbook in front of her.

"I tried calling yesterday," Garrett said suddenly, softly, leaning over to her, his voice much too close for comfort. "I wanted to see the boys."

"We were out," Mya whispered tersely. And she had no intentions of telling him where they had gone. He had lost that right to know her whereabouts when he had locked mouths with Miss Cheerleader. Mya had made sure she wasn't at home when he had come to see the boys on Thursday and again on Friday. Although she wanted him to maintain a close relationship with their sons, she had not counted on him coming by the house every single day.

After talking to Maxi that Wednesday night, she had done what Maxi had suggested and had taken a shower, gone to bed, then ended up crying herself to sleep. She had cried so hard, at one time she had thought that her heart would burst open. Never before had she felt such pain, such heartache.

She had awakened on Thursday morning physically exhausted and mentally drained. She didn't think she had any tears left and found that not to be true when she began crying all over again. By the time Mrs. Butler had arrived with the boys she had looked a sight. After the boys had eaten their breakfast and were settled in front of the television watching *Sesame Street*, she had called Mrs. Butler aside and told her that Garrett was no longer residing in the house and that, although he was welcome to visit the boys at any time, they were not to ever leave with him without her permission. She knew she had placed her children's nanny in an awkward situation since it was Garrett who was paying her salary. However, it was important to Mya that the woman understood things between her and Garrett had changed and that he was no longer a permanent fixture in the Rivers's household.

Trying to ignore the man sitting next to her, Mya glanced around church. A lot of the people there were members who had followed Reverend Stonewall from Dayspring Baptist. She had remembered how upset Garrett had become when those members had "defected," as he had called it. And he hadn't had any kind words to say about Reverend Stonewall either. Therefore, she had been a little surprised when Reverend Stonewall had mentioned on Wednesday night that Garrett had come to see him for consultation. And now he was here in church on Sunday. It was sad that most people, including her, turned to God only when they encountered bad times.

Mya brought her attention back toward the front of the church when Reverend Stonewall came to the pulpit and his booming voice filled the sanctuary. "All have sinned and come short of the glory of God. All of us know that particular scripture. It pretty much lets us know that none of us are perfect. And as imperfect human beings, any of us, all of us, are subject at some time or another to mistakes. Some mistakes may be considered bigger than others, but still, no matter how you size it or weight it, a mistake is a mistake. It could be a mistake in judgment, a mistake of one's actions or a mistake of one's inactions. Today I want to talk about forgiving one's mistakes."

Mya shifted in her seat, thinking the last thing she wanted to hear about was forgiving someone for their mistakes. For the past five days she had been feeling pretty scornful, and her motto was more like—give pain to others like they have given pain to you. She sighed inwardly. Here she was in the Lord's House having such thoughts. And as far as she was concerned it was all Garrett's fault.

"Yes, I want to talk about forgiving," Reverend Stonewall was saying. "None of us like to forgive another person's mistakes. But if we are going to be in keeping with the scriptures, and if we are going to follow God's Holy Word, we must do as God has commanded us to do. Now I ask you. Is it easy? Is it easy to put aside the pain someone has caused you and throw your arms around that person and forgive him or her? No. I just said we are human. And as human beings we want to lash out. We want to hold grudges. We want to not forgive and we certainly don't want to forget. But in the book of Colossians, the third chapter and the thirteenth verse, it says, *Be gentle and ready to forgive; never hold grudges. Remember the Lord forgave you, so you must forgive others.* So just what does this mean? It means that we must forgive those who wrong us. We must forgive those who persecute us and say all manner of evil things against us, even those who try to spitefully use us. But because we are human, forgiving doesn't come easy. It is something we must work at and pray at. We must let love, not bitterness, rule our hearts."

Reverend Stonewall went further and spoke of several scriptures that supported forgiveness. He told the congregation of a number of wrongdoings to Jesus and how in all situations, He forgave those who had tried to harm him. Reverend Stonewall then wrapped up his sermon by calling on everyone to love each other as God loves.

After church was over, everyone began spilling out, shaking Reverend Stonewall's hand as they passed through the doors. When Mya made it to where the reverend stood, he shook her hand and thanked her for coming and said that he hoped to see her next Sunday. He then turned to Garrett and reaffirmed their meeting at the church for Tuesday night.

"I can manage the boys now," she said to Garrett as she took her sleeping sons out of his arms when it was apparent he was about to walk them to her car. And she didn't want him to do that. Even with Reverend Stonewall's sermon on forgiveness, the pain of Garrett's betrayal was still too raw. But he didn't take her hint and followed, determined to walk them to her car anyway.

She ignored him while she put both boys in the back seat and snapped their seatbelts in place. She then walked around the other side of the SUV and opened the door and got in. When Garrett stood at the car window she adjusted her seat and placed the key in the ignition.

"I'm going to meet with Reverend Stonewall on Tuesday

night, Mya. Would you come with me?" he asked softly. He didn't want to wake the boys who were still asleep.

Mya flipped the sun visor down to shield her eyes from the blazing sun before glancing up at Garrett. "Why should I accompany you to meet with Reverend Stonewall, Garrett? You're the one who messed around, not me," she whispered harshly. "You're the one who threw away everything precious we had just to lock mouths with a woman who has probably locked mouths with every guy on your team. No, Garrett, I don't want to meet with Reverend Stonewall with you. In fact, I don't want to do anything with you. You hurt me, so much that I ache all over. And although I understand everything Reverend Stonewall said today about forgiveness, I *ain't there* yet. And chances are I may never be."

"Mya, please I—."

"No, there's nothing left to say, Garrett."

"And you're willing to throw away everything that we have, everything that we mean to each other because of your inability to forgive me?"

Mya narrowed her eyes at him. "Yes, because you were quite willing to throw away everything we have and everything we mean to each other during what you term as a moment of weakness in another woman's arms."

Silence hung between them and a few moments later Garrett's shoulders slumped against the car. Then in a low, weary voice he said, "I know I screwed up, Mya. I know I hurt you. If I could I would erase that night from our lives, but I can't. I love you, Mya, with all my heart. I always have and I always will, and I believe that deep down in your heart you know that. Please tell me what I can do to make things up to you. What do I have to do for you to forgive me? What do I have to do to get my sons and wife back?"

Mya fought back tears when she gazed into Garrett's eyes and said. "There's nothing you can do, Garrett." Taking a deep breath she said softly. "I'll be leaving town Wednesday morning for Orlando. I've made arrangements with Mrs. Butler to stay at the house while I'm gone. When I return on Thursday I'll work on putting a schedule together as to when you can come by. I prefer not being home when you do."

She tried ignoring the look of pain she saw in his eyes. "Please call Mrs. Butler and give her a number where you can be reached if something comes up while I'm gone. Goodbye, Garrett." Then without saying anything else she turned the key in her ignition.

Garrett stepped back and watched as she pulled out of the church's parking lot. No wonder Lee Jenkins had felt the need to pray for him on the cruise. As a man of God Lee had known the rough waters he would be facing. Garrett breathed in deeply. Yes, the waters were rough and even a bit choppy but he had no intentions of drowning. He didn't care what it took, he intended to get his family back.

CHAPTER THIRTY-EIGHT

Maxi woke to find Christopher propped up in bed on his elbow, gazing down at her. She smiled at him as she stretched out her body in bed, liking the feel of coming into such close contact with his. His body felt firm, solid, hard.

"Good morning," she purred softly as she remembered the evening before which had been the day they had arrived in Las Vegas.

"And good *afternoon* to you. It's after one o'clock," he responded, returning her smile.

"Oh, did I wake up late?"

He shook his head. "No, in fact I think your timing is perfect." He then leaned over and captured her mouth with his.

When he ended the kiss she drew in a deep breath and slowly eased it out. "Umm," she said softly, licking her lips. "There's nothing like a kiss to get a person's blood stimulated. What do you have planned for us to do today?"

"Make a baby."

She rubbed the sleep out of her eyes. "Oh, I think we may have done that last night."

He chuckled when he remembered that they had come straight from the airport to the hotel and had gone to bed.

Sometime during the night they had eaten after ordering room service. Then they had returned to bed. "Yes, that's a possibility but I want to cover all bases."

"That's not all you like to cover, Christopher." She couldn't help but yawn and quickly apologize. "Sorry, I don't function well before I have my first cup of coffee."

"You don't function well or you don't function at all?" he asked, slowly raking his fingers down her bare shoulder toward her naked chest.

Maxi inhaled sharply when she felt his fingers gently caress her breast. "I, uhh, don't function well," she got out, but barely.

"But you do function?"

"Yes."

"Good." And with that one word he shifted position and let his body cover hers as his lips covered her lips.

The sounds of their breathing blended in with the other sounds around them. Somewhere outside their hotel room a church bell rang, a car horn blew, and there was even the sound of an airplane flying overhead. Yet all those sounds were lost to the groaning sighs of pleasure from Maxi's lips the moment Christopher buried himself deep inside her body. And when they began to move together, smoothly, fluidly, in perfect harmony with each other, he pulled his mouth away from hers and looked down at her.

"I've never wanted anything like I want this," he whispered huskily as he increased the pace of his hips that ground into hers, and lifting hers to meet his next thrust.

And then, like always, everything exploded. Their minds. Their bodies. Wanting even more, he hooked the inside bend of his elbows behind her knees and lifted her hips higher, closer, as he drove one final time into her, knowing that at that very moment, if it hadn't done so before, his seed had hit its mark. He could feel all the feminine muscles inside her body react, clenching, milking, pulling everything out of him, and the more she pulled the more his testicles seemed to produce just what she wanted and in the amount she wanted. That thought drove him over the edge and into an orgasm that rammed every nerve in his body.

And when he felt her body strain against him in her own orgasm, he recaptured her mouth, groaning deep into it when he felt the milking sensation of her body intensify as she demanded and got every single ounce of baby-making fluid out of him. He felt drained, then renewed, then drained again. It was as if their reproductive organs had minds of their own and they knew they had a job to do, and today, at that very moment, they were hard at work doing it.

When there was nothing left in his body to give, Christopher collapsed on Maxi, totally limp, languid, empty. He felt her breath on his neck, then felt the moisture of her tongue as she licked sweat from his cheek. What they had just gone through had to be what some people called "mind-boggling." He wondered if his brain would ever be able to function again. And he didn't want to think about the lower part of his body that was still planted deep within her. Just where he wanted it to be for the moment. Just where he intended to stay . . . at least for a while yet.

A tired chuckle escaped his lips as he shifted their positions in bed, but keeping himself planted inside of her.

"What's so funny," she murmured, sounding out of breath.

He leaned down and kissed her cheek before answering. "I was just thinking that you were wrong. You function very well without your first cup of coffee."

Putting the canvas bag on the desk in their hotel room, Maxi began pulling out the souvenir items she had purchased. Since they had missed lunch, she and Christopher had showered and gotten dressed and had gone to the hotel's restaurant for an early dinner. Then they had taken a tour of Las Vegas, enjoying all the sights and sounds around them.

She watched as Christopher pulled off his shoes and stretched out on the bed. "I think I'm going to give Mya a call to see how she's doing. I haven't talked to her since Friday before I left for Atlanta."

Christopher nodded. "I hope things work out for her and Garrett. They have been together too long to let something like this tear them apart."

Maxi nodded in agreement. But then she also knew just how much Mya was hurting. Half an hour later after talking to Mya, she hung up the phone, troubled.

"Well, what's the verdict?" Christopher asked her.

"Mya's still bitter. She said Garrett was at church when she went today and they sat together, only because the boys left her no choice. She said that after church he suggested they meet with the minister to try and work things out, but that she refused him. I think it would be best if he gave her some time and space. Mya is going through a difficult time right now but I believe that once she thinks about it, she will come to realize that Garrett does love her."

Tears pricked Maxi's eyes. "It just doesn't seem fair, Christopher," she said, barely getting the words out. "Now I'm happy but she's not."

"Maxi." He quickly crossed the room and pulled her into his arms. "Everything is going to be fine."

"But it should have stayed fine, Christopher. She's hurting and there's nothing I can do. Garrett and Mya are two people who love each other. Everybody knows that. They shouldn't be going through this."

"Yes, but they are going through it. And because they are two people who love each other I believe things will eventually work out. As her friend the only thing you can do is be there for her if she needs you. But this is something Mya is going to have to work out for herself and with Garrett. Somehow, some way, she's going to have to forgive him in order for them to get beyond this."

Maxi nodded in agreement. "You know the boys must be confused by all of this."

"Yes, I'm sure they are." He kissed her lightly on the lips. Deciding to switch subjects, he asked, "How soon will you know if you're pregnant?"

"In about three weeks." Maxi pulled out of his arms and looked up at him. "Are you anxious to get rid of me and go back to your old lifestyle that involves all those women?" The thought of another woman sharing his bed after what they had shared for the past two weeks brought pain to her heart. But she couldn't let him know that.

He smiled down at her. "No, I like making babies with you. And you haven't forgotten our agreement?"

"And I like making babies with you, too, and no, I haven't forgotten," she said as the pain in her heart deepened.

CHAPTER THIRTY-NINE

Christopher was on his way home when he received a call on his cell phone. "Yes?"

"It's me, Christopher. Tori."

He lifted a brow. He hadn't heard from her since their conversation nearly two weeks ago. Nor had he received any more photographs. "And what did you find out?"

"It wasn't my husband who was having me investigated. It was my stepson. He thinks I'm nothing but a golddigger who only married his father for his money."

"Seems he had you pegged right?"

"I wanted more than just money. I also wanted respectability."

"A respectable married woman doesn't commit adultery. My God, Tori, you hadn't been married six months, not to mention that your husband is a well-known political figure. You should have been more cautious."

"And I'm paying for my mistake, trust me. My stepson has threatened to give his father that photograph unless I file for divorce and leave quietly with only the clothes on my back."

"Are you going to do that?"

"What choice do I have?"

"How about the truth? You can always go to your husband and tell him the truth. He might surprise you and be forgiving."

"If I were your wife, would you forgive me?"

Christopher didn't have to think long or hard for an answer. "No. But then I wouldn't have been so trusting of you in the first place, so who knows, he might surprise you. I wouldn't let your stepson have the upper hand if I were you."

"I don't know if I want to fight him. He's hard as nails, and to make matters worse he's a divorce attorney."

"It's your decision but I didn't think you were the type of person to give in to anyone without a fight."

"On what defense? I committed adultery."

"Yeah, and you had me committing it right along with you, which I'm still pissed off about."

"I'm sorry I got you involved."

"I'm sorry you got me involved too. But as usual I learn from my mistakes." After a long moment he said, "I hope things work out for you."

"I hope things work out for you, too."

After turning off the phone he swung his car onto Madison Avenue as he headed for home. Once he got there he saw the light blinking on his answering machine and walked over to turn it on.

"Christopher, this is Maxi, please call me when you get in."

He checked his watch before picking up the phone to return Maxi's call. He hadn't spoken with her since their weekend in Las Vegas.

"Hello."

"Maxi? This is Christopher."

"Christopher! We did it! I'm pregnant!"

Christopher couldn't help but smile. "Are you sure? I thought you couldn't find out for another two weeks or so."

"That's what I thought too, but the pharmacist told me that I could find out as early as one day after a missed period. Since I was four days late already, I decided to give it a shot and it turned blue. Oh, Christopher, I am so happy."

He was happy, too, and if the truth were known he was pretty damn pleased with himself. "When do you go see a regular doctor?"

"Not until next month. Would you like to come with me?"

Christopher hesitated. Hell, yeah, a part of him wanted to go, but this is where he was supposed to cut out and let her go solo. His part in her pregnancy was over until the baby came. Then he would begin providing support for his child the way the two of them had agreed on. "No, I'm sure you'll do fine from here on out without me, Maxi. Just let me know when the kid's born so I can start sending those child support payments."

There was a quiet pause before she said, "All right."

When there was another pause, Christopher said, "I'm happy for you, Maxi."

"You made it all possible, Christopher. Thank you."

"Don't mention it. You deserved it. Take care."

"I will. Goodbye, Christopher."

"Goodbye, Maxi."

A little later Gabe dropped by and Christopher told him the news. "Congratulations, man. A baby. Hey, that's deep."

A part of Christopher didn't want to think about just how deep he'd gone inside Maxi to plant that seed. That was the first and last time he would have unprotected sex with a woman and it had felt good only because it had been Maxi. He couldn't describe the feeling he got exploding inside her.

"Have you thought of any names?"

Christopher took a sip of his wine. "That's up to Maxi. I'm technically out of the picture from here on out."

"That's the way you want it to be?"

Christopher frowned. "Yes." He leaned back in his chair and eyed his best friend, seeing his frown. "And why are you trippin'? You knew it was going to be this way with me and Maxi."

"Yeah, but I thought you had changed your mind?"

"Since when?"

"Since the two of you started sleeping together. Especially after you told me about the great time the two of you had in Vegas. Can't you see she's different?"

"Yes, but Maxi's always been different." Christopher then thought about all those times they had made love. They had been explosive. "And whenever we made love it was to make a baby."

"Oh, and you didn't enjoy it?"

Like hell he didn't. It had been the best experience of his life. "It doesn't matter whether I enjoyed it or not. I have no intention of getting involved in any sort of a relationship with any woman and that includes Maxi."

"Why?"

"You know why. The baby was a gift to her."

"And you weren't included in the package?"

"That's right."

"I think you were included, Christopher."

Christopher stood and walked over to the bar and poured another glass of wine. "You think too damn much, Blackwell."

"Possibly, but hear me out, will you?" he asked stretching his legs out in front of him. "You raced off to see Maxi in Savannah, a town you swore you would never return to, when you thought you would be involved in some sort of scandal. Why? To protect her from possible embarrassment if word got out that she was having your baby."

"Yeah? So?"

"Yet, you're letting her face having a baby alone."

Christopher rolled his eyes to the ceiling. "She won't be alone. She has family in Savannah."

"But what about the baby's father? What will the good citizens of Savannah think of her when word gets out that bad boy Christopher Chandler is the father of her unborn child?"

"And your point is?"

"My point is that most people, I imagine, will shake their heads thinking it's a sin and a shame that for once you didn't have the decency to do the right thing and marry Maxi and give your child a name. It will sound like history repeating itself to them."

Christopher frowned. "My child will have a name; whatever name Maxi decides to give it. She wanted a baby and I gave her one. No one has to know I'm the child's father. I told Maxi that."

"Yes, they do. I get the distinct impression that Maxi isn't the type of woman to deny any man the right to his child. And I refuse to believe you're the type of man who will father a child and not want to play a major role in his life. I refuse to believe that you would treat your child the way your father treated you."

Christopher glared across the room at Gabe before slamming down his glass of wine, spilling some of it on the floor. "It's way past my bedtime. Feel free to let yourself out," he said leaving the room.

Over the next couple of months Christopher tried not to let the conversation he'd had with Gabe get to him but found it hard to do. He also tried to get back into his old routine but found that hard to do as well. Oh, the women were willing but he was beginning to find them downright boring as well as annoying. Such was the case with the woman who was presently in his bed. He had looked forward to their date all week and hadn't been disappointed as far as sex went. But a part of him felt he was still missing something, something vital.

"So, that's the reason I plan to quit my job and open my own printing company."

"Hmmm," he responded absently.

The woman, whose name was Barbara, turned over and gave him a hard nudge in the side with her elbow. "You haven't been listening to anything I've said, Christopher."

He glared at her. He would be royally pissed if he had a bruised side tomorrow. "I didn't invite you here to talk, so why bother?"

Barbara sat up in bed and glared back at him. "Haven't you ever heard of pillow talk?"

"I heard about it but never bought into it. Takes up too much energy. Energy I can use for other things."

"Like screwing my brains out."

He looked at her and wondered if that was the reason she was now acting like someone who had lost her friggin' mind— since her brains were now missing. "Yes. You got everything you asked for." He heard her deep sigh of indignation, then felt the bed dip when she got out of it.

"There was a time you used to be a lot of fun."

"And there was a time you didn't talk so damn much."

He heard another sigh of indignation. "I'm leaving."

"Fine. I'll call you next week." Even when he said the words he knew that he wouldn't.

"Why bother?"

"For sex. I like screwing your brains out and you like having them screwed out." A few minutes later he heard his door slam shut with enough force to wake up the entire neighborhood. He got up to make sure she had locked the door behind her and wasn't surprised to discover she hadn't.

Going back into his bedroom he got back into bed and stared up at the ceiling, quickly forgetting about Barbara and thinking of Maxi. Had she told anyone she was pregnant yet? Was she showing? Had she listened to the baby's heartbeat? Did she know if she was having a boy or a girl? Was it too early to find out?

He thought of her often, every day, in fact. He even thought about her during those times when he wasn't supposed to be doing so, like tonight while screwing Barbara's brains out. Barbara and other women had lacked something. To be totally honest there hadn't been a woman who could hold a candle to Maxi in bed. With her it had been more than just sex. And it had been more than flexing their muscles and bodies to make a baby. He didn't know of any other woman who could make him feel the way Maxi did both in bed and out. No other woman could look at him and make him feel that he was somebody special, someone on top of the world, someone she desired with a passion as well as trusted with her life. And because of it his mind, soul, and body craved her in a way that was downright abnormal. When they had shared a bed the more he made love to her, the more he had wanted her.

He wanted to see Maxi. He wanted to talk to her. And he wanted to make love to her again, this time without a reason or purpose.

Because he loved her.

"Damn!" He ran his hand over his face wondering where that thought had come from. And then he knew. It had come from a place where Maxi had always been, ever since the first grade, and reinforced on the cruise. His heart. There was no sense being a fool any longer and wasting his time with other women. Maxi was and always would be the only woman he wanted. He wanted her and he wanted their baby.

An hour or so later he reached over and picked up the phone. He smiled when Gabe's sleepy voice came on the line. Why should Gabe sleep when he couldn't?

"Yeah?"

"I'm taking some time off, Blackwell. I'm going to Savannah."

"It's about time. I'll handle things until you get back. And I suggest that you see the folks before you leave, especially if you're thinking about getting married. Mom will be upset if you don't. She feels it's her God-given right to know every blasted thing. The last thing you want is to get out of her good graces. It can make life a living hell for both of us."

"Good point."

"I always knew you were a smart man, Chandler. Slow but smart."

"Goodnight, Blackwell."

"Goodnight."

CHAPTER FORTY

Maxi dropped her mother off at home after the two of them had returned from church. Ever since she had told her mother about her pregnancy, Gwen Chandler had been on cloud nine knowing she had a grandchild on the way.

Maxi hadn't had to tell her mother who the baby's father was. The wise older woman had figured it out for herself, and assumed her daughter had gotten pregnant from Christopher on the class reunion cruise. When she had asked Maxi if she needed to plan a wedding anytime soon, Maxi had said no and Gwen had left it at that with no lectures and no disappointed or disapproving looks.

Maxi had seen Dr. Frazier for a checkup and he'd informed her that her pregnancy was progressing nicely and there was no reason she couldn't have a problem-free delivery. However, because of her fibroids he would need to keep her under close observation for a while.

"Hi, sweeties, Mommy is here," she cooed softly to her plants when she entered her home. She had gotten into the habit of holding conversations with them every day. They'd almost died while she'd been on the cruise and after nursing them back to health she had promised never to neglect them again. Believing her word as the gospel, the plants had decided to give her another chance and were now huge, healthy looking, and growing all over the place.

Thinking about the cruise made her think about Christopher. Who was she kidding? Everything single thing made her think about Christopher, especially when she noticed her stomach was showing signs of expansion. And it didn't help matters that she had a photograph of the two of them on the cruise in a picture frame on her dresser. The more she looked at his handsome, smiling face the more she loved him. At first a part of her believed that deep down he truly loved her, too, but since she hadn't heard from him in two months—not even a phone call to see how she was doing—had made her realize, that no matter how wonderful the time had been when they'd been together, the only thing he felt toward her was gratitude and friendship, nothing more. And those were the reasons he had unselfishly given her the child she had wanted.

She had made the mistake of calling him one night a few weeks ago, to tell him about her first visit to Dr. Frazier. A woman had answered his phone. His female visitor had enjoyed letting her know he was in the shower at the moment and couldn't possibly come to the phone. That night she'd finally accepted what he had told her all along. He didn't want a relationship, serious or otherwise, with anyone.

Her thoughts then drifted to Mya. They had talked that morning and she knew things between Mya and Garrett hadn't gotten any better. Mya still refused to talk to Garrett about anything, yet he hadn't given up trying. Maxi couldn't help but admire his determination in getting his family back although Mya was making it downright difficult for him. She and Mya made a point to talk at least two or three times a week. A lot had happened in both of their lives and they needed each other more than ever.

Maxi was about to go into the bedroom to change into more comfortable clothing when the doorbell rang. "Must be the pizza I had Mom order for me," she told her plants as she passed them on her way to the door. But still out of habit she glanced through the peephole.

She blinked. Taken aback. It definitely wasn't the pizza man. "Christopher!"

Taking a deep breath she opened the door and there he was, standing less than three feet away. "How are you?"

"I couldn't be better now that I see you."

Maxi swallowed and held his gaze, not ready to buy into anything he said—not when he hadn't called in two months. "Would you like to come in?"

Christopher immediately picked up on the coolness of Maxi's tone. The coolness, he noted, was also there in her forced smile. His gaze shifted from her face to her stomach and noted she wasn't showing yet. What did he expect? She was only two months along. He moved his gaze back to her face. "Yes. I'd like to come in."

She stepped aside and when he entered and glanced around the first thing he noted was that she had a number of large plants all over the place. He hadn't noticed the plants the last time he had visited. "Looks like a greenhouse in here," he commented just to have something to say. A part of him tensed. In all the years he had known Maxi he had never felt this uncomfortable around her.

"I like the effect they give," she said, closing the door and walking pass him to the living room. "What brings you back to Savannah, Christopher? Another scandal?"

Christopher lifted a brow. Only a dumb person would not pick up on the fact that she was angry with him about something. Like Blackwell had said, he was smart, although slow at times. "No. I came to see you."

"Why?"

His brow raised a little higher. "You have to ask me that?"

"Yes," she said lifting her chin high and proud.

"Because I care."

Some of the bitterness left Maxi. "Yes, I'd buy that. If you didn't care I wouldn't be pregnant."

Christopher crossed the room to stand before her. "I do more than care, Maxi. I love you."

Maxi's heart gave a funny little lurch at his words. If he had said them two months ago she would have been overjoyed. Now she was only filled with doubt. "And when did you decide that you love me, Christopher? I know it wasn't on the cruise and I know it wasn't during the time we were making a baby. Heavens forbid it was that evening I called to let you know I was pregnant. And I know for certain it couldn't have been two weeks ago when I called you and some woman answered your phone and told me, quite gleefully I might add, that you were in the shower and couldn't possibly come to the phone."

"Maxi, I—"

"No, it doesn't matter because I'm the fool, Christopher. You told me all along what the score was but a part of me didn't want to believe it. But now I do," she said wearily.

Christopher became angry, not with Maxi but with himself. He should have been man enough to face his feelings for her long ago but he hadn't. And now it could possibly be too late. No, he refused to believe that. If ten years hadn't destroyed what was once between them, he refused to believe that two months could.

"Can we sit and talk about it?"

She glanced up at him. "What is there to talk about?"

"I can think of a number of things. How about let's give it a try?"

Sighing, Maxi sat down on the sofa and Christopher sat down beside her. "First, I want to know if you're feeling all right?"

She looked at him and decided not to make some smart remark about it taking two months for him to ask. "Yes, I'm fine."

"And the baby?"

"He or she is fine, too."

"I'm glad."

Maxi studied his features. He was handsome as ever and a part of her wanted to trace the tip of her finger around his lips before kissing them. She held her hands together tight in her lap, not believing she could think such a thing. But then, having such thoughts was normal. She and Christopher had spent some hot and heavy days and nights together while making their baby. Just thinking about those times made heat pass through her body. "Why are you here, Christopher?"

"I've told you already. I love—"

"Besides that."

"There's no other reason why I'm here."

His statement had been blunt. "So, I'm to believe that you woke up this morning and decided that you loved me?"

"I wish it would have been that simple. It would have saved me a lot of time and expense."

"Not to mention a lot of condoms, I bet," Maxi remarked with bitter humor.

Christopher looked at her, surprised at her apparent anger. He'd been upfront with her from the beginning that his life was filled with fast women and meaningless affairs. "Is that what has you upset, Maxi? The fact that I haven't been celibate since the last time we were together? You knew I was into women. You also knew I would resume my lifestyle once I had given you a child."

"Yes, but I—I thought . . ."

"You thought what? That a man who'd been a loner all his life could miraculously fall in love overnight? I had loved you for twelve long years, Maxi. Twelve long years. Do you know that on most days the only reason I went to school every day, rain or shine, was because I knew you would be there. When I left Savannah ten years ago, the only way I could survive without having you in my life was to forget you and get involved with other women. And for the past ten years that's what I've done." He knew he had to make her understand.

"But a part of me knew I could never treat you like I treated them. In my mind, the only reason we slept together—no matter how enjoyable it was—was to give you my child. It wasn't until later, that I realized it was for more. It was only recently that I realized that each and every time I made love to you, that you became a part of me because I shared a part of myself with you that I hadn't shared with any woman. I finally admitted to myself that I still loved you, the same way I had loved you in school, which was with a possessiveness and an insane longing I couldn't get rid of. Do you know I carved your name on every damn tree in the Vines?"

She shook her head. "No, I didn't know that."

"Did you know that I used to dare the other boys to go near you and ended up kicking a few behinds because one or two did it anyway?"

"No, I didn't know that—at least not until the cruise."

"Did you know that the day I left Savannah, for an entire hour I stood in your backyard underneath your bedroom window, hoping that I would see you one last time before I left?"

She wiped a lone tear from her cheek. "No, I didn't know that."

"Did you know that the first major chain store that Gabe and I built and owned in Detroit I had the honor of naming *Maxi*?"

Maxi lifted a brow. The *Maxi* department stores were sprouting up all over the country and were on the same scale as a Bloomingdales—very elite and high class. "No, I didn't know that either."

He slid a little closer to her. "And do you know how hard it was for me to tell you I didn't want to be a part of my child's life? Especially when you would be that child's mother? So don't tell me that I don't love you, Maxi. I've had other women, true enough, but none of them has ever meant what you mean to me. The condition you're in proves that."

He stood. "I hope I've given you something to think about. I love you and I want to marry you." Ignoring the shocked look on her face when he mentioned marriage, he continued. "I'll be in town for the rest of the week and will be staying at the Marriott on the ocean if you want to talk."

Maxi then watched as he crossed the room and walked out of her house.

CHAPTER FORTY-ONE

"You're asking the wrong person if you want advice on love and happiness, Maxi."

Maxi shook her head. "No, I think you're the perfect person to ask, Mya. No matter what has happened between you and Garrett, you can't convince me that you don't still love him."

"Of course I still love him but I can't live with him, not with anger eating away at me like it is."

"And you still haven't gone back to see your minister?"

"No."

Maxi decided not to push Mya on the issue. She was still hoping and praying that things would work out between her and Garrett.

"At least he's as miserable as I am," Mya said softly. "I talked to his mom the other day and the family is really concerned." She inhaled deeply. "They ought to be concerned because a part of me isn't sure Garrett and I will be able to work through this."

"You will, it will just take some time."

"It's been three months and I still can't stand the sight of him, Maxi. When I see him I envision him kissing her."

"Then envision him kissing you."

"I tried that but it doesn't work. The thought that he let another woman—"

"Don't think about it, Mya. It won't do you any good. Try putting it behind you."

"It's hard, Maxi."

Maxi heard the tears in Mya's voice. "I know, but you're going to have to let it go sometime. There are women who have patched things up with their husbands for more serious charges. I read in a book where a woman actually caught her husband in bed with another man and forgave him."

"She had a bigger heart than I have then."

Maxi giggled. "Bigger than mine too."

After a long moment, Mya asked. "So what are you going to do about, Christopher?"

"I don't know."

"Do you love him, Maxi?"

"Yes, with all my heart."

"Do you want to marry him?"

"Yes, with all my soul."

"Then what are you waiting for? Your child to grow up and plan the wedding for you? No matter what happens between us, I'd never regret marrying Garrett."

Maxi smiled. "I'm glad to hear you say that."

"Yeah, me too. Look, I better end our call. I have to get up early tomorrow. I'm flying to Orlando. I'll call you when I get there and leave my hotel number on your answering machine just in case you need to talk."

"All right. Take care, Mya, and have a safe trip. Love you."

"And I love you, too."

The next day when Maxi left work, instead of going home as usual, she took the scenic road that lead to the ocean and the Marriott Hotel where Christopher was staying. He had been in town only two days and already news had spread around town about his return.

Her mother had phoned her at work to inform her everyone was curious to know why bad boy Christopher Chandler was back after ten years. And of course, everyone wanted to know what he was up to since rumor had it that he'd met with the mayor yesterday. And according to her mother, everyone was shocked to find out that he hadn't been in jail during the ten years he'd been gone but was a highly successful and wealthy businessman living in Detroit. Her mother had also indicated that she'd heard Ronald Swindel was still in shock; especially after he'd used the tax payers' money to do a background check that revealed the state of Christopher's finances were more fact than rumor.

After parking her car and walking into the hotel Maxi wondered what she would say to Christopher when she saw him, but in her heart she knew.

"I wondered if you would come."

She turned at the sound of Christopher's voice and noticed he had just stepped off the elevator. "Hi," she said studying the features that were also studying hers just as intently. "Going someplace?"

"Yes, to get something to eat. Want to join me?"

She nodded. "Yes, I'd like that." She didn't bother to ask where they were going. And when he automatically slipped his hand in hers, she didn't resist, not caring that a number of local people who worked at the hotel were watching them with keen interest.

They went to a seafood restaurant not far from the hotel and enjoyed their meal. During dinner they talked about a lot of things, mostly how much Savannah had changed. The last time he had come to visit her, he had come at night and had left early the following morning, without seeing much of the city in the daylight hours.

"I remember when an old shack used to sit on this very spot," he said while they waited for the waiter to bring him their check.

"Yeah, I remember that shack, too. I also remember Lover's Cove wasn't too far from here."

He raised a brow. "And what do you know about Lover's Cove?"

She chuckled as she glanced over at him. "Not much, since you managed to scare all the guys away from me. But thanks to Mya, I knew enough. Lover's Cove used to be one of her and Garrett's favorite hot spots."

Christopher chuckled. "Yeah, I bet it was." He leaned back in his chair. "I understand they still aren't back together."

Maxi nodded. "How do you know that?"

"From Garrett. I talk to him occasionally."

Maxi looked at him, surprised. "You do?"

"Yes, and he's pretty torn up about it still. Mya refuses to give him any slack or any forgiveness. But he is determined to get his family back." He then looked at her intently. "So am I, Maxi. I am determined to have you and the baby in my life. The two of you are my family."

She lowered her head for a second then lifted her gaze back up to him. "Are we, Christopher?"

"Yes."

A short while later they had arrived back at the hotel. "Would you like to come up to my room a while?"

"Umm, I don't know. It might cause a scandal."

"But it's a scandal I think we can handle."

Maxi thought he could handle just about anything. At least a lot better than she could. All during dinner she could feel sexual tension radiating between them and he hadn't seemed particularly bothered by it. However, she had almost been tempted to jump his bones.

"So, do you want to go to my room for a while to talk?"

Maxi doubted they would get much talking done. At least not tonight. "Yes."

Once in his room, as soon as he closed the door Christopher

gathered her into his arms and kissed her. Moments later when he ended it she looked up at him. "I thought we were going to talk."

"We are. Don't you know that kissing is the best form of communication between two people who love each other?"

"And do we love each other?"

"I believe so. Am I right?"

"Yes, you are right. I do love you, Christopher, and your baby loves you, too."

He stared down at her, with such deep emotion in his eyes that it nearly brought tears to hers. "How can you be so sure my baby loves me?" he asked huskily, in a voice that trembled slightly.

"Because the baby feels what I feel and right now I feel so much love for you I can't stand it."

He studied her features. "And can you handle the fact that there have been other women?" he asked softly, watching her reaction to his question.

Maxi knew why he was asking her that. "Yes, because in my heart I know that none of them meant anything to you. I'm the only one you cared enough about to give such a precious gift to. I'm the only one."

"Yes, you are the only one because I love you." He reached out and cradled her face in the palms of his hands. "Will you marry me?"

She stared at him as tears formed in her eyes. "Yes, I'll marry you."

And then he kissed her again before taking her to bed and making love to her. Tender, passionate love. Afterwards, they lay wrapped up in each other's arms, glorying in being together. "Everyone is wondering why you're back," Maxi whispered softly, in the quiet stillness of the room.

"You're the reason I'm back. You and the baby," he said without hesitation. He felt her smile against his chest and pulled her body closer to his.

"They're also wondering why you met with the mayor yesterday."

Christopher chuckled. Evidently some things about Savannah hadn't changed. It was still filled with a lot of inquisitive minds and big eyes. "I met with the mayor to make him an offer that I hope he can't refuse."

Maxi lifted her head slightly and looked at him. "Really?"

"Yes."

"What?"

"I want to purchase the Vines."

Maxi sat up in bed and looked down at him. "The Vines?" At his nod she asked. "Why?"

"Because it was such a part of my childhood and because your name is carved on every tree and because I agree with what you said on the cruise. The Vines should be a place where people can continue to live, but it should be nice and affordable. If the mayor sells me the land, I plan to tear down all those old homes and build a new residential area of single dwelling homes. I'm committed to making sure the Vines never becomes an eyesore to the city again."

"Oh, Christopher, that's a wonderful idea."

He reached out and pulled her on top of him. "But not as wonderful as your loving me, agreeing to become my wife and having my baby. I don't think anything is as wonderful as that, Maxi."

She smiled at him. "Do you really believe that?"

"Yes." He then proceeded to show her how much he did believe it.

CHAPTER FORTY-TWO

Mya tried to keep her spirits high when she met Robert Noble in the lobby of her hotel on Wednesday afternoon. They had a meeting with Simon Prentice at Noble Technology at three o'clock.

"Sorry we couldn't finish up this business a few weeks ago, Mya, but something unexpected came up," he explained as he escorted her out of the hotel to his car.

"That's fine and I understand. And in a way it worked out better. The stock market has been doing some unbelievable things in the past week."

"Good things, I hope," he said with a broad smile as he opened his car door for her.

"Yes, and did you notice that the price of your stock escalated once word got out you're now doing business with us?"

He chuckled. "In my arrogance, I assumed the upward climb in stock prices was because of that calendar getting turned to the month of August."

Mya couldn't help but laugh. Although she hadn't seen the calendar, she had definitely heard about it. Twelve highly successful black businessmen from across the country had come together in rare form to pose for a calendar where each month one of them was highlighted as the man of the month. Appropriately dressed in designer business suits and looking the epitome of successful businessmen, the calendar told of their accomplishments and the roads that they had traveled to achieve their success. From what she was hearing the calendars were selling like hotcakes and Robert Noble was Mr. August. All the proceeds from the sale of the calendars were being donated to radio celebrity Tom Joyner's scholarship fund to aid historically black colleges from which all twelve of the businessmen had graduated.

Mya and Robert's meeting with Simon Prentice lasted until six that evening. When the meeting was over she felt good about it. She had covered a lot of ground with the two men and felt confident that she was slowly winning Mr. Prentice over, although he still tried to maintain a reserved attitude.

"It's late and you must be starving," Robert Noble said to her after checking his watch. "How about if I treat you to dinner?"

"You don't have to," she said, although she was hungry.

"No, I want to. I think I heard the ice around Simon's heart cracking," he said whispering to her. "In no time at all, I believe you will have him eating out of your hand, Mya."

She smiled. "Instead of having him eating out of my hand, I'll gladly settle for him being receptive to all of my ideas," she said.

"And in time he will. Simon is a very intelligent man. That's the main reason I have him running things."

When they were on their way to the restaurant Robert remembered he needed to go by his house to pick up a package he wanted to deliver to Simon later. Mya wasn't surprised when he turned his car into the driveway of a very beautiful home that sat on at least ten acres of land.

"Your home is gorgeous, Robert," she said when he pulled the car into a four-car garage.

"Thanks. Come inside and have a look around while I grab the information for Simon. Then I won't feel so guilty when I also make an important phone call," he said sheepishly. "I hope you don't mind."

"Of course I don't mind."

His home was a decorator's showcase, she thought, as she moved around looking at things while he chatted on the phone with a business associate in London. She picked up a photograph that was sitting on his fireplace mantel when she heard him hanging up the phone.

"Her face looks familiar," she said of the beautiful woman in the photograph. She then noticed the resemblance. "Is this your sister?"

He walked over to her and looked at the framed photograph Mya held in her hands. "Yes, that's my sister, Katherine. My one and only. There were only two of us and we're very close."

"Where does she live?"

"In Atlanta and she runs her own pharmaceutical company. You may have seen her in an issue of *Essence* last year. She was featured in an article that highlighted a number of successful business women."

"Your parents must be proud of the two of you."

"Yes, the only thing they aren't proud of is the fact that neither Katherine nor I are married." He chuckled. "They want grandchildren real bad."

Mya smiled as she thought of Garrett's parents. "Grandparents are special. My grandmother raised me after my parents were killed when I was only six. And my husband's parents have been wonderful grandparents to my sons."

"You are blessed to have them."

She nodded knowing what Robert said was true. She was blessed to have the Rivers in her life as well as in her sons' lives.

"You and your husband have been together a long time, haven't you?"

His question caught her by surprise and it was then that she noticed just how close the two of them were standing. "Yes. We began dating in junior high school and got married in college."

"So you've never dated another man in your entire life?"

"Yes, that's right. Garrett has been the only one."

Robert was staring at her with such intensity she suddenly felt heated . . . a tad uncomfortable. "Then he is a lucky man," he said huskily.

Her heart began thundering when she noticed Robert had moved to stand closer. So close it would seem almost natural for the two of them to kiss. But even with the problems she was having in her marriage, she still physically and emotionally belonged to Garrett.

"And what about you, Robert? Is there a lucky lady in your life?" she asked taking a step back as she placed the photograph of his sister back on the fireplace mantel.

Robert sighed deeply, getting the message with her movement. "No."

She turned and met his gaze, which was a soft caress. "I'm sure one day there will be." She then checked her watch. "Shouldn't we be leaving for dinner now?"

Later that night back in her hotel room she thought about Robert and how easily it would have been to have an affair with him. She knew from his body language that he would have been more than willing if she'd shown the least bit of interest. A part of her wanted to feel that she didn't owe Garrett anything, especially not her faithfulness. But another part of her knew that wasn't true. She still loved Garrett and she wouldn't get involved with someone else just for spite. Two wrongs didn't make a right.

Mya wiped a lone tear from her eye when she thought about how much history she and Garrett had together. She remembered the first day that she had seen Garrett at school and how he had walked her home that day. She remembered the first time they had made love, teenagers satisfying their curiosity about sex, and how gentle and responsible he had been with her. But what stuck out most in her mind was that summer when she thought she had gotten pregnant. All it had taken was a phone call and within forty-eight hours he had returned to Savannah to be there with her and to take care of her. Without wasting any time and running the risk of losing a football scholarship, he had married her and had given her his name. There had never been a time that she had doubted his love for her.

She wiped another tear from her eye. She loved her husband with all her heart. Was there any way she could find it in that same heart to forgive him?

Tomorrow when she returned to Dallas, she would call to see if Reverend Stonewall could meet with her, counsel her, and pray with her. And she wanted to meet with Sister Stonewall as well. She wanted to know how the two of them had moved beyond his infidelity to hold on to the love they had.

When Mya drifted off to sleep moments later, her mind was filled with thoughts of Garret and how they could resolve the problems between them.

The next day Mya started shaking her head in disbelief as she glanced around her living room. The placed looked like a florist shop. Vases of flowers were everywhere.

"They are beautiful, aren't they?" Mrs. Butler said behind her. "They were delivered this morning."

"Yes, they are beautiful," Mya said as she continued looking around her living room. She had just arrived back in town and had been met by the fragrance of various flowers the moment she had walked in the door.

"The card is on the table, Mrs. Rivers."

"Thanks."

Mya crossed the room to the table to pick up the card. Her breath caught when she pulled it out of the envelope and read it:

To the woman who has always had my heart. A different arrangement of flowers for every year we've been together. I love you, Mya. And I will love you until the day I die.
    Garrett

Mya read the card again. And again. She then smiled through her tears.

CHAPTER FORTY-THREE

Mya stretched her body when she became awake and then remembered she was not in her own bed. She and the boys had caught a flight from Dallas midday on Friday for Savannah to attend Maxi's wedding.

The sun was already flooding through the bedroom window indicating it was going to be a beautiful day. She was happy for Maxi and wanted only the best for her and Christopher. She and Maxi had spent some time together last night and had talked about a lot of things, but mostly they had talked about what the two of them had had to endure this year and how they had become stronger women because of it.

There was a knock on the bedroom door and Mya pulled herself up in bed. "Come in."

"You're awake, sweetheart?"

The older woman who entered the room still looked good for her sixty-one years. Her hair was styled like Mya had always known her to wear it, long and loose around her shoulders. And it was beautiful hair, thick and black, with only a sprinkle of gray at the temples.

The one thing Mya had always liked about Garrett's mom was her smile. From the first time Garrett had brought her home to meet his parents when she was a shy girl of fourteen, his mother had made her feel welcome with that smile. And another thing she had always liked about her was that she was fair. She never took sides. Mya knew that although she was Garrett's mother, from the day Garrett had declared to his family that Mya would always be his girl, his mother had accepted that and had made Mya feel like the daughter she'd never had. That's why, even with the problems she and Garrett were having, she felt comfortable in coming here to stay during the time she was in Savannah. To her, the Rivers's house had been her home, too.

"Yes, ma'am, I'm awake, Ma Rivers." Mya sat up in bed. Pa Rivers had been the one to pick her and the boys up from the airport yesterday afternoon. Ma Rivers had been at choir practice. One of Garrett's sisters-in-law had come by before Mya could unpack and got the boys, eager for them to spend the night at her house with her three kids. By the time Mya had finished unpacking and had changed into something comfortable, Ma Rivers had come home. Mya had been in the bedroom putting things away when she had looked up to see the woman standing in the doorway. As if she had immediately known what Mya needed, she had held out her arms to her. Mya had quickly gone into the older woman's embrace and cried what she hoped were the last of her tears.

Joanne Rivers looked at the woman her son had always loved to distraction and continued smiling. "Did you sleep well?"

"Yes, I slept fine." Mya glanced around. She was in Garrett's old room. His football trophies took up one entire area of the room and on the other side of the room was a wall he had dedicated to her. Mya believed every single picture she had ever taken while in high school was somehow plastered on Garrett's bedroom wall. Looking at them made her remember what everyone had said— Mya and football were Garrett's two passions in life.

"Well, Pa wanted me to let you know that breakfast is ready. You know how he is. He wants to spend time with his baby girl."

Mya chuckled. The Rivers had a total of six children, all boys. At twenty-eight, Garrett was the baby in the family and when he had married her that had automatically made her the baby, too. "Tell Pa Rivers I wouldn't miss a chance to eat breakfast with my favorite guy."

Ma Rivers nodded and turned to leave the room. She turned back around as if to say something, shook her head, decided not to, and left the room, closing the door behind her.

Mya pondered Ma Rivers's actions. Was there something she had wanted to say? Breathing deeply she pushed the covers aside and grabbed her robe. The bathroom was at the end of the hall and she needed to use it and to get dressed for breakfast.

A few moments later, dressed in a pair of jeans and a T-shirt, Mya entered the Rivers's kitchen and stopped. Garrett was sitting at the table talking to his father. She placed her hand on her chest, surprised to see him. He sensed her presence and looked up. She held his gaze for several seconds as she tried to get herself together. She noticed that the room had gotten quiet. Also sitting at the breakfast table besides Ma and Pa Rivers was Garrett's oldest brother, Randy. At six-foot-eight-inches tall, Randy had a love for basketball and for a while had played in the pros before a severe ankle injury ended that career.

Taking a deep breath, Mya continued walking into the room. "Good morning, everyone." As expected Randy stood and gave her a big brotherly hug. "You need to stop growing, Randy."

He laughed. "Mya, at thirty-six I'm too old to still be growing. You, Mya Ki'Shae, on the other hand, need to stop getting shorter."

She smiled. "How's Andrea and the kids?"

"Everybody's fine. They'll be by later."

When he released her Mya took the only chair not occupied at the breakfast table, which just happened to be next to Garrett. She only hesitated for just a second before sitting down.

"Good morning, Mya."

"Good morning, Garrett. I didn't know you were coming here."

"I got a call from Christopher inviting me to the wedding."

Mya nodded. "Where did you sleep last night, since I used your room?"

He shrugged. "I didn't get in until five this morning so I haven't done much sleeping. But I did crash for a little while in Randy's old room. I felt like a midget in a room made for a giant."

Mya couldn't help but laugh. And she could tell by everyone's expressions that her laughter was what was needed to make everyone at the table relax. Evidently Ma and Pa Rivers had not been sure how she would react upon seeing Garrett.

Breakfast had always been a special time at the Rivers's house and this day wasn't an exception. Ma Rivers brought everyone up to date on everyone at church and Pa Rivers talked about all the fishing he and Deacon Matthews were doing now since both men had retired. After breakfast Mya helped Ma Rivers clear the table and load the dishes in the dishwasher her five sons had chipped in to buy her a few Mother's Days ago. In fact they had purchased her all new appliances that year since it was no secret how much she liked to cook.

"I hope you're not too upset with seeing Garrett here, Mya," Ma Rivers said to her after they had loaded the last dish.

"No, this is Garrett's home. I just didn't know he was going to be here."

Ma Rivers smiled. "Neither did we until he called from the airport saying he was on his way."

Mya nodded. So it had been an unplanned trip for Garrett just like she had thought. "I'm fine with it. Like I told you last night, I feel better after talking to Reverend Stonewall. I still hurt but I love Garrett."

Ma Rivers smiled. "And everyone knows that he loves you. He always has."

"And I think that had me worried most of all, Ma Rivers. The possibility that Garrett didn't love me as much as he always had. A part of me was convinced that I was no longer woman enough to satisfy him. I never had to worry about other women before but then I suddenly found that I had to worry."

Ma Rivers waved her hand. "You still don't have to worry. If you could have only seen the expression on Garrett's face when you walked into the kitchen for breakfast you would definitely know that. Love was written all over it for everyone to see. And it's always been that way. Garrett has never been ashamed of loving you and admitting to anyone that he did." She chuckled. "I remember one time he almost knocked Elgin's head off because Elgin told him that it wasn't cool for a guy to admit to liking a girl. Garrett had gotten all in Elgin's face and said that was too bad because he wanted everyone to know that he loved you and just how much."

Mya smiled. Elgin was Garrett's thirty-three-year-old brother who was as big as a locomotive. Not too many people messed with him because of his size. She couldn't imagine Garrett being that bold as to get in Elgin's face.

"What Garrett did was wrong," his mother continued as she took Mya by the shoulders. "But as painful as it is, you and Garrett have too much history, too many years behind you, to let something like this come in and destroy such a beautiful relationship. And I know in my heart the two of you will work this out. It will take giving on both your parts."

The two women embraced, then looked up a few moments later when they heard a sound behind them. It was Garrett. He looked at Mya, unsure of himself. He then spoke. "I was about to go over to Ben and Nina's house to get the boys and was wondering if you wanted to ride over there with me?"

Mya inhaled deeply, not sure she was ready to be alone with Garrett just yet. But then she knew they had to start somewhere. Things couldn't continue like this. She couldn't have his family feeling uncomfortable around them because of their situation. She nodded slowly. "Yes, I'll go. Just give me a second to grab my purse."

At first, they rode the first couple of miles and didn't say anything to each other. Then Garrett spoke. "Mark called last night. He's been picked up by the Jacksonville Jaguars and he's excited about it."

Mya nodded. "I'm glad. I know how much he wanted to continue playing football." After a few moments she then said, "Thanks for the flowers, Garrett. They've been beautiful." He had been sending her a beautiful arrangement of flowers every week for the past month.

"You're welcome, and I mean everything I write on those cards."

She glanced over at him but didn't say anything. When she looked at him, the person she saw was the man who had always had her heart. The man who had given her two beautiful sons and the man who had always loved her. He was also the man who was romancing her by sending her beautiful arrangements of flowers. But. . . .

She turned away and looked out the window. There was that "but" lurking in the back of her mind. Reminding her.

"What do you have planned for the rest of the day?" Garrett asked her moments later.

"I told Maxi that she could use me in whatever capacity that she needed to. I think I'm the one who's going to pick up the flowers from the florist to save Mrs. Chandler a trip. I think Maxi thought this would be just a small affair but it seems her mother had other ideas."

Garrett nodded. "I told Christopher I would help him do some things today as well."

Mya nodded. The car then became silent for the rest of the way to Garrett's brother's home.

CHAPTER FORTY-FOUR

Everything was beautiful, Maxi thought, as she glanced around her mother's living room. Because of all the extravagance that had gone into her and Jason's planned wedding, she hadn't wanted anything elaborate. All she wanted was a small wedding in her mother's home with just family and friends. And she'd gotten just what she'd wanted.

Her mother, Ms. Bessie, and some of the other ladies from the church had gone out of their way to make her and Christopher's wedding one they would remember for a long time.

She knew Christopher had been filled with emotion when a number of people had hugged him and told him how glad they were to see him again. She also knew he had become even more emotional when the Blackwells had arrived and Joella Blackwell, being the very friendly person that she was, had gone around the room introducing herself as the proud mother of the groom. Maxi had met the woman last month when Christopher had taken her home to meet the couple that he considered as his adopted parents. She knew the Joella was a jewel and was glad she had been the mother Christopher never had.

Maxi also had a another reason to be happy. Her mother had

confided to her earlier that she and Jim planned to marry over the Christmas holidays.

Maxi glanced across the room at her husband talking to Gabe and Garrett. Every so often she would notice how Garrett's attention would shift from the conversation and move around the room, no doubt looking for Mya. Maxi smiled. She had an idea just where her best friend was.

Leaving the living room she walked through the open French doors that led to her mother's beautiful flower garden. And there, like she knew she would, she saw Mya sitting on a bench underneath a magnolia tree.

Maxi couldn't help but remember the many summer afternoons she and Mya had spent sitting on that bench under that same tree sharing secrets like only two best friends could. She couldn't help but smile at the memories as she walked slowly toward her.

"Why are you so sad?" She asked the same question she had asked Mya that day in the schoolyard twenty-one years ago.

Mya looked up when she saw her. "I want my husband," she replied in a voice that sounded very much like the one she had used that day, just like she was about to cry.

"Where is he?" Maxi asked, pretending not to know the answer.

"Inside."

"Then why don't you go to him?"

"Because I still hurt," Mya replied softly.

"Then let him take the hurt away."

Mya met Maxi's gaze as she tossed her words around in her mind. She blinked back tears. During the wedding when Maxi and Christopher were exchanging vows, her gaze had found Garrett's across the room and held. The force of his gaze had been like a soft caress, and she had read profound love in his eyes.

"Can we be friends?" Maxi asked in that same serious voice that she had that day.

Mya smiled. "Yes, we can be friends."

"Best friends?"

Mya's smile widened. "Yes, the very best. For the rest of our lives."

The two women embraced, knowing that they would indeed be best friends forever.

Maxi felt the presence of someone behind them and turned around. It was Garrett. She had wondered how long it would take before he came looking for his wife. She smiled at him. "Hi, Garrett. I think I'll go back inside and ask that husband of mine to dance with me. I'll see you two later." She then turned and walked away, leaving Garrett and Mya alone.

For the longest time Garrett and Mya didn't say anything to each other. Then Garrett reached out and touched the wetness he saw forming around her eyes. "You're crying," he said softly.

Mya couldn't do anything but nod. She held his eyes, then suddenly saw the mistiness that appeared there. She reached up and her fingers slowly traced the lines around his eyes. "So are you."

He breathed deeply. "Yes, because I know how much I hurt you and I never wanted to hurt you, Mya. I love you so much and you mean everything to me. You always have. Please believe that."

He took a step closer to her and then, with unsure movements, he reached his hand out to her. Mya looked at it for the longest time before placing her hand in his. He then took another step to stand directly in front of her. He leaned forward to capture her lips with his, but she pulled back. After a few hesitant moments she brought her hands to his face. And then she leaned in closer, slowly bringing her lips to his.

It was at that moment Garrett understood what she was doing as her tongue entered his mouth and instantly did a thorough sweep of the insides as if removing any trace of the other woman. He fought to hold himself in check while Mya plundered his mouth, doing what she felt she needed to do to erase what still held them apart.

Moments later when he felt the intensity of the kiss change, he joined his tongue to hers. He felt her shudder in his arms and heard the moan that sounded from low within her throat as he took charge, repairing what he had damaged. He kissed her with all the love he had in his heart. He kissed her with all the need in his soul, silently conveying to her just how much she meant to him.

She broke off the kiss and leaned back in his arms and gazed up at him. "I liked that," she said conversationally.

He held her gaze when he said, "So did I."

Mya drew a deep breath. She knew that under the circumstances Garrett wouldn't suggest anything to her so she decided to take the initiative and make the suggestion to him. "Are you going to continue to kiss me out here or are you going to take me some place private?"

She watched his eyes darken, and saw the slow, shallow breath that eased from between his lips. "I would love to take you some place private. Would you go with me?" he asked huskily.

Her lips curved into a smile. "Yes, I'd go."

He smiled. It was irresistible, seductive. "Will you leave now?"

"Yes."

He took her hand in his. "Let's go."

He thought about taking her to Lover's Cove, where they had made out the very first time, to relive the memories of that beautiful night. Then he decided this night deserved its own memories. So he headed for the Bowman Hotel, which was one of the most elegant hotels in the historic section of Savannah.

He had told himself not to pounce on her the moment they were alone in the room, but he couldn't help it. The instant the door closed behind them, he pulled her into his arms and kissed her like a starving man who was getting his first real meal in a long time. He feasted on her mouth and his hands were everywhere on her, as if verifying that she was real and there with him. Evidently she also felt the same need because her hands were all over him as well, and within minutes both of them were completely undressed.

He reached out and his hand slowly slid up her body, touching her everywhere as he realized just how close he had come to losing her, and thanking God he had not. "I love you," he whispered as he picked her up in his arms and carried her over to the bed.

After placing her there, settling her head on the pillow, he began brushing kisses all over her body, nibbling gently, tasting, and teasing. He was desperate to show her how much he loved her, needed her, and wanted her. Only her.

He slid his hands between her thighs and discovered she was ready for him and the thought of that made his breath quicken and his body ache. "I love you," he whispered again, thinking he could never tell her enough, intent on showing her just how much.

The mattress dipped under his weight when he joined her, placing his body over her, settling between her legs. He kissed her as his hands continued to skim over her, eliciting soft moans from deep within her throat.

He broke off the kiss when he began easing into her, wanting to see her, wanting her to look into his eyes to see just what she meant to him. He knew it was there in his face. Emotions he refused to hide.

Mya let out her breath in a rush when she gazed into Garrett's eyes, reveling in the knowledge that he wanted her and most of all that he loved her. His eyes told her everything. Their separation had been hard on him. She looped her arms around his neck wanting to feel connected to him in every way she could. Slowly, gently, he continued to ease into her and she raised her hips to take him in. And when he reached a point where he couldn't go anymore, he stopped.

A long moment passed and still he didn't move. He just looked at her. It was as if he wanted to always remember this time, tonight, when they had recaptured what they had almost lost. His eyes were locked on hers as if mesmerized. Her body quivered with need. She craved his mating. Wanted it with a passion.

And then he began moving. His strokes into her body were complete, hard, all consuming and she willingly surrendered to him as their passion for each other escalated. She cried out softly when the rhythm he'd set sent shudders of pure pleasure through her. This, she thought, was the kind of love they had always shared. Total, complete, fulfilling, and no one could ever take that away from them. She was his and he was hers. Always had been and always would be. He had branded her, claimed her long ago, just like she had him and tonight both of them were affirming what they had together. A special love that had survived high school, college, and beyond that—against all odds.

"I love you, Garrett," she whispered to him softly.

It was as if her words were just what he had needed to hear. He leaned down and kissed her long, hard, and deep and his body continued to make love to her, sliding in and out of her body. Rocking her. Pleasing her. Loving her.

They came. Together. Their orgasm flooding through both of their bodies simultaneously, emptying their minds, filling their hearts and beckoning them to partake in such beautiful and powerful passion shared by a man and woman who love each other deeply. The pleasure was heightened by the sounds of their satisfied sighs as they reached the highest peak of total ecstasy.

Later when both of their breathing was under control, Garrett managed to reach for the telephone to make a call.

"Mom? Hi, this is Garrett. Are the boys okay? Oh, they did? All right." He reached out and pulled Mya closer into his arms. "Mya and I have decided to stay out tonight. We won't be back until morning." He smiled. "Maybe even lunch time." He then glanced down at Mya who was watching him. "Yes, Mom, she's okay. We're both okay. Everything is fine. Yes, Mom, I'll tell her. Bye." He then hung up the phone.

He turned and slipped his hands under Mya's hips, lifted her and placed her atop him. "Mom said Terry and Dawn came by and got the boys to spend the night at their place."

Mya nodded. Terry was Garrett's thirty-year-old brother and Dawn was his wife. They were expecting their first child in a few months. His other brother Daryl, who was thirty-four, and his wife Tonya were also expecting in a few months. Christmas this year in Savannah with the Rivers would be pretty joyous with new babies to spoil.

"Mom also said to tell you," Garrett continued, "that she loves you and is happy for us."

Mya smiled. "She's been worried."

"Yeah, the entire family has. They all love you, Mya."

She smiled. "And I love all of them. I was very lucky when you came into my life, Garrett."

"No, I'm the one who was lucky. But then I never believed it was luck that brought us together. It was our destiny." He slipped his hand behind her head and brought her mouth down to him. He wanted to kiss her, to mate his mouth with hers and to make love to her all over again.

So he did.

EPILOGUE

Maxi and Christopher

Maxi watched Christopher's reaction as she slowly slipped the buttons from out of his shirt one by one. She felt blessed.

"I think tonight calls for a celebration," she said when the last button had been undone. She then went for the belt on his pants.

"And just what are we celebrating?" he asked huskily. Not that he thought they needed a reason to get naked.

"Christopher Max is eight months old today."

"Oh, I thought we were celebrating something else."

She lifted a brow. "Something else like what?"

He smiled. "Like last night. You broke a record."

She blushed as she remembered. While making love last night she'd had so many orgasms she had stopped counting. "You did that on purpose."

"Yeah, I did. I like watching you come. It does something to me."

She laughed. "Oh, it does something to you all right. I believe it increases your sex drive," she said slipping the belt from his jeans. She then went for his zipper.

"Possibly," he murmured huskily. "Probably," he further added on a deep sigh when he felt her hand reach inside his pants to free him. "Don't you want me to take off my jeans?"

She looked up at him. "No need. I got just what I want in my hands." And then she slowly eased it into her already naked, hot, wet, body. "Ahh," she moaned softly. "Perfect." She then spread her legs more.

"Perfect timing," Christopher said, enjoying the feel of being so deeply embedded within her.

"Do it, Christopher. On the wall."

He took her spread legs and wrapped them around his waist. Keeping their bodies joined he carried her across the room and pressed her back up against the wall. And then he made love to her, the way she liked. Wall style.

He liked doing it this way, too.

While standing he could go deep inside her, pushing in and pulling out, over and over again in a way and at an angle that could drive him over the edge. He watched her eyes close as she savored the sensations and the feeling of him inside her and the friction of her thighs as they rubbed against the denim of his jeans.

"Open your eyes, Maxi. I want to see you come."

She opened them and locked with his when he gave one final thrust into her body. She screamed out his name when he climaxed, flooding her with the thick, hot essence of his fluid. The feel of him shooting off inside her always made her climax as well. She tightened her legs around him, clenching her muscles, milking him for all it was worth. For all she could get. She wanted everything.

Moments later when there was nothing left to give—at least for the moment—Christopher eased her body down his. "Now I take off my pants and we continue this in bed like normal people."

She nodded, too weak to respond.

"Do you think Christopher Max will sleep for a while?" he asked as he gently placed her on the bed.

She smiled up at him when she thought of their son. "He'll sleep long enough."

When he had removed his pants and joined her in bed, he smiled and said, "Damn, I hope so."

Garrett and Mya

From his position on the field, Garrett could see it was a packed stadium but he had expected no less. Whenever the Cowboys played it was football at its best. He had taken a few hard knocks already but then, that was all part of the game. A game he loved.

Thinking about something else he loved, he looked over his shoulder into the stands, to a certain area to find a particular woman who was sitting where she normally sat. During this time last year they were having major problems in their marriage but they had worked through them and now once again their marriage was solid as a rock.

His gaze found Mya, along with his sons who were sitting next to her. And in her arms she held the newest member of their family, their three-month-old daughter whom they had named Destiny.

They had decided to have another baby after Mya had brought her career in the financial arena to an end. The boys, she had told him, were getting older and they needed her at home. The decision had been totally hers and he had been happy with it because so was she.

He caught his wife's gaze, gave her a thumbs up and smiled. She smiled back and threw him a kiss. He felt like a man on top of the world. Now if they could only kick the opposing team's butt. But then he knew, win or lose, he would have a treat when he got home.

A very sensuous treat.

**If you loved *Perfect Timing*, read on for more
by Brenda Jackson . . .**

PERFECT FIT

**In this sexy, heartfelt classic from *New York Times* bestselling
romance legend Brenda Jackson, one woman's run of bad luck
may end in the sweetest kind of windfall . . .**

Sage Dunbar is dealt a shattering double blow when she discovers
that her fiancé has depleted her bank accounts and her father
has been having an affair. Reeling with shock, she accepts a job
promotion that involves relocating to Anchorage, Alaska. She
never expects to cross paths with a man who will challenge
everything she thought she knew about love.

Gabe's "sex-only" relationship policy has been working just fine,
keeping him free of messy entanglements and emotional baggage.
Then he meets Sage, and his no-commitment ways start to lose
their appeal. But Sage isn't ready to give her heart and trust to
another man any time soon. With a single-minded determination
that surprises even him, Gabe resolves to convince her that true
love can erase every obstacle—real or imagined—in its path . . .

*Available from Kensington Publishing Corp.
wherever books are sold.*

CHAPTER ONE

Gabe
Detroit, Michigan

Gabriel Blackwell had a low tolerance level for women who constantly tripped on excess emotional baggage, and the one sitting across from him had bags packed so heavy he wondered how she was lugging them around.

After listening to her moan, weep and groan for the past hour, he'd just about had it. There were only so many burdens a mortal man could take from a woman who refused to see the light of day because her lover of the past two years had made one mistake too many.

He lifted the wineglass to his lips and took a sip as he continued to listen to her whine. Since this was their first date, she was evidently clueless that this was not the way to go about establishing a new relationship with someone. When he'd picked her up for dinner, he'd been truly impressed since she definitely was a looker who had everything in all the right places. For once he had thought his mother, who'd harassed him into going out on this blind date, had finally done something right. It didn't take long for him to change his mind and decide that instead she'd definitely done something wrong. En route to the restaurant, when a certain song by Luther Vandross began playing on the car's radio, the woman had begun crying her eyes out over what she'd tearfully described to him as "painful memories." Evidently the pain only got worse, because she'd been sobbing ever since. Several times he had offered to take her back home, but she'd refused, saying that at some point she had to get on with her life. And each time he'd come close to telling her that she was exhibiting a piss-poor job of doing so.

He knew of very few men who needed or wanted the stress of getting involved with someone who couldn't regain control of her emotions and let go. He'd found out the hard way three years ago that some women actually enjoyed bemoaning a lost cause. He had fancied himself in love with such a woman. After they had dated exclusively for ten months, she broke things off between them the moment her ex-lover returned to town and decided he wanted her back. The scars from that encounter had been slow to heal.

"I guess I'm not making a good impression tonight with it being our first date and all, but I can't help it," the woman said, breaking into Gabe's thoughts as she sniffed into the handkerchief he'd given to her earlier.

When he didn't say anything, she continued by saying, "I can't believe I'm still upset over the fact that he left me. He was nothing but a total jerk anyway." A few minutes later she added, "But still, after what we used to mean to each other, you'd think he would have the decency to at least return my phone calls."

Gabe lifted a brow, wondering if she really thought a jerk would actually do something decent. Then, belatedly, what she'd said caught his attention. "You've tried calling him?" he asked, more in astonishment than interest. She had spent the past hour telling him how she'd discovered the guy had hocked her jewelry to pay his gambling debts, as well as the fact that he'd been carrying on an illicit affair with a woman in the office where he worked. As far as Gabe was concerned, the man had two strikes against him. She was definitely better off without him and had said so herself several times during the course of the evening. Yet in the same breath, she'd just admitted that she'd tried contacting him. Gabe determined she was a glutton for punishment and was taking obsessive love to an all-new high . . . or in his opinion, a very disgusting low.

"Yes, I've been trying to reach him for the past two days, ever since I found out about my condition," she finally answered as fresh tears appeared in her eyes.

Gabe inhaled sharply, almost choking on the wine he'd just sipped. He cleared his throat and shifted uneasily in his chair, then inquired as calmly as he could, "Your condition?"

Red, swollen, tear-soaked eyes met his gaze. She again put his handkerchief to use as she sobbingly replied, "I'm pregnant."

The next day

Joella Blackwell looked at her son and said calmly, "The situation you described doesn't sound like a major crisis to me, Gabriel."

Gabe shook his head in disbelief, clearly stunned. After a brief moment of recovery, he was almost certain he had misunderstood his mother's response, so he decided to tell her again.

"I said the woman who you talked me into taking out last night announced over dinner that she's pregnant."

And just in case his mother still didn't get it, he clarified by saying, "She's going to have a baby, and before you give me an all-accusing stare, just remember that last night was our first date and under the circumstances it was definitely our last."

Joella Blackwell raised a dark brow as she continued the task of setting the table for dinner. Christopher Chandler, Gabe's best friend and business partner, whom she considered her surrogate son, and his wife and their ten-month-old son would be coming, and she looked forward to seeing them. She was pleased that at least one of her sons had finally put aside his whoring ways to marry and start a family.

"I know what being pregnant means, Gabriel. All I'm saying is that at least she was honest and up front with you. So the way I see it, to decide you won't be seeing her again is acting rather hastily. I would think you could put the issue of her pregnancy behind you and move on."

Gabe leaned in the doorway that separated the kitchen from the dining room, wondering if his mother actually thought such a thing was possible. But then, he knew she really did. Everyone who knew Joella Blackwell was well aware that she had a soft, loving and forgiving heart. She was a good Christian woman who saw good in everyone and believed a positive spin could be derived from any negative situation. In this case, she was dead wrong. "You're expecting too much if you assume I'll consider asking her out again," he finally said.

Joella Blackwell shrugged. "I see no reason why you shouldn't. Being pregnant is not the end of the world. Men date pregnant women all the time."

Gabe frowned. "Yeah, and usually when they do it's because they have a vested interest, like being the father of that child. Don't you see the problems that can develop if I become involved with Keri Morton?"

"No, I don't see the problems since she's made you aware of her condition. It's not as if she's trying to pass the child off as yours. I think you're being too judgmental. Your name may be Gabriel, but you're far from being an angel yourself."

Gabe shook his head. "I happen to like children, no matter whose they are, but there's a lot more to it than the pregnancy issue. She's still hung up on her baby's father."

"She actually told you that?"

"She didn't have to. She talked about him enough over dinner for me to tell, and I refuse to get involved again with a woman carrying around excess emotional baggage. And trust me, Keri Morton is up to her ying-ying in it. I'm not interested in dating a woman with issues."

Joella Blackwell didn't say anything for the longest moment.

She remembered how a few years back Gabe had fallen in love; a woman he had practically offered everything—his time, his money and most important, his heart. The day before he was going to ask her to marry him, she broke off things between them to get back together with her old boyfriend and had even had the gall to send Gabe an invitation to their wedding. Since that fateful time, he had refused to date women who he thought had personal problems they couldn't let go of. What she'd tried to get him to see was that everyone had some sort of issues. No one lived a completely carefree life.

"There's no such thing as a perfect woman, Gabriel."

Gabe met his mother's gaze. "I'm not looking for one, but any relationship I get seriously involved in again has to be uncomplicated and straightforward."

Joella shook her head. "I hate to disappoint you, but there's nothing uncomplicated or straightforward about any woman. God made us unique and he gave us emotions and I do thank him for that. Otherwise, this world would have ended long ago if it was left up to a man. Your gender on occasion has shown to be rather heartless. And heaven forbid if anything has to be done. Men take forever to do nothing. Women are known not to beat around the bush. And we are a nurturing breed. We're sensitive, understanding, and luckily for the male, we're also compassionate. That's the reason we can't let go of things as easily as a man. Then there are some of us who can't seem to let go at all. They're the ones in need of more personal growth and healing, along with tender, loving care. But in due time they'll learn there is life after a love that's ended."

Gabe heard everything his mother said, but still he felt women like Keri were the ones to watch out for and avoid. As far as he was concerned, the best way to handle those types of women was to put concrete and solid rules into place. And his number one rule was to not become involved with a woman who obviously sweated the small stuff and who refused to let go and move on.

"Is it wrong for me to want a woman who'll complement me in every way?" he finally asked. "A woman who I'll consider as my soul mate, my perfect fit? Until that time comes, I have no intention of getting seriously involved with anyone with issues."

"And what if you fall in love with her first?"

Gabe frowned. "Trust me, that won't happen. I may not be an angel, but neither am I a fool. I've learned from past mistakes." He then turned and walked away.

Joella watched her son leave and shook her head sadly. She wondered when it would occur to him that in addition to not being an angel or a fool, he lived in a glass house and shouldn't throw stones because it was quite obvious that he had issues of his own.

Late that evening Gabe entered his apartment, went straight to the kitchen, grabbed a beer out of the refrigerator and took a swig. His mother had been too busy lavishing her attention on her surrogate grandchild to remember to harass him any more that afternoon. But he wasn't crazy enough to think she was through with him. With Christopher married that meant Gabe was now the recipient of all of her attention. As soon as she could, she would try playing matchmaker again.

Walking down the hall to his bedroom, he smiled as his thoughts fell on his partner and best friend. Christopher had begun working for Gabe's father's construction company at eighteen. Omar Blackwell had taken the young, hard-working loner under his wing and become not only Christopher's boss, but a mentor and father figure. The Blackwells had offered Christopher things he'd never had before, family ties, trust, respect and complete love.

Gabe knew his parents considered Christopher their other son, and since the two boys were the same age, they had talked Christopher into furthering his education right along with Gabe. They both had graduated with MBAs at the top of their class. Christopher had a degree in industrial design, and Gabe had earned a degree in structural engineering. And when Omar Blackwell retired six years ago, signing ownership of the company over to Gabe and Christopher, they had taken it in a whole new direction, one that was now world known. The Regency Corporation had built numerous upscale shopping malls, industrial office parks and department stores all over the United States in the past five years. Their biggest contract to date was the Landmark Project, which involved building a multimillion-dollar ski resort near Anchorage, Alaska. Plans were to start on it by the first of the year.

The fact that a deal of that magnitude had been awarded to a company owned by two African-American men had made headlines. He and Christopher had been featured in several newspapers and magazines, and had even made the covers of *Black Enterprise* and *Ebony*, as well as being the recent recipients of *Black Enterprise*'s prestigious Minority Businessmen of the Year Award a few months ago. At the age of thirty-two, they were the youngest individuals to receive such recognition.

As Gabe began stripping off his clothes, he thought about his mother's fixation with marrying him off. It was as if she was on some sort of mission. Unfortunately, it was one he was having no part of. He had tried placating her by dating a few of the single women from her church, but since it seemed the majority of them had issues that he refused to deal with, he continued to make his work the top priority in his life.

Now that Christopher was a family man, their roles in the company had switched. Gabe did the majority of the traveling these days as well as working most of the international deals. Christopher was the one who stayed in the office and ran things on the home front, and the few times he did travel, he took his wife, Maxi, and the baby with him.

Gabe sighed deeply. The new demands of the job had taken over his life. He didn't have time to develop any sort of serious relationship with a woman other than a brief fling, which was just fine and dandy with him. Anything else took time and energy he couldn't spare.

Stepping into the shower, he couldn't help but appreciate his ongoing affair with Debbie Wells. Like him, she was a successful professional who preferred a sex-only relationship; no romance, no commitment—just raw physical contact and sexual release, which was an invigorating way to work off stress.

Over the past three years, after his disaster with Lindsey Jefferson, he'd found that a nice, unencumbered, noncommitted sort of relationship with a woman was what he needed. It definitely had its advantages. There wasn't a chance you would fall in love, and neither party had expectations of anything turning serious. There was no room for jealousy or possessiveness or broken hearts. And best of all, you could walk away at any time without looking back. Debbie was great in bed, and like him, she played by the rules. He couldn't ask for more, nor did he want to. He liked things just the way they were.

He heard the doorbell the moment he'd stepped out of the shower and had begun drying off. Tucking the towel around his waist, he walked barefoot to the door. Glancing through the peephole, he smiled as he opened the door. It seemed his thoughts of Debbie had conjured her up on his doorstep.

She entered his home after placing a chaste brush of her lips across his cheek. He closed the door behind her. "How was your trip?" he asked, knowing she had been out of town on business for the past week.

"Atlanta was fun as usual," she replied, tracing a polished fingertip along his earlobe. "I know this visit is rather unexpected, but I hope you're in a position to help me out with something."

Her voice was low and seductive, and he liked that. "Something like what?" he prompted, although he had a fairly good idea. He watched her eyes grow dark and sensuous which caused a deep stirring in his body.

She leaned forward, and after reaching around him to re-

lease the towel covering his body, she moved into a position
that placed a silken-clad thigh between his nude legs. It was obvious she felt his erection when her lips tilted into a smile. Her
mouth was mere inches from touching his. He let his gaze
linger on that mouth, thinking how well practiced it was in
pleasing him.

She then grinned wryly. "I need to be screwed senseless
tonight, Gabe."

He couldn't help the smile that tugged at his lips. The one
thing he liked most about Debbie was her honesty, her candid-
ness and more importantly, her hearty sexual appetite. He felt
a hard throbbing that started low and deep in his groin. "That
makes two of us. I need to be screwed senseless tonight myself."

Her smile widened. "Oh, yeah?"

"Hell, yeah." He lowered his head and claimed her mouth,
nibbling, sucking and tasting, creating the level of intimacy
they both needed and wanted. As always, her enthusiasm and
hunger thrilled him and took his sexual cravings to a whole
new level.

Picking her up into his arms and taking her into his bedroom, he knew that before the night was over, they would get
what they both wanted.

The sun was setting low in the sky when Gabe and Christopher completed their final inspection of the job site, a small yet
upscale shopping mall on the outskirts of Detroit. Everything
was on target with plans for the opening by the first of October.
After a brief discussion with their building foreman, they removed their hard hats and safety glasses and walked back toward their cars.

"Dinner's at six if you want to drop by," Christopher invited
before opening the door to his vehicle.

Gabe shook his head. Even after a full year, it was hard seeing
his best friend as a happily married family man when Christopher had always sworn to never marry. He had been the ulti-

mate bachelor, a ladies' man, and one who strongly believed in sex-only relationships. But Maxi, a woman from Christopher's past, had reentered his life and changed all of that, which proved there were such things as miracles. Hell, Chris had even traded his Mercedes sports car in for . . . of all things . . . a minivan.

Gabe silently grinned. *A minivan.* He was ashamed for Christopher since Christopher was too happy with life to be ashamed for himself. "Thanks, Chris, but I need to get prepared for that trip to Anchorage next week. Since the Landmark deal was originally your baby, I have to make sure I'm up on everything about it."

Christopher nodded. He knew that John Landmark intended for his exclusive ski resort to be the largest in the world, as well as the most renowned. It would be nestled among miles and miles of snow-covered mountain slopes and scenic wood trails; a project that would take a year to complete, maybe longer if the weather wasn't cooperative. Landmark had handpicked a firm in Charlotte to handle the resort's marketing and advertising, and a firm from California to take care of the landscape designs. With an undertaking of this magnitude it was important that all three entities work together if the end result was to be successful. "All right, but if you change your mind, you know you're welcome."

Back in his car Gabe began his journey home. A part of him was eager to start work on the ski resort. Being awarded the contract had literally opened doors, and business was booming. Recently, he and Christopher had discussed hiring an additional building crew just to handle the new business they were acquiring.

Gabe looked forward to the two weeks he would spend in Anchorage, a city that was vastly different from Detroit. He needed to get away for a while, especially because of his mother's overzealous matchmaking schemes. She had called earlier that day, telling him about another young woman that she wanted him to meet. He had come up with an excuse why he couldn't meet the woman any time soon and had quickly ended the conversation.

His thoughts turned back to Anchorage and all the work he had to pack into the two weeks he would be there, including finding suitable temporary housing for his men. Because of the length of time many of them would be staying there, some had decided to take their families with them, an option he and Christopher had offered them. The last thing the company needed was any member of the work crew getting homesick or pining for companionship. And those who decided to leave their families behind could fly home at least four times, which included the major holidays.

Gabe planned to make time to check out the city while he was there. He'd heard that Anchorage was beautiful and the perfect place to fish, which was something he enjoyed doing. And since he would eventually be spending a lot of his time there, he may as well look for temporary housing for himself as well.

Less than twenty minutes later, Gabe had arrived home. The first thing he did was check his phone messages. He wasn't surprised to find several from his mother, but he *was* surprised to find one from Keri Morton. She had called to thank him for dinner and to let him know that she and her ex-boyfriend had decided to try and work things out for the baby's sake. Gabe shook his head as he made his way to the refrigerator for a beer. After the earful Keri had given him, he truly wished them the best.

She had been a woman on the rebound, and he had to remember that type of woman was nothing but trouble.

Connect with

Visit us online at
KensingtonBooks.com
to read more from your favorite authors, see books
by series, view reading group guides, and more.

for sneak peeks, chances to win books and prize packs,
and to share your thoughts with other readers.

facebook.com/kensingtonpublishing
twitter.com/kensingtonbooks

Tell us what you think!

To share your thoughts, submit a review,
or sign up for our eNewsletters, please visit:
KensingtonBooks.com/TellUs.